THE STORM

THE STORM

COLLEEN WINTER

To my parents, Patricia and Stewart,
for showing me how to follow my dreams and take chances.

"The day science begins to study non-physical phenomena; it will make more progress in a decade than in all the previous centuries of its existence."

—Nikola Tesla

ONE

STORM

Storm stumbled on the path, the vision of what she had witnessed in the clearing blocking out all else. There had been an excruciating, searing burn as the Gatherer's corrupted field had stripped away her energy, leaving her bare and raw. She could feel the damage that underlay the wonder and the sheer awe of what she had seen.

It had been a glimpse of what had brought all the people to the clearing. It wasn't a path or a channel or even the Gatherer, but an awareness of something bigger. Something so infinite it had shut out all else. Part of her wanted to go back to it, for even the slightest touch of it again. Yet the part of her that wanted to live kept her stumbling down the path.

She struggled to find the trail in the dark forest and used the rough bark of the trees as guideposts. She anchored herself to the wetness of the ferns against her legs, the strike of water drops on her face. When she reached the log they had climbed over on the way in, she pressed her hands into the wet sponginess of the moss and turned to let Maria and Amanda catch up.

A new rush of rain pattered on the empty path. When had they last been behind her? She had no memory of their footsteps or their breath. She had seen only the spectacle of the Gatherer, the exquisite up-front view of a tiger's face before it eats you alive.

Rain ran onto the back of her hands and formed rivers over her skull.

She leaned against the log, not knowing whether to go forward or back. Maria had drilled into their heads that if they were separated, she was to return to the vehicle. Yet it made no sense that they weren't here with her. They had only been steps behind.

She was saved from her indecision by a movement further back on the trail, a bobbing light coming towards her. A white flash raced in front of the light that formed into the shape of a dog, darting silent and fast through the ferns. It stopped abruptly in front of her, its head held high, the short rhythm of its panting crowding in between the sound of the rain.

It was a beautiful creature, with long white hair and a patch on its face; no hint of aggression, simply the joy of running free in the woods.

She felt a short ache for Blue, her sole companion for so many months in the Yukon.

"Hey, bud."

The dog gave a short wag of its tail, before a single high-pitched bark.

"Yeah, yeah. We know. You found me."

The dog looked back to the lights that had almost reached them. One of the figures holding them was tall and male, the other short, the underbrush at the side of the trail as high as her waist.

The dog barked again; its ears perked forward.

"Sasha!"

The woman's voice split the quiet of the forest.

The dog pranced backwards and the woman rested her hand on its back, her short stoutness at odds with the elegance of the dog.

Gwyneth, the smiling, self-proclaimed spiritual leader of the retreat that was home to the corrupted Gatherer, was breathing hard, her dark curls plastered to her head. The man shone his flashlight in Storm's eyes, and she raised her hand to block the light.

Gwyneth stepped closer. The dog took it as a cue to say hello and Storm opened her free hand to it, and carefully rubbed behind its ears. Its wagging tail thumped against the log as it pressed its body against her knees.

"Is it really you?"

Storm could see nothing beyond the flashlight shining in her eyes.

"Can you point that somewhere else?"

The light moved down, highlighting the dog pressed against her legs.

"Sash, come here!" The pressure on Storm's legs eased, the dog's ears tuned to something in the woods. "Come here!"

With a casual leap, Sasha cleared the log and raced into the woods.

Gwyneth frowned as she watched the dog go, before her focus returned to Storm.

"How can you be here?"

Gwyneth had partially recovered, suspicion replacing the reverent awe. The man stayed behind her, holding something in his hand that she couldn't see. She sat down on the log, a sudden, deep exhaustion swirling around her feet.

"I came to see your Gatherer."

The water from the moss was seeping into her pants, but she didn't have the energy to stand.

"Why would you do that?"

Storm searched the path for Maria, wished for her strong competence to deal with this woman.

"So I could understand it."

There had been that moment when she had understood everything, beyond the Gatherer, beyond this isolated place.

"Didn't you invent it?"

The man's voice was deep and hostile. Gwyneth raised her hand to silence him, with a control far better than she had over her dog.

"I was told this one was different."

She thought she might lie down on the log, let herself drift towards the vision she had only glimpsed.

"And is it?"

Gwyneth's expression had gone flat, her tone smug.

"I didn't get close enough."

The man shifted beside Gwyneth, the beam of the flashlight having crept up to Storm's chest. Storm drew back at the sight of what he held in his hand: the smooth plastic of a taser, the tip pointed to the ground. The perfect weapon to terrorize the afflicted.

Gwyneth stepped closer.

"We're having a ceremony tomorrow night. You should come. I can give you full access to the Gatherer."

Storm inched sideways along the log. "I can't be that close."

"You were just in our clearing. Why not show yourself? The congregation would love to see you."

"Congregation?"

Storm slid further down the log, stopping when her hip pushed up against the stub of a broken branch.

Gwyneth was smiling, with the same pandering she had used when Storm had watched her dealing with the man in the clearing whose suffering had been so acute. She waved her arm to take in the wet forest and the clearing behind it.

"I know you witnessed the truth tonight." An undercurrent of reverence ran through her words. "Because you are the person who delivered it to us. Showed us the path to that higher place."

Storm tried to scramble over the log, except the man was too fast. The hard plastic of the taser pressed into the tender skin of her neck.

She froze.

"I can't go back there."

Gwyneth clapped twice, like a primary school teacher.

"Nonsense. You were sent to us for a reason. This is not the time to be a coward."

Storm saw the expanse of it again, its emptiness. She wouldn't survive prolonged contact. She couldn't help but see the irony, that she would be killed by the Gatherer not when she tried to stop it, but because some zealot still believed she was the savior.

There was a strike on her shoulder and the taser scraped down her neck. The man grunted as he hit the ground. Storm caught a flash of Maria's ponytail and vest, and then she was standing above him, the taser pointed at his face, the flashlight on the ground at her feet.

He lifted his hands to shield his face.

Gwyneth stared, her expression changing to that of someone who had just witnessed a miracle.

"Of course, you are here too." Her voice rose with excitement. "You both have to come tomorrow. Truly. This has to be a sign."

"You okay?" asked Maria.

She picked up the flashlight and stood between Storm and Gwyneth. "Yeah."

The forest had changed, the rain quieter, withdrawn into the simple potential of a spring evening.

"Hop over the log," said Maria.

"No. No. No." Gwyneth came forward, her hands held up in supplication. "You need to come back with us." She stopped within reach of Maria, her self-assurance bullet-proof.

"That Gatherer isn't what you think it is," said Storm.

There was the sound of shouting in the distance, like an angry mob coming towards them. Storm climbed over the log but halfway over she stopped, the cries turning into words. There was a level of panic to them that could only mean fear.

Gwyneth's eyes widened. Her head turned to the voices, even as her hands were still held out to them.

Fire. The barn is on fire.

Gwyneth whirled back on them, her face wide with shock and confusion. Storm almost felt sorry for her.

Maria lifted the taser. Blocked her path to Storm.

The man was already running back towards the growing cries as the first smell of smoke reached them.

Gwyneth hesitated and took a step towards them.

The smell of charred wood thickened, and the first trace of doubt broke through her forced benevolence. She gave a small gasp, almost a choke, before she turned and ran.

There was more shouting now, a glow of orange visible in the sky. Gwyneth's outline blurred the further she got from them; her short legs not able to carry her fast enough.

Maria hurried Storm over the log.

"Should we go?" asked Storm.

"Only if you want to take the blame."

Maria climbed over behind her.

"Was it you?" asked Storm.

Maria looked back towards the fire.

"No." Though there was hesitancy there. Concern.

She shone the light in front so Storm could see the path. Storm started walking, listening to the cries of fear behind them. Within a few minutes, they no longer heard the commune, the rain muffling the cries, the forest floor calm and quiet. Storm struggled to walk, the strength of her fatigue too much to overcome.

Maria slipped beneath Storm's arm and held her around the waist. Storm was grateful for it, the final hold of the Gatherer peeling away as they moved further from the barn.

"Where's Amanda?" Storm asked as they splashed through a puddle. There was the barest return of strength in her legs from the water, the agitation in her nerves calming.

She felt Maria stiffen, her grip around Storm's waist tighter.

"I don't know."

Storm tried to stop but Maria kept moving her forward.

"Is she okay?"

Maria shook her head, her stride never faltering.

"She knows how to look after herself."

There was more hope than conviction in the words.

Storm tried to look over their shoulder, back the way they'd come, but the woods were too dark. They wouldn't know if Amanda was there until she was on top of them.

"You should go back," said Storm.

Maria pushed a branch out of the path.

"Gwyneth will make damn sure that the world knows we were here. What better publicity for her spiritual retreat than having the inventor of the Gatherer show up?"

"That's not what's happening there."

"It doesn't matter. That's how she'll play it. Our job is to get as far away from here as possible."

"What about Amanda?"

There was the barest hesitation in Maria's stride.

"We can't worry about that right now."

Storm twisted her head for a final glance behind them. They had known they could be separated, or worse; she just hadn't expected it to happen so soon.

TWO

ADAMS

Two long wings ran out from the main building that held the entrance, the white stone discoloured with age and the rows of windows looking as empty and haunted as when they had first transported the afflicted from the dark zone to this forgotten place.

Great Bear Hospital read the sign at the gate, the painted letters as faded and gone as the lives that had once been destroyed here: a hospital for indigenous children with tuberculosis in the 1940s and 1950s that had been more about abuse and torture than healing. The patients Adams had delivered would have added to that history of suffering, the walls and the air itself inseparable from that legacy.

Adams' mouth was dry, his grip on the wheel so strong it felt as if it might snap, every face he imagined on those neglected children that of his daughter Camille.

"Are the afflicted even here?"

Hamel's voice pulled him back, like an echo in a tunnel far behind him.

The old hospital came back into focus, the overgrown shrubs and the sagging roof line. It was no place to bring anyone, let alone the sick.

"They're here."

Adams unbuckled his seat belt and turned off the minivan.

"There will be a woman with long gray hair in charge, named Marty, and then a taller, dark-haired guy, Romero, but it was the little girl who had the web."

He stepped out of the vehicle into the morning air, the chill off the ocean bitter enough to reach his bones.

"Will they be armed?"

"Unlikely, but Romero will be protective." He couldn't blame the guy. He had only been trying to protect the people in his care.

Adams checked for his SIG in his holster. It was ridiculous to be bringing it here, against people who could barely stand.

The gravel crunched under their feet as they approached the entrance, the roof a domed arch over the double doors, the three steps littered with years of forest debris. There was a movement in the window on the second floor, and his hand moved to his pistol before it had even registered.

"Easy," said Hamel. It wasn't something he would have said in their unit when Adams had the higher rank. Now they had no titles, no roles, only the skills they had come away with and a need to find a little girl with wings.

He forced his hand to his side, tried the deep breathing that was supposed to help his focus. It didn't work. Nothing had since — well, he didn't think about that, preferring to let the rage consume him.

The door opened as they reached the bottom of the steps. They spread out, ready for whatever came at them, but it was only Marty, more haggard and drawn than she had been at the warehouse.

"Have you brought supplies?"

She didn't recognize him. He had been one of a dozen soldiers, the trauma of that night erasing everything else.

"We've been sending requests."

There was little hope in her voice. The words trailed off, recognizing that neither they nor the vehicle were what she needed.

"Who is it?"

Romero's voice rang out behind her, his protectiveness as strong as it had been that night.

"We'd like to ask you a few questions."

Adams kept his voice measured and professional, the perfect soldier. But was he even that guy anymore?

There was a movement to the side and both he and Hamel tensed as a bird burst from the branches of an old oak above the tangled, overgrown garden. The puff of its flapping wings pushed over them before fading towards the ocean.

"We can't take any more people," said Romero. "We already can't care for the ones we have."

Romero maneuvered around Marty and came out the door. His hair was longer, his clothes dirty and creased, like he had been living rough.

"We aren't bringing more people."

It made Adams ill to think of rounding up more of the afflicted and dumping them here like discarded clothes.

"Then what is it you want?" said Marty.

What did he want? Other than the impossibility of having his wife and child returned to him. The images came unbidden, harsh and bright, of finding Valerie and Camille cocooned in the black body bags. His entire life zipped up and as easily discarded as these people here. What he *wanted* was to not have found them there and to have never arranged their arrival at the treatment facility. For them to still be safe in Quebec, far from here.

"There was a network at the warehouse, that was brought here," said Adams. "We'd like to see it."

"Why?"

Because it had been the only bit of hope in all the darkness. A moment of light and openness that his mind kept returning to.

"The girl said it helped cure the afflicted."

"You were there," said Marty. "That night." Her gray eyes didn't leave his. He expected anger and recrimination, not the compassion that softened her gaze. Shame overwhelmed him and he looked away.

There was movement in the garden, the slightest shift of the high ferns. He nodded to Hamel, and Hamel slipped away, his movements as fluid as the air itself.

"There's no one here but us."

"We know," said Adams. No one would willingly come to this remote place, far from resources and support.

Romero crossed his arms.

"I'm not handing it over to the government. To see it just disappear. Or worse."

The worse was what had been done to the original Gatherers, once a miracle delivered to save the world and now something that was killing and corrupting the very essence of the earth.

"We're not with the government."

Marty tilted her head to the side, appearing to consider. He knew that all she would see was the weapon, and not the person behind it.

"We just need to see the network," said Adams.

He didn't know why, only that in those weeks of blind grief the only thought that had broken through the shock had been the little girl and the device she had clutched to her chest.

"We need supplies before you see it," said Marty.

Their desperation was throwing him off-balance, their scrambling no different than the growing number of the afflicted on the streets, begging for whatever they could get before they were shipped away.

"We can do that. Whatever you need." It was a promise he couldn't keep. "But we see the network first."

A vine ran up the door frame, countless tiny spikes branching off in search of new holds.

"Once they see it, they won't be back," said Romero.

Adams didn't deny it. This was probably a waste of time, him grasping at straws.

And then she was there, being ushered unwillingly in front of Hamel, her fairy wings more tattered, the strands of copper wire hanging off like falling feathers.

Her expression was defiant and angry, and it so strongly reminded him of Camille that he was dizzy, his knees weak. Hamel was suddenly at his side and everyone was watching him. He had the sense that a chunk of time had passed.

The girl stood next to Marty, holding the older woman's hand. Her tutu had disintegrated to a single layer, the mesh hanging down in shreds over her jeans. Her blonde hair hung in matted curls and her blue eyes gazed at him with the same clarity that had disarmed him when they had first met.

"Do you remember me?" he said.

"You killed Mr. Nakamura."

His first response was to deny it, for he didn't know the name. Yet there had been that older man, who hadn't wanted to be moved and Adams had carried him to the truck and laid him among the others.

"I'm sorry. I didn't know he died."

Marty and Romero stood with the girl, as would a family: the child drawn to the mother for comfort, the father apart and without the skills or knowledge to protect his family. Except it wasn't a family, but three people thrown together by the Gatherer, the same way it had torn his family apart.

"No network until we get our supplies," said Romero.

Adams shook his head in irritation. He was done with people standing in his way, making catastrophic decisions about things that were too important to mess up. Hamel waited for a signal, as willing as Adams to move.

It was the girl's watchful gaze that stopped him, taking in everything that he and her adults were doing. The same way she had watched him carry Nakamura into the truck.

"No supplies until we see the network."

He heard the weariness in his own voice, at the pointless back and forth.

Bits of cracked concrete spread out from a hole in the top step, small stones embedded in the pieces.

"The network doesn't work."

The girl stood ramrod straight, arms crossed, a fierce strength in her thin arms and legs.

"It does," said Romero. "It's just taking longer to establish itself here because of—" He gestured to the building. "—the structure."

He could have meant the building or the history that lay within it.

"How do we know you won't trick us?"

The girl's forehead was pinched in a frown, her uncontrolled hair a tangle above her thin face.

He considered lying to her, the same way he would have once lied to Camille, so she wouldn't be afraid or know the truth.

"Because if we'd wanted to take it, we could have by now. Without you ever knowing."

He saw the flash of fear in her eyes but didn't regret it. She wouldn't survive without the truth, no matter how much it hurt.

He and Hamel remained still; it was the family that was restless, as if only now realizing the danger.

"Megan can show you where it is," said Marty, putting a hand out to appease Romero. He remembered the calmness of that voice from the night he had brought them here.

Megan hesitated, watched him with that disarming clarity before letting go of Marty's hand and turning towards the door. Adams followed them inside, Hamel bringing up the rear.

A wide stone staircase led up from the foyer, the lines severe and unadorned. The space felt colder than the outside, like it guarded a deep chill within its foundation.

Megan ran ahead of them. A window stretched the height of the stairwell, flooding the white stone with pale morning light. It smelled of age and decay, and dirt was embedded in the stone from decades of wear.

A man stood on the third step, his brown hair cut short, his shirt wrinkled and torn. He stared down at them, his gaze too direct, and Adams adjusted his stance, reacting to the inherent threat.

Megan swerved towards the man and Adams instinctively moved to protect her. He had his foot on the first step when Megan took the man's hand, the touch breaking his focus so that he turned away as meek as a scared child.

He hadn't been looking at them at all but had been trapped by whatever was going on in his head. Adams shook himself. The mental symptoms were the worst kind of torture.

The man shuffled down the stairs, continuing from where he had been interrupted. Marty laid a hand gently on the man's arm as she passed and Adams looked away, pity for the man threatening to overwhelm him.

Megan was already on the first landing, and he climbed towards her, refusing to look behind.

At the first landing, he stopped, waiting for Marty to catch up. She climbed slowly and he wondered if she had taken on the affliction of those she treated or if the toll was from months of providing care. A corridor ran off the landing and the silhouettes of more patients shuffled through the thick dusk, the corridors darker than the daylight of the stairwell. There was no electricity here, like the warehouse, and there was the faint smell of burnt candles.

One of the patients looked up. She had the same gauntness as Valerie and Camille, and her skin had been robbed of color. He had a memory of Valerie sitting in bed at the treatment facility, and her whispered words for him to "take her home."

"How many people are here?" asked Hamel, his words dragging Adams back.

Megan stood above them, already waiting at the top of the next flight. He looked again to the patient, but the woman had turned away.

"We started at a hundred and thirty," said Marty.

She didn't expand on what had happened since then, who had died or survived, or how many more had been dumped there. He reminded himself that this was a good place, where they tried to help. For all the good it did.

On the second flight, Marty lagged further, and Adams moved back to help. She allowed him to take her arm and support her up the final few steps.

"You'll be carrying me if you take any more of my weight, Sergeant."

"Adams is fine."

At the top step, she was breathing hard, and she paused, watching a mother and toddler cross the landing below.

"Is Megan's mother here?" he asked.

Megan's mother had been one of the afflicted at the warehouse, and the reason Megan had been there, a healthy child among the sick.

"Yes—"

There was a hesitancy to Marty's words, and he saw the worry in the small shake of her head. He would have asked more but Romero ushered them into a large common area. An empty counter ran along one wall with a row of utility cupboards above, and large discolored windows looked out over the tops of trees to the turbulence of the ocean.

Megan stood in the middle of the open space, looking down at what was the center of several dozen wire spokes running to the edge of the room and either extending up the wall to the ceiling or disappearing into the floor. The wire closest to him went into a hole drilled into the wall. The wood chips from the drill bit still lay on the floor below it.

The space had a calmness to it, and for a moment he imagined Megan glowed, the light from the windows catching in her curls. The beauty of it caught him off-guard and he had the urge to be far from there, in a peaceful place, even if he didn't know where that would be.

He followed a path between two spokes, the wires converging as they approached the hub. By the time he stood next to Megan, that calmness had overtaken him, allowing him, for once, to breathe. Megan looked up at him.

"How does it do that?" he asked.

She squatted down so that her hands hovered above the hub, and she drew them along the path of a wire.

"Pulses are sent out along the wires and it creates a web of energy. If it works, it can help repair damaged nerves and cells."

She moved her hand above the next.

"But you said it doesn't work."

She moved her hand back above the original wire.

"Not like it did at the warehouse. There, you could actually *feel* it working."

"Can you feel it now?"

She snatched her hands back, but it was too late. He had seen her holding her palm to the wire as you would to a fire, gauging whatever she felt.

She wiped her hands on her dirty jeans. Her gaze flitted to where Marty stood.

"What do you feel?"

He said it so that Marty and Romero wouldn't hear. But she simply glared up at him before moving back several feet, stopping halfway out on the spokes as if in some spot of safety he couldn't see.

Hamel approached the hub from the opposite side. His arrival fractured something that had been there, and the loss of it filled Adams with regret.

"Is that what I think it is?"

Hamel was on his knees, looking into the tiny Gatherer at the center, the crystals so small they looked like diamonds.

"It sends out small signals along the wires, so that it creates some kind of web of energy," said Adams.

"But it's a Gatherer. Doesn't it cause—"

Hamel tore his gaze from the tiny device. Adams understood the reluctance to look away, its power hard to fathom.

Megan stepped closer.

"The Gatherer connects things." Her voice sounded like a song he knew well. "When it's working, it heals the people inside it."

Both he and Hamel lifted their gaze to the ceiling, as if seeing the energy that would encompass the entire structure, making it more than it really was.

"Can you fix it?"

"We've tried."

Romero had arrived behind them while Marty was being drawn from the room by a frail young man. "But we don't understand the technology enough to know what is different. Why it seemed to work at the warehouse and not here."

"So, you don't know if it worked at all," said Hamel.

Romero gestured to the corridor and the entire building. "People we thought it had helped have died." He rubbed the back of his neck, the gesture rife with fatigue and frustration.

Hamel gave Adams a quick look. They had hoped for so much more than this, for a tool they could use to push back the spread of the plague.

Hamel rose from his knees and spoke to Romero. "Can you explain to me how it works?" He walked towards the wider spaces between the spokes and drew Romero with him.

Adams approached the hub and sank down. The crystals were small and fragile. He had so needed this to be real and not just a child's experiment. That moment when he had been able to breathe had been nothing more than wishful thinking.

"Did it make your mom better?"

Megan nudged one of the wires with her toe, the once-white canvas of her shoe smudged near-black with dirt.

"Why did you come here?"

He brushed a layer of dust away from the hub. He had told her the truth earlier even when it had frightened her, and he wouldn't break that small kernel of trust.

"I remembered you from that night when we brought you here. How you were so much more alive than anyone else. I was hoping it was because of the web, and I could use it to make people better."

She pushed the wire further out of alignment, more of its length pulled from the straight line of the spoke.

"Do you have someone who is sick?"

The beat of his heart rose. He looked to see if she noticed. She held his gaze, the blue unflinching.

"I did." His voice was a croak, hardly a voice at all.

A cloud darkened the blue of her eyes and there was the slightest crease between her brows.

"They died," she said and simply nodded. He wondered how the world and his life had come to this. Where he took solace from a child who had suffered as much as him.

"I tried to use it to fix my mom."

He swallowed, pushing down everything this child and this place had drawn out.

"Did it help?"

The wire outline of her fairy wings was bent, and several large holes broke the mesh. The tiny crystals lay between them, the whole device small enough to fit in her palm.

"Not yet."

She tilted her head and he saw the shift in focus. She was concentrating as if hearing something far away.

"What is it?"

Her calmness crumbled, her courage breaking into tiny pieces so that when her gaze lifted her eyes were wide with shock. She darted past him, running between the wire spokes, reaching the door when Marty returned and tried to stop her but Megan was panicked, veering around the woman at full speed. Adams ran after her, her panic igniting his own irrational need to get to Valerie and Camille before it was too late.

Marty held up her hand, and the heartbreak in her face stopped him. Megan's wings retreated into the hallway, her thin legs barreling her tiny body down the corridor as if she flew.

"What happened?"

His heart pounded, the stark plainness of the room out of sync with his body's alarm.

Marty lowered herself onto a bench that sat against the wall of the corridor, a pained, sorrowful movement. The lines on her face were suddenly deeper, her shoulders more stooped. Her defeat let the air out of his alarm, her sorrow too complete.

"What is it?"

Marty rubbed her face. It was the first time he had seen her anything less than stoic.

Hamel and Romero silently joined them.

Romero looked older too, in the dusk, as he laid a hand on Marty's shoulder.

"Is it Beverley?"

Marty nodded, as she lifted her face from her hands. She looked to the ceiling as tears glistened in her eyes.

Adams felt like an intruder, coming here and asking something of people that were already overloaded.

"Is she Megan's mother?" Hamel asked. He stood a step back from Romero as if he meant to retreat. He had lost his own mother to the Gatherer and had seen the connection Adams had missed.

"She had been with us the longest," said Marty. "I thought—"

Adams fought the tightness in his chest.

"I should go to her." Marty rose and sat heavily back down.

"I'll go," said Romero. He nodded to Hamel and Adams before following in the direction Megan had gone. In the distance there was the sound of raised, distressed voices.

"Can I get you anything?" Hamel asked.

Marty drew in a long breath. "Not unless you can make this all go away." She half-heartedly lifted her hand to encompass the floors above and below them.

They stood in the futility of it, their failure to find what they were looking for and their inability to make any of it go away.

"I wish we could," said Adams.

Marty pushed her hair back from her face and seemed to gather herself. Hamel and Adams supported her as she rose but she was steadier now, solid. She moved a few steps in the direction Romero and Megan had gone.

"What will happen to Megan now?" asked Hamel.

The lull of the hospital surrounded them, hundreds of murmured voices combining into an unsettled hum.

"There are other children here who are unattended."

More parents that had died, leaving children behind.

"So, she won't be sent away?"

Marty turned, the flesh of her elbow visible through where her shirt had split.

"She will always have a place here."

Her conviction startled him, for surrounded with so much death, how could anyone be certain of anything?

THREE

MARIA

WATER DRIPPED INTO MARIA'S eyes as they reached the road, the rain falling harder since they had left the clearing. It would help to contain the fire and hopefully keep everyone safe. Her first instinct had been to run towards it, to help in any way she could, and it had pained her to turn away.

She and Storm walked side-by-side across the streaming pavement, Storm's stride stable, if slow. Maria sought out the gleam of the bumper, wanting Amanda's cocky, unrepentant silhouette to be leaning against it, maddeningly smoking a cigarette.

She cast the flashlight beam across the tree boughs that shielded the pickup, the green buds gleaming wet.

"Is she here?" asked Storm.

Maria had waited for Amanda to show up as they fled, either suddenly stepping in front of them or coming up from behind. Smelling of smoke. Or gasoline. Or whatever she had used to start the fire. Her worry had flipped to irritation and back again, that Amanda had chosen this point in time to act on some perceived injustice.

Storm pushed back a branch that blocked the passenger's side of the pickup. Maria expected to see Amanda inside, tossing her hair off her shoulders with a self-satisfied grin.

Maria climbed into the driver's seat, the air cold and still. Amanda's cigarettes lay on the dash and Maria flipped them open, checked that Amanda's lighter was slipped in the slot left by a cigarette.

It didn't mean she didn't have one with her, or that she hadn't found another way to set the barn on fire. She'd always been resourceful when she set her mind to it.

"Do we wait?"

Storm's hair was wet against her scalp, her skin white in the darkness.

No was the correct answer. She should get Storm far away. There would be no photo evidence, but it didn't mean Gwyneth wouldn't be believed. She had seen Storm Freeman alive and investigating a Gatherer. Even without the fire, that would be news enough. With it, news crews would arrive quickly, and they wouldn't be the only ones.

"People will know you were here by now."

Maria's hand was on the key in the ignition, but she couldn't bring herself to turn it.

"She'll be here," said Storm.

The branches hung too close; her view of their surroundings cut off.

"You should get in the back," said Maria.

Storm held the crumpled emergency blanket in her fist.

"Did she set the fire?"

Maria had ignored the edge in Amanda's voice when they had left her at the clearing. Maria had thought a squeeze of her hand would be enough to appease her.

"People will be arriving soon. You have to get in the back. If they find you—"

Stanton would lock Storm away someplace where she wouldn't be able to contradict him or do anything to harm the Gatherers. Maria would be ... she couldn't be court-martialed, because officially she already had been dishonorably discharged, but she too would be made to disappear.

"I couldn't have destroyed it," said Storm. Her words were flat, muted inside the tin shell.

"That's not what we came for," said Maria.

She had seen the shocked wonder on Storm's face when she had been in the thrall of the Gatherer and recognized that Storm had experienced something other than just pain. She had thought she had been remembering some of the original wonder of the device. A connection that would have made it hard to destroy.

"It's what we'll have to do eventually."

"You'll do it when the time comes."

If they ever managed to get out of there.

Maria's leg bounced in agitation. Gwyneth's people could easily have found Amanda.

She turned the key to the first stop, and the dash lights came on, the seat belt alert buzzing.

"Okay, I'm going," said Storm, a note of alarm in her voice at the idea of being in the cab when the engine turned on, immersed in its electromagnetic fields.

Maria turned the key to *off*. "Sorry." She had been too focused, forgotten where she was.

Storm gathered the blanket around her and stepped out of the truck.

"Will you be warm enough?"

The door thudded shut.

The cab was quieter, and darker. Storm's outline moved along the bed of the truck, vulnerable to whoever might be in the woods.

Maria was out the door, the light from the cab spilling on the ground before she closed the door. She met Storm at the tailgate. Rain pattered around them, the darkness filling in the spaces between trees, so Maria felt as isolated and vulnerable as they had been at the hunt camp.

She helped Storm into the shielded box Amanda had installed near the tailgate, as she kept her eye on the surrounding wetness. How long until troops or media swarmed around them?

There was the slap of a shoe on asphalt, and she ushered Storm into the box and gestured for her to stay low. She moved beside the front bumper, using the truck as cover. The footsteps were uneven, intermixed with the sound of rain, as if the person hesitated, or stumbled. She imagined the man with the beard who had been so conflicted, wet, and struggling to make his escape.

She peered beneath the trees, saw the flat black expanse of pavement with its faded yellow line.

The footsteps had stopped, and Maria strained further. Whoever was there blended too well with the dark. The footsteps started again, faster this time, and Maria pushed closer to the fender, trying to be as unseen as the pickup.

There was a stumble and a muted curse, and Maria was on her feet moving fast into the road.

"What the hell are you doing?"

Amanda jumped back.

"Oh, thank God." Amanda waved her arm at the trees. "These all look the same, I had no idea where you were."

Maria pulled her off the road.

"Hey! That hurts!"

"Get in the truck."

She held the door for her, closed it harder than necessary. Maria had the truck started almost before her butt hit the seat. The dim glow of the running lights moved with them as they rolled forward out of the shelter onto the road. She checked the rear-view mirror; Storm was already cocooned in the copper blanket.

Amanda craned her neck to see Storm in the back as she pulled her wet hair off her neck. There was movement from the shiny pile of copper that could have been a wave. Amanda waved back.

"I was worried you had left."

The truck slid on mud.

"We should have."

The tires finally gripped the road, the water spraying off the sides as they accelerated. She squeezed the wheel.

"I had to come out the driveway and back track along the road. I thought I had missed you."

Amanda wedged her hands between her knees and hunched her shoulders in cold. She looked again at Storm in the back.

"Is she okay?"

"What the hell were you thinking?"

The heater blew cold air on their feet, the engine not ready yet to provide any warmth.

"It needed to be stopped."

She was unrepentant, her certainty unshakable.

"We could have been caught."

Amanda had her face turned to watch the tree trunks flash by in the headlights. A sudden burst of rain clattered onto the roof and onto Storm's small shelter. Maria drove faster.

"You didn't have to wait."

The coolness of Amanda's voice made Maria wild with fury.

"You think I would just leave?"

There was no hiding her anger or the worry of everything she had imagined happening to Amanda while she and Storm had walked out. Amanda didn't bother to respond, the accusation that Maria had left once before hanging between them.

"There's more at stake here than your need to stir things up."

"Did you not see those people?"

Amanda grabbed her cigarettes off the dash, opened the tray and snapped it shut without drawing out a cigarette.

"I'm not saying it didn't need to be destroyed. Everything was wrong about that place. But you put Storm and those people at risk."

"Those people were already at risk, and the fire wasn't going to spread in the rain. It was only the barn that burned."

"Did it? Burn?"

The air blowing on her feet started to warm, as if it carried traces of the fire.

Amanda smiled. "That dead white stuff along the bottom of the walls, it burns like kindling. I barely had to use the lighter fuel."

"You had lighter fluid?"

"Always."

The warm, dry air had started to push into the cab though Storm was still exposed to the onslaught of the cold and wind.

The sides of the road were solid forest, unbroken by the opening of a road or a space carved for a house. They needed a place to stop, where Storm could once again regain her strength. The familiarity of it was daunting; their ability to take only a few steps forward before needing to stop and rest. Maria drove faster, until the slip of the old tires on the wet pavement forced her to slow.

Gwyneth's benevolent, saccharine need to be the focus of attention would have her talking and posting to anyone that would listen. And that would be many.

"Is there a way to bring Storm into the cab?" said Maria.

Amanda had helped Storm create a sheltered space at the cabin, and understood some of how electromagnetic fields propagated from a source. They hadn't had that option when they'd stolen the truck, the need to travel fast balanced against the reduced risk of fields from a carbureted engine.

Amanda looked back at the dark lump that was Storm. There wasn't much to see.

"Maybe … there isn't much to work with."

"You don't have some copper shielding tucked in beside your lighter fluid?"

Amanda grunted, as she wrung the water out of her black hair.

"That would have been a good idea."

Amanda searched the glove box and then forced Maria to lean forward so she could look behind the seat. There was the clatter of metal on metal, and the scrape of things pushed to the side. Amanda turned on the overhead light, making it harder for Maria to see in front of them. She sat down with a thud, with nothing in her hands.

"We're going to have to stop," said Amanda.

"We can't."

Maria didn't know where to stop. Where could possibly be safe.

The wipers thudded on the windshield, the headlights tracking the yellow line. Water from the road drummed on the underside of the cab.

Maria braked hard and pulled onto the gravel shoulder. The noise of the rain eased, the world suddenly quiet.

Storm was half sitting by the time they reached her.

"Where are we?"

In the glow from the running lights, she looked dazed, and seemed to struggle to focus.

"You need to come into the truck."

Storm looked alarmed and searched the forest for a threat.

"You'll get hypothermia out here."

Storm looked down at her clothes and the copper blanket she had pushed back.

"What Maria is trying to say," said Amanda, as she joined them, "is do you need to come into the cab? Or are you okay out here?"

Storm looked irritated and Maria knew she had made a mistake. She had forgotten how capable Storm was of looking after herself.

"I'm dry." Storm touched her hand to the front of the oilskin. "And this—" She lifted the crinkling copper material wrapped around her legs. "—is an emergency blanket." She said the last words slowly, directing them at Maria.

Amanda laughed, a loud bark of glee.

"Fine," said Maria, "Let us know if that changes."

She retreated to the cab, and almost missed Storm asking Amanda.

"Did you destroy it?"

Maria paused, her foot on the running board.

"Yes."

The rain had eased to a drizzle, the vibration of it filling the air.

"Good," said Storm, as she settled the copper blanket around her legs. "One down. Thousands more to go."

FOUR

ADAMS

ARTY, ADAMS, AND HAMEL stopped at the top of the long staircase that led down to the main entrance of the hospital. The steps were dusty, cobwebs staked out on almost every corner, and a discolored oil lamp sat at their feet.

"Where will you go now?"

Marty sounded beyond weary, her sorrow resonating in every word.

The sound of cutlery and the murmur of voices filtered from a door at the bottom of the stairs, and he wondered how many of the patients he had delivered, unwillingly, to this isolated place.

"Back to the city," said Hamel. His answer surprised Adams, since he hadn't even thought of what they would do next; he'd had too much invested in a mythical web. "It's our best place to learn more of what's happening. See where we can offer help."

Bits of dust floated in the light from the window, and he watched their slow weave, until a movement from one of the corridors drew his attention. Small groups of patients watched them, more like ghosts than people.

"Why do they hide like that?"

Marty regarded the group that stood just inside the shadows: three women with clothes that hung on wasted frames and a man not much older than Adams who leaned on a walker.

"Most of them were dropped off by the military. Plus, everyone who comes from the outside is too casual with their technology. The residents assume you have a cell phone."

He and Hamel had left their phones in the van so the transmissions wouldn't harm the patients. Though it hadn't mattered. There was no service in this part of the province, no place they could connect even if they wanted to.

"Does anyone visit?"

The group seemed unable to settle, hovering half in and half out of the light.

Marty's expression was quiet, a screen blocking the movement behind.

"No."

They started down the stairs, and he wanted to wipe at his arms and shake his head, anything to stop the pull of their suffering. At the bottom, he was out of breath, gulping for air.

Marty paused two steps above him. Her running shoes were a faded blue, the neatly tied laces a dull gray.

"Is everything alright?"

Her voice was too compassionate, too kind.

"Yeah. Fine."

She watched him for a long moment, as he struggled to stay composed. After an eternity, she handed him a folded piece of paper.

"We need fresh food, bedding, all the anti-seizure meds you can find, cortisol cream…"

He was relieved his hand didn't shake when he accepted the list.

"We'll get what we can."

It was a promise he couldn't keep, and he was ashamed at how little he could help. There was a crash from inside the cafeteria, and the hum of conversation paused before it continued. The two small windows that looked into the room were embedded with a mesh of wire that prevented him from seeing inside.

Hamel opened the main door and a gust of dirt and twigs burst in over the tiles. A storm was coming, the unsettled air already pushing through the cracks in the old building.

"I appreciate it," said Marty.

"It's the least we can do."

Her gray hair was pulled back from her face, her pants and shirt ill-fitting and worn. It was the same outfit she had worn each time he'd seen her. She smiled at him, and he marveled at her ability to care for those around her.

Above them, the light shifted, and a long shadow fell over the stairs.

Megan stood on the top step, the blurred light of the skylights washing her of color so she appeared as an outline. She had lost her wings, the elastics that had held them on replaced by the straps of a backpack. Romero hovered behind her, trying to hold her back, his voice quietly pleading.

Her eyes were red and swollen, and she walked with all the poise of a belle at the ball.

Romero tried once or twice to stop her, but she pushed off his hands, barely seeming to have noticed the touch.

She stopped next to Marty, even more ethereal next to the older woman's solidity.

She had changed into a deep blue dress that matched her eyes and replaced her sneakers with a pair of black patent leather shoes.

"I'm coming with you."

The conversation from the cafeteria surged into the sudden silence, the shocked look on Marty's face mirroring his own. The door thudded as Hamel let it shut, the turbulence from outside cut short.

"Oh, sweetie." Marty reached for Megan's hand.

She didn't let her take it, kept her gaze locked on Adams.

"You said you wanted to make people better."

Adams could barely speak, the impossibility of taking her with them, her audacity already tearing out his heart.

"I do."

"Then I can help."

Dirt covered the steps behind her, and the walls were scuffed and cracked.

Hamel returned to stand beside him and knelt in front of Megan. Her hands were curled into fists.

"I think it's great you want to help." His voice was gentle, filled with compassion and concern. "But how do you think you would do that?"

"I know how the Gatherer works."

"We can't take you with us," said Adams. His agitation rose at the idea of it, at his inability to protect her.

There was no hint of hurt in her eyes, only determination. She turned to Hamel.

"You know I'm right. That I understand it better than both of you."

She had been the one to bring the small device here, and Adams had seen the way she held her hand above the wire as if sensing it.

"That's not the point," said Adams. "You're just a child. We can't take care of you."

Marty again tried, unsuccessfully, to take Megan's hand. Romero hovered behind her.

"I can look after myself," said Megan. "I could help."

No one spoke, none of them knowing what to do with this girl whose grief had led her to this crazy, impossible decision.

"You don't know these men," said Marty. "I don't know them. You can't just go with them."

"I do too." Megan's voice was rising, strident. "Hamel is good with technology, understands it like me. And Adams lost people. Like me."

The patients had gathered on the landing above them, drawn by the echoes of Megan's voice. They were worn and trembling.

"All of that is true," said Hamel. "But we're two ex-soldiers sleeping in a van. It wouldn't be safe for you."

"I understand it better than Romero. I'm the one who built it."

She looked at Romero for confirmation. He still held his hands in front of him as if he would stop her, but he nodded, and let his hands fall to his sides.

"Your mother would want you to stay here," said Marty.

Megan flinched at the mention of her mother, but it only seemed to make her more insistent.

"No, she wouldn't. She said as soon as I had the chance, I should leave."

A thread on one of her buttons had come unraveled, the string forming a thin line on the blue.

"I think she meant when you were older. Once things have—"

Marty didn't seem to be able to finish because the world wasn't going to settle down, not for a long time.

"It cured me," said Megan. "When I was at the warehouse."

The world stopped, with Megan at the center of it.

"Is that true?" Adams looked to Romero.

He was shaking his head and frowning.

"I had the shakes. Like my mom." Megan held up her hand, the fingers steady and strong. "After being at the warehouse, they were gone."

"I thought you said it didn't work," said Adams.

"I'm the only one."

A silence grew around them, filled with hope and suspicion, all of them fixated on her small unwavering hand.

"Why didn't you tell us this before?" said Hamel.

His words were cautious, tiptoeing around the trap, or the lie.

"My mom said not to. She said they would take me away."

A woman in a hijab exited the cafeteria. She nodded at Marty before slipping around them and up the stairs, her tread on the steps light.

"You never showed me," said Marty, once the woman was out of earshot.

"My mom—"

"Told you not to," finished Hamel.

Sadness crossed Megan's face, and a flash of something deeper before she tucked it away. There had been someone else she'd kept the secret from, someone close enough that it pained her.

"I never saw your tremors," said Romero. He spoke carefully as if trying to gently uncover the lie. Megan looked up at him, her poise that of an adult.

"Nobody did. Except my mom. They started on my right side and only spread to one leg before they went away."

Romero nodding, confirming the progression of the symptoms.

"And I have this."

She hiked up the hem of her skirt, exposing her long skinny leg. At the top, at her outer hip, a splash of white marred her smooth skin.

"It used to be a rash."

The pattern matched the rash he had seen on Camille, except hers had been red and weeping. This one was the white iridescence of a scar.

Marty touched the white spots, tracing the outline that would have covered half her thigh.

"No one's ever recovered," said Romero.

Megan let the hem drop.

"Which is why I should go with you."

"Or stay here," said Romero. He moved beside Megan and rested his hand on her shoulder. Perhaps he was who her mother had been trying to protect her from. The man who would cure the plague.

She stepped away from him and walked down the final two steps to stand beside Adams. She slipped her hand into his. He felt that same calmness again, a momentary ability to breathe.

"You can't leave now," said Romero. "Not when there's finally hope."

There was a smudge of dirt on her hairline that she had missed in her rush to get there. The zippers on her backpack bulged from where she had shoved everything she owned into the bag, in preparation for going with them.

Romero stepped towards them.

"We could cure people." His plea was quick and breathless. "This is the breakthrough we've been waiting for."

A breakthrough she had kept secret from him even when she knew how much it would mean. Her mother had been right to keep her hidden.

Adams squeezed Megan's hand in reassurance, and she held tight in return.

"It has to be her decision," said Adams.

Marty was frowning, her mouth open in shock. Megan had been smart enough to keep her sickness and her health from all of them. He wondered what other secrets she had hidden.

"You can't just take her," said Romero. "It's irresponsible." He was blustering, his voice rising so it echoed against the bare walls. A larger crowd had gathered, and Adams hoped the underlying echoes had obscured Megan's announcement. He understood the power of what she was and the need to protect it.

Hamel rose from his crouch and stood on Megan's other side.

Marty only had eyes for Megan. She walked stiffly down the two steps and Adams wondered if she too would be a threat. Yet Megan's hand remained relaxed in his, her face uplifted when Marty placed her hands on either side of her face and kissed her forehead.

"Your mom would be so proud of you."

There were tears in her eyes, and she looked as if she would weep.

Megan smiled, her nostrils flaring as she struggled not to cry.

"I promise I'll come back."

Marty's smile was bittersweet. "I would love that. But only when you're ready. There will be lots to do."

"You can't just let them take her," said Romero.

Hamel had moved in between Romero and Megan. Romero was at least smart enough to know when he was outmatched.

"It's her decision," said Marty, running her hand over Megan's curls. There was sorrow in the gesture, and pride.

The front doors flew open and a young man with black hair and skin ran in, bringing wind and leaves with him. He was out of breath, his eyes wide and he looked wildly from Adams to Hamel until his gaze found Marty.

"Two more buses have arrived. Some of them look bad."

The yellow of the school buses was visible through the open doors, and the first of the passengers were descending the steps into the growing storm.

"Bring them to the cafeteria," said Marty. "We'll get them sorted from there."

The young man braced himself at the door against the wind, the lawn already filling with people, the sky above it near black.

Romero and Marty didn't move.

"Promise me—" said Marty.

Romero's cheeks were sunken as if losing Megan would take the last of him.

In the end it was Megan who went to them, the same way she had taken charge of all of them since the start.

Her hug with Marty was long and tight. In front of Romero, she hesitated. Yet Adams had to re-adjust his opinion of Romero when he bent his head to her.

"You'll tell me everything when you come back, so we can fix everyone here?"

She gave him a tight hug and Romero met Adams' eyes over her head.

It was a demand he gave, that he return her to him, not as a miracle or a phenomenon but as a young girl he had grown to love.

Adams nodded.

"You'll send updates?" Marty asked.

"Of course," said Hamel. "And supplies."

The grip of Marty's hand was strong when she took Adams' hand, the force of it reflecting the trust she was putting in him.

He returned the strength, unsure whether he could make good on any of it.

Marty moved into the arriving patients with Romero behind her, greeting the sick and frightened, assisting in any way they could.

"Should we help?" asked Hamel.

As he said it, patients flowed from inside the building, some struggling, others stronger, all of them reaching out to the new arrivals. Patients with rashes reached out to the new arrivals whose suffering matched theirs. Trembling hands reached to stop the shaking of others. Marty and Romero were at the head of all of it, drawing those that suffered into the fold.

"Looks like they have it covered."

They stood on the step, the sick and the sicker flowing around them, Megan between them.

"It will be dangerous," said Adams. "The places we will need to go and the things we will need to do." Romero reached to catch a woman who had stumbled. "I may not be able to protect you."

Megan pulled him through the crowd towards the van that sat on its own, outside the flow of people.

"That's okay."

Her words were faint, whisked away in the wind that ripped through the crowd, lashing leaves and small twigs against their faces.

"I won't be able to protect you either."

He laughed, the barest breath, almost a gasp. He felt the openness widen.

"As long as we're clear on that."

FIVE

AMANDA

AMANDA WOKE WITH A start, bracing her hand against the dashboard as the truck bounced over a rough section of road.

"Sorry," said Maria, "that hole was deeper than I thought."

It was early morning, the sky just beginning to lighten, the woods lining the narrow road still in darkness. Amanda's mouth was dry and her neck ached from sleeping sitting up.

Maria looked wrecked. She sat straight like a good soldier, her focus complete, but by the light of the dashboard Amanda could see the strain around her eyes and the heaviness of her arms on the wheel.

Amanda checked the back of the truck where Storm traveled inside the shielded box. Her hand gripped the top edge and Amanda could see nothing but the faint outline of her face in the narrow opening.

Amanda reached for her cigarettes and, after lighting one, drew a long, slow pull into her lungs. The edge of her headache eased.

They hit another hole and Amanda lifted off her seat.

"Why are you driving so fast?" The trees flew past and the truck rattled as if it would fall apart.

"No reason."

"Did you see something?"

"Not sure."

"Not *sure?*"

Amanda checked farther behind them, to the gravel road emerging in the morning dusk.

"I had to change the route."

"Shit."

Amanda stubbed out her cigarette as she craned her neck to see the sky. The lightening strip above them was clear, though the soft blue was suddenly threatening.

"Why didn't you wake me?"

"You needed sleep."

Amanda opened the glove compartment where she had stowed her Glock and slipped it into her pocket.

"You need to stop being the hero all the time."

The engine geared down for a hill and they roared upwards.

"I wasn't. I took care of it."

"Like hell."

Amanda gripped the handle above the door as they veered around a corner, the truck slowing suddenly as Maria navigated the tight turn.

In a brief open section, she caught a flash of Storm's alarmed face.

It's okay, she mouthed, not knowing whether she could even see her.

"There was a vehicle following us for a while, matching our speed. I couldn't see much because of the headlights but I didn't want to take any chances."

"Are they still following?"

The wall of conifers loomed behind them, the base still trapped in darkness.

"I don't think so."

Amanda searched for the flash of headlights, the glow on the eastern horizon the only source of light. She checked the sky.

"Any drones?"

Maria shrugged as they accelerated down a hill, gravel flying up against the bottom of the truck.

"It was dark."

"Did you keep your hat on?"

Maria's ball cap was low over her eyes, a shield against any facial recognition.

"Of course, plus we've been on back roads the whole time."

"Which makes that car even more suspicious."

They passed a gate across an overgrown driveway. Maria leaned forward to see deeper into the property.

"How far out are we?" asked Amanda.

Maria veered into the center of the road and Amanda swore as they plunged into the wall of trees, only seeing the opening once they were in it.

They bumped down a rutted road, branches scraping at the sides of the truck, Amanda's arms braced on the dash and window.

The headlights flashed on something, a reflection off metal or glass. Maria slowed, the engine quieter as the shape of a low cabin emerged ahead of them. It was made of logs, the white mortar between the logs cracked and falling out. Behind it, through a sea of tall grass, the barn was in worse shape: one side of the roof had caved in and the door hung on a single hinge.

Maria steered towards the cabin, the path smooth through the grass, and stopped in front of the doors.

"Can you open it?"

Amanda hopped out and in the beam of the headlights pulled at the door. Dirt had accumulated at its base and she struggled against it, kicking at the hardened earth that blocked the edge.

She pulled again and got nowhere, her gaze moving back to the sky as she anticipated the buzz of a drone.

Storm was out of the truck, unsteady on her feet as she came towards her. She had her hood up, her hands tucked in the pockets of her oilskin, an apparition arriving out of the gloom.

"You okay?" asked Amanda.

Storm picked a fallen board out of the grass and used the end to scrape away the earth. Within moments they were pulling open the door, and Storm helped her lift so it scraped along the ground.

It was a sweet relief when Maria pulled the truck into the barn and parked between a corroded tractor and an unidentifiable piece of rusted equipment half-buried by the collapsed roof. Maria turned off the engine and the silence that followed was like a blanket around them, even as they all strained to hear disturbances in the quiet.

Maria dragged the door closed, and Amanda peered through a crack between the weathered boards. The sticks and moss on the cabin roof were coming into detail in the growing light, the decay and abandonment of the place a comfort.

Storm flipped over a dented bucket and sat heavily on it. She pushed back her hood.

"What was that about?"

Maria had the truck cab open and loaded a pack with the food Amanda had bought at a charge station a few hours back. Her fatigue showed in a loss of precision, several of the energy bars falling into the dirt on the bowed wood floor.

"Maria thought someone was following us."

"Who was it?"

Maria bent to pick up one of the bars. She seemed stiff, almost drunk with fatigue.

"I couldn't see in the dark." Maria jammed a water bottle into the top of the bag. "We're not far from the trail head." She placed the full pack on the ground and used her sleeve to wipe down the inside of the truck.

Storm walked unsteadily to the bed of the truck, the toll of riding in the back in each step. She started wiping.

"They'll still be able to find our DNA," said Storm.

"By the time they figure it out, we'll be long gone."

"We could just burn it," said Amanda.

"No!" said Maria and Storm together, and Amanda grinned. A fire would be too much of a beacon, but she still liked the reaction.

She moved to the passenger's side and wiped surfaces with a crusted old rag she found in the hay. Before she closed the door, she slipped her cigarettes into her pocket.

Storm and Maria stood just inside the barn door, light showing through the gaps in the boards. A row of cracked and twisted leads or reins hung on the wall, though there was little else to show that animals had ever been there. The barn smelled of rotting hay and the faintest trace of diesel.

"There's an extension of the coastal trail that reaches this far north," said Maria, as she cracked open the door. Amanda stepped close behind her and looked out over top of her head. There were tracks in the grass where they had driven the truck, but otherwise the clearing was as they had found it. A door was missing on the back of the cabin, one of the windowpanes had broken, and something had built a nest in the chimney.

A bird called, and after a pause there was a response in the distance. Amanda felt Maria's body go rigid.

"Was that a signal?" Storm whispered.

It sounded again, a high, shrill call, and the line of Maria's shoulders eased.

"That's one hell of an imitation," said Amanda.

"It's a bird," said Maria.

She eased open the door further, in time to see the flash of chrome through the trees.

Amanda stumbled as Maria stepped into her and shut the door. She held onto Maria's back so she wouldn't fall. By the time she righted herself and looked through one of the cracks, the chrome had turned into a bumper on a white truck. Whoever was driving was taking their time navigating the potted drive.

Maria pushed Amanda back and shoved the pack into her hands.

"You and Storm go out the back. I'll slow them down."

She already had her gun in her hand and was checking the bullets.

"Three has to be better than one," said Amanda.

The brown of Maria's eyes was like flint, all focus and action.

"We talked about this."

"But—"

"There are no buts." Maria gave the briefest of squeezes on Amanda's arm before she pushed her away.

The whine of the electric engine had stopped outside the door. They had wasted whatever lead they had. Storm still pressed her eye to a crack in the wall.

"It's the Ministry."

"What?" said Amanda, but Storm held a finger to her lips as they heard the sound of the vehicle's door opening and shutting.

Maria pushed Amanda again and tried to pull Storm away from the wall.

Amanda laid her hand on Maria, pressed hard enough for it to get her attention. She pointed at herself and then towards the closed door.

Maria shook her head vehemently but before she could do anything, Amanda slipped outside.

She squinted in the brightness, pulling the door shut behind her even as a young man who had been examining their tracks jumped back. He was clean-cut with pressed jeans and his neatly ironed shirt carried the logo of the Ministry. She swore under her breath at the sight of the pistol on his belt.

"Good morning," she said.

He frowned, looking suspiciously between her and the barn.

"I know you have the diesel in there. I can smell it from here."

"It's nice to meet you too."

She took her cigarettes out of her pocket and took her time lighting one. It was a magnificent clearing, bordered by towering trees and in the distance the burble of water.

"You shouldn't smoke here. You could start a fire."

The grass was soaked from the rain overnight, and most of the trees still gleamed with moisture. It would take an effort to start a fire here, not that she wasn't up for it.

"I'm going to need to see your vehicle," he said.

"I don't think so."

Every bit of her wanted to scream for Storm and Maria to run. He was too competent, too measured in the way he watched her.

"It's a federal offense to be in possession of a vehicle that operates on fossil fuels."

"I have a permit."

"Do you?"

This plan didn't seem so smart anymore. The isolation of the clearing was more threatening now than magnificent.

"Stand aside."

She blew smoke in his direction and picked a piece of tobacco off her teeth as fear spread down her back.

"How about you get in your truck and leave, and I'll save you a lot of trouble."

He wasn't looking at her anymore, focused instead on the barn.

"Is anyone else with you?"

He was within arm's reach and she hadn't been aware of him moving. She backed in front of the doors, blocked the place where they would open.

"I prefer to break my laws solo."

One corner of his mouth turned up, and her breathing narrowed.

She dropped the cigarette into the grass and crushed it with her toe, trying to use the movement to step away, but the door blocked her retreat.

"Bullshit. I saw her at the charge station."

Amanda had been in and out in five minutes. They had been careful with the face recognition, but of course people recognized faces too.

"You're too late," she said, relieved even as fear for herself rose. "She's already gone."

His attention flicked from the opening to the loft above the door.

"I doubt that."

His chest was muscular beneath his shirt, his movements sharper now, and with considerable strength. Maria would have seen the signs, recognized him for what he was.

"Hands above your head," he said and patted her down. She didn't fight, knew that she would lose that battle. His face was blank when he removed the Glock and placed it in his holster. He threw her cigarettes on the ground.

"She's not coming back."

She should have let Maria handle it. First the fire, now this.

"She can't have gone far."

She clenched her fists to stop them from shaking.

He checked his watch and she saw his impatience.

"Mind if I take a look?" he said.

The sky had brightened to a rich blue, the rumble of the stream so idyllic it was ridiculous.

"Do I have a choice?"

She opened the door carefully, fumbling with it to give herself time to think.

The reek of rotting hay overflowed from the interior. The pickup ticked quietly and looked entirely at home next to the rusted tractor and the half-buried equipment. The collapsed boards were gray with age, the splinters where the ends had sheared from the roof smooth and round.

She stepped aside as he tapped on the side of Storm's shielded box, taking several long moments to examine the copper inlay and the care with which the box had been bolted to the frame.

When he had it fully open and pressed his hand onto the mattress, his head jerked upright.

It had still been warm, the foam Amanda had so carefully selected retaining the heat of Storm's body.

"Don't move."

He had his pistol drawn, and yanked open the cab door, every movement and gesture controlled and powerful.

"So — not from the Ministry."

"Quiet."

He was coming around the truck, moving towards the back of the barn, when he stopped, his mouth opening in shock before he remembered himself. He stared behind her and Amanda's heart fell.

Maria couldn't be this stupid, saving Amanda from another rash move. But when she turned, it was Storm who stood at the entrance to the back room. Her oilskin was open, her red hair brilliant against the gray of the barn, her gaze as focused and composed as his.

There was a grunt and a thud, and Amanda whirled back to see two bodies hit the concrete. There was a brief tussle and Maria was on top of him, tossing the Glock to Amanda as she pointed his revolver in his face.

"Get up."

His face was flushed red, his lips pressed tight together.

"I knew it was you."

The loathing in his voice was clear.

"Congratulations," said Maria. "Storm, grab me the reins." Storm reached for the reins hanging on the wall and returned with a mittful of cracked leather.

Maria bound his hands quickly, and his feet. He didn't resist. Which was too bad because Amanda thought she would shoot this time if she needed.

"You know Stanton will find you," he said. "It's only a matter of time."

"Good," said Maria, as she pulled one of the reins tight enough that he winced. "Because time is all we need."

"He couldn't send a signal," said Amanda. "There's no service."

"I would have felt it," said Storm.

"You were that close?"

"Open the tailgate," said Maria. "Amanda, take his feet."

He struggled as they tried to lift him, kicking out with his feet so that Amanda dropped his legs. Maria dug her thumb into a pressure point on his neck and he stiffened in pain.

Storm had the shielded box open. A dent showed in the mattress, the white painted walls showing scuff marks from Storm's boots. It seemed too nice for him; the place had been designed for Storm. They loaded him in.

"You won't get away," he said.

Maria undid his watch and handed it to Amanda.

There was a warning sign on the screen saying a message had failed to send.

"It's not military."

He didn't say anything, only kicked at the box, the plywood giving a crack on impact.

"Should we tie him up more securely?" asked Storm. She was watching him curiously, always the scientist, everything a specimen.

"Do we know who he is?" asked Amanda.

"We know enough," said Maria.

She patted him down and drew out a knife strapped to his leg, a tablet from his back pocket, and a wallet. She piled them on the tailgate.

"You know what they do to traitors?" he asked before he spit on Maria's coat.

Amanda froze, waiting to see what Maria would do. There was a time when the backlash would have been violent, and vicious.

Maria gave a strange half-smile, as she picked the crusty rag off the ground. She used it to wipe away the spit and then shoved it into his mouth.

He looked less certain with the rag in his mouth, fear beginning to work its way through the hate.

Amanda picked up the tablet, and her sadness fled.

A 'message sent' window showed at the center of the screen.

She must have gasped because Storm and Maria crowded around her.

"Can you see what it says?"

Amanda tapped the icon.

Maria Kowalski sighted at 3:23 a.m. at Terrace Charge Station. Currently in pursuit on Highway 16 going south. Advise.

The number it had been sent to could have been any cell phone in the province.

"Military?" asked Storm.

Amanda flipped the tablet over and pulled out the battery. She did the same with the watch.

"Put them inside your coat."

Amanda had sewn copper shielding into Storm's oilskin to prevent signals from getting through.

Storm slid both into a deep inside pocket as Maria used his knife to slash the tires.

"What about—" asked Storm, nodding to where he squirmed inside the box. The skin on his wrists was already red where he strained against the leather.

Amanda flipped up the side of the box, so they no longer saw him.

"They'll find him soon enough," said Maria.

"How much time do we have?" asked Storm.

They were already moving, Maria leading, checking the clearing before they crossed the open space. Storm followed as she did up her coat, and Amanda came at the end, the pack over her shoulder.

"It depends on who's at the other end of that number."

Instead of going south towards the trail head, Maria turned north and skirted around the cabin. The peacefulness of the clearing was suddenly so much more fragile. In the distance, above the pound of their running feet, was the rush of water over stones.

SIX

ADAMS

DAMS SAT BESIDE MEGAN on the warped, wooden floor, the pieces of a small Gatherer laid out before them. The rest of the room was bare but for a rickety single bed in the corner and a chipped bedside table. Megan had removed the shell of the Gatherer and taken apart the outer connections, including the bundle of wires that ran out the bottom of the concave dish. She worked methodically and without words, ministering to the device that had killed her mother with the delicate cuts of a surgeon.

"How much do you need to take?"

Adams had asked her several questions since she started, his words registering no more than the dozens of other questions he and Hamel had asked her since they had left the old hospital. She had been strangely silent after advocating for herself, as if it had been her final outlay before grief overtook her. The Gatherer they had stolen from the side of a boarded-up business had been the first thing to raise her from her resolute silence, a flicker of the life he had seen in her eyes sparking when he had placed the device in front of her.

She sat back on her heels, her hands resting on the outer rim of the dish.

"Can we use the whole crystal structure for the hub?" Adams asked.

He had little understanding of how the Gatherer worked, beyond its simple operation of drawing energy from the air through a crystal lattice.

Megan shook her head and leaned forward, her hands moving over the crystals the way they had over the wires in the web at the hospital.

"I need something to break it with." Her face was above the lattice.

"Are you sure?"

She tilted her head towards the dish and closed her eyes.

After several minutes, Adams got up and left the room. He tried to stay in the back room as much as possible, to reassure her in some way, but most of the time she barely registered he was there, her focus on the small crystals.

He paused at the window. Their cottage was one of a dozen on the edge of a small, swampy lake, the others empty this early in the season. A weathered boat house was attached to a dock that extended into the lake, where small white caps were already forming at the center, where the wind was strongest.

"You'll want to see this."

Hamel sat at the small laminate table, his laptop hooked to the VHF/UHF radio and modem. He had been on there all morning, unsuccessfully trying to get a view into the Gatherer Corporation's compound and to pinpoint Stanton's exact location. He tilted the screen for Adams to see.

The video of a newscast came up on the display, an anchorwoman leading the broadcast. "Breaking News" read across the top, followed by "Storm Freeman reported alive and well." His pulse ratcheted up as he pulled the laptop closer. There had been earlier news reports, interviews with Stanton on Storm's mental breakdown and the care she had been receiving. He had thought Stanton still had her at the compound and that Maria's rescue attempt had failed.

"—appears that Storm Freeman, the original inventor of the Gatherer who had reportedly been having mental health issues, has returned to the world."

A video of a half-burned barn showed on the screen, the melted husk of what must have once been a Gatherer inside.

"—a large model version of the Gatherer was destroyed at a health resort located in north-western British Columbia. The resort's owner, Gwyneth Sween, claims Storm Freeman and her accomplice, former Special Agent Maria Kowalski, started a fire in the barn that held the newest version of the device. The resort was full at the time and had been preparing for a special celebration the following night."

They were alive. He searched the video for the slightest image of them, anything to confirm they had really been there.

The image switched to the round, chubby face of a woman with bright spots of indignation on her cheeks.

"We are grateful that none of our members were hurt. Storm Freeman has destroyed the heart of our community and her actions have put the health of everyone at risk."

The woman seemed about to say more when the view switched back to the anchorwoman.

"Ms. Sween claims to have seen Ms. Freeman, yet there is little proof that the infamous inventor actually visited the remote retreat."

Stanton's smug face filled the screen and Adams tasted the bitterness that came with his rage. There was the same white hair swept back from the high forehead and his remorseless eyes stared into the camera. He looked leaner, his wide cheekbones more prominent, and the sagging skin on his neck showing signs of age. Adams felt a rush of vindication, that even Stanton couldn't escape the passage of time.

"This supposed sighting is a hoax and undermines the progress that Ms. Freeman has made towards recovery. It is shameful that this group believes it can use Ms. Freeman's name to further their own ends."

"How is Ms. Freeman doing?" The anchorwoman oozed earnestness and concern, asking the question everyone wanted to know.

Stanton took a moment before responding, his act one of gravity and regret.

"She continues to improve though it will be a long road back. The pressure of inventing the Gatherer and bringing it to the world, and the challenges that she has had, were too much for her. We need to be careful with her recovery and blatantly false incidents like this only extend the time it will be before it is safe for her to return to public life."

The view switched back to the anchorwoman.

"Storm's mother, Alicia Freeman, who hasn't been seen publicly for several months, but reportedly still runs the Gatherer corporation, issued a press release saying that her priority is for Storm to have the time and space she needs to recover and asks that everyone respect her privacy.

"In other news, the headquarters of a rebel group that called themselves the Diesel Train was raided this morning. An entire warehouse of the banned diesel fuel has been confiscated—"

Adams stopped the video. Clicked back so he could see the footage again.

"I don't see how they believe her. There's nothing showing her there," said Hamel.

He opened another news report highlighting Freeman's re-emergence. The same location, same footage, except this one went longer and panned over a large crowd of what could only be the afflicted, in matching white tunics.

"What the hell is that?"

"It's the Wellness Retreat. Their website says it's 'where people can restore and rejuvenate'."

He watched the footage again. He had served under Stanton, taken orders. Listening to him had been like sitting in his office again waiting to be betrayed. He stood, banged out the screen door and inhaled the cool air. Hamel followed, quiet at his side.

"It could have simply been a chance to be in the limelight," said Hamel.

"But if they were seen, it means Storm got out. And Maria."

The hope was exquisite, an energy flowing through him that he hadn't felt since he had watched the door closing behind Maria and Storm in the compound. He had thought he was on his own, that a cure with Megan might be the only solution he could act on until he found a chink in Stanton's armor.

"So where have they been?"

He tried not to put too much stock in it because he didn't know if he could handle it being false.

The white caps pushed faster over the lake, crashing against the foundation of the boathouse and dock.

Yet there had been something about the woman's face, the reverence he had seen in others who criticized Storm even as they treated her like a God.

If they were alive, and free, it changed everything. He could sense the realization in Hamel as well, an energy that mirrored his. The cabin suddenly seemed too remote, too far from where they needed to be.

"We need to find them."

He followed Hamel inside and within moments had a satellite map of the province up on the laptop. A red dot showed the location of the wellness retreat, far up the coast, north of Rima. Maria would be as far from there as possible by now. Wanting to be out of the public eye. Then why set the fire?

He felt Megan's presence before he saw her. A confused sadness that floated into the room. She stood at the bedroom door, her mess of curls seeming too big for her small shoulders.

"Are you okay?"

She had blood on her fingers, as if she had been clawing at the crystals. He had forgotten she wanted something to break them with.

Both he and Hamel made to go to her, but she was already moving towards them.

"Is that where Storm is?"

She was so thin, a smudge of blood on her jeans.

They turned to all face the laptop; the tiny red dot lost amid an endless expanse of green. Megan moved closer, leaned in to see the details of the terrain around the dot.

"Can we go there?"

SEVEN

MARIA

MARIA BROKE FROM THE trail, the carpet of pine needles soft and quiet beneath her feet, the tall cedars towering overhead. She longed to lie down and sleep, but they were too close to the trail and the dusk was not full enough yet to provide cover.

"You okay?" Maria asked Storm as she held back a branch to stop it from snapping into her face.

Storm nodded as she passed under, though it was automatic after months of Maria's inquiries.

"There's a brighter spot through the trees." Maria pointed in a direct line away from the trail. "Head for that."

She held the branch as Amanda passed, a half-dozen steps behind.

"Did you see anything?" asked Maria.

Amanda had pulled her hair back in a ponytail, the line of her cheeks sharp in the dim light.

"Birds and small animals, and the occasional crash of waves. I don't think there's anyone here but us."

Maria scanned the sea of ferns and the thick trunks. There was only the nagging quiet that had trailed them all day. She was grateful for it, but it didn't make sense. The entire trail should have been swarming with troops. From the moment they had left the barn she had expected to be found.

She held her breath and listened deeper, and succeeded only in hearing the wash of waves and the creak of two trees as they rubbed together.

Storm and Amanda's outlines were weaving their way towards the patch of brightness. She checked the trail to the north and south before following, unable to trust its quiet emptiness.

The brightness, as she had hoped, came from an open area of rock. It overlooked the ocean where the sun was just touching the horizon, the bleed of orange blurring the line between water and sky.

Amanda dropped onto a rounded boulder and Storm already sat against the base of a tree, unscrewing the lid on the water bottle.

"We can stay here tonight," said Maria. The sound of waves rose up the cliff, though it was more of a steep hill, the shrubs and trees dense along its side.

Storm took a long slow drink and handed the bottle to Amanda. They looked worn and ragged, and she marveled at their audacity. That they believed they could face down Stanton and the Gatherer, and win.

"Do you think they found him?" asked Storm.

Amanda lighted a cigarette, the burnt smell of smoke a dry breath in the dampness.

"Probably."

Maria lowered the pack to the ground and handed each of them a slightly compressed sandwich from the top.

"Then why aren't they here?"

Maria unwrapped her sandwich, her hunger rising fast at the smell of tuna. The first bite was heaven and she tried not to inhale the whole thing.

"I don't know."

"Maybe we don't matter anymore," said Storm, examining her sandwich suspiciously.

"You saw how Gwyneth reacted," said Maria.

Storm nodded as she chewed.

"She had a beautiful dog."

"That's what you remember about her?" said Amanda, flicking ashes. The embers bounced on the rock before flaring out.

"What? I like dogs."

"She wanted you to preside over whatever ceremony she was having," said Maria. "I don't think you've been forgotten."

"Nor you."

Maria licked a bit of butter from her finger. The hate in the man at the barn had been fanatical. She still felt the shock of it. There would be others, military and otherwise, who didn't understand what she was trying to do.

"Which still leaves the question of why we've been allowed to enjoy this walk through the woods," said Amanda. Her sandwich lay on her knee, untouched.

Fatigue was crowding into Maria's thoughts, the warmth of the food spreading through her like a drug.

"They might already know where we are," said Storm.

The sky was a deep blue, the chill of night riding on the evening air. They could be watching from a distance, yet her gut said they weren't. It was only them, the trees, and the ocean. Maria stretched open her eyes to shake off the heaviness and clear the dullness from her thoughts.

"And waiting to see what we're going to do?" said Amanda.

"It's possible."

Amanda lifted her arm and waved her hand as if beckoning people towards them.

"Come on, don't be shy! Join us. There's lots of room."

"Don't do that," said Maria. "There is still a chance they haven't found us."

Amanda paced to the side of the clearing.

"I hate the feeling that they're watching." She glared at the rocks below and the forest behind them. "I'd rather just get it over with."

"Be careful what you wish for."

Maria accepted the water bottle from Storm and took a long pull. There had been a time when people had shunned contact with the afflicted, when they still believed it could be spread through touch.

"We need to move faster," said Maria. "At this pace Storm will be compromised or we'll be fully seen before we get anywhere close to Rima."

"Vehicles are out," said Storm. The city would be flush with everything electric, cars, buses, scooters. There would be no safe transport.

"They'll be watching for any thefts."

Maria looked pointedly at Amanda.

"Why do you always think the worst of me?" Amanda held her arms wide in exasperation.

"When do you ever prove me wrong?"

Storm smiled smugly, the same way she did every time the two of them argued, as if she were enjoying it.

"Fine," said Amanda. "I won't steal any cars."

"Or boats."

Amanda pulled the elastic out of her hair and shook it free.

"So what are we going to do? Run?"

Maria rubbed the back of her neck, closing her eyes for a moments rest. The loss of the pickup had been a blow; their plan was already compromised.

"We'll figure something out," said Maria. The sun sunk further, the orange spreading into yellow across the horizon, and the blue of the sky above them darker. "I'll take the first watch."

Maria lifted her head when Amanda let out a bark of laughter. Storm's grin was wide.

"You're kidding, right?" said Amanda.

She was beautiful standing there, her hair a mess and her clothes scuffed with dirt. And annoying as hell when she challenged Maria at every step.

"I have more experience."

"When was the last time you slept?"

Maria tried to remember to before the barn, the commune, to sometime at the hunt cabin.

"I'm trained for this."

"And I'm trained to know when you're being an idiot."

Storm stifled a laugh.

"Fine. I'm not going to fight you on this."

"Good. And then I'll wake Storm up."

"I should do the middle watch," said Maria.

"That's fine," said Storm, standing and brushing off the seat of her pants. "I'm happy for the extra sleep."

Amanda had opened her mouth to respond but closed it when she and Storm exchanged a look. Maria bristled. What she wouldn't do for subordinates who listened and didn't question an order.

"Make sure you wake me."

"We will," said Amanda, far too pleasantly.

"At midnight."

"Yep."

Frustrated, but too tired to fight, Maria lay down where she was, using the pack as a pillow. She wondered whether the bright spot on the horizon was a star or a planet before she fell into a deep obliviating sleep.

She woke with a start hours later, damp with cold, and her body aching. The sky was as she had last seen it, the glow now coming from the east, instead of west. She sat up.

Her head was groggy, the clearing taking a moment to slide into place.

Storm sat with her back against the tree, her knees bent in front of her and her hands deep in her pockets.

"Morning."

"You didn't—" Maria's voice was a croak and she had to clear her throat before she could finish. "—wake me."

Storm stretched her legs and flexed her feet. Her nose was pink on the end and her skin pale.

"Didn't need to."

"Where's Amanda?"

A low fog covered the ocean, wisps of it floating past their heads.

"She'll be back."

"Where did she go?"

Maria could see very little through the density of trees back towards the path, the other directions ending in open air where the slope dropped away to the water.

"Let's go to the water," said Storm, standing, a towel already in her hand. She moved stiffly, Maria not the only one feeling the cold. "I found a way down over here."

There had been no one keeping watch, yet they still hadn't been found.

"Was there any trouble?" Maria asked as she stood, still feeling disoriented.

The ground sloped steeply down at the edge of the clearing, disappearing into the fog. The new shoots of grass were already bent from where Storm had previously passed.

"We would have woken you if there was."

Storm walked carefully, one hand on the upward slope, traversing the terrain at an angle. At a thick patch of shrubs she turned back, continuing down on an opposite track, the first of what would be many switchbacks if she meant to reach the water.

"You're going in?"

Storm navigated around a fallen log.

"I thought it would help. Before we get to the city."

Maria shook her head, trying to clear the fog that was as thick as that around them. "Are you sure it's safe?"

Storm's response was to keep going, slowly and carefully, every step taking her closer to the fog.

With a look at the trees, and confusion over where the hell Amanda had gone, Maria followed. The slope eased as the fog grew thicker and the walking came easier as larger trees were able to perch on the hill. Maria repeatedly looked back up to the clearing but it soon became veiled in fog, its exact point hard to discern.

"Where did Amanda go?"

"I told her where we'd be."

"That doesn't answer the question."

They stood above a short stretch of sand, the waves washing quietly against it.

"It's a surprise."

"I hate surprises."

Their visibility was limited to the short stretch of sand. Sounds barely penetrated the fog and they stood in a strange, eerie quiet.

"You were here already?"

Storm picked her way down the final few steps and jumped onto the sand, landing with two feet.

"I thought I should wait for you before I went in."

Storm untied her boots.

"That's something at least."

Storm pulled off her stocks and shoved them into the top of her boots, her toes bony and white on the sand.

"They should have found us," said Maria.

The sand gave beneath her feet as she stepped onto the beach, the ground not as firm as it appeared.

"It could be the fog." Storm gestured to the wall of white where the ocean should be. "Or that message never sent."

"You said you didn't feel it."

"Maybe he sent it before he got to us."

Maria pulled her coat closer around her as Storm folded her oil-skin and placed it on top of her boots. The fog clung to Maria's skin, making the air colder than it was.

"Someone would have followed up."

He'd known Stanton, and had despised her in a way reserved for those who had served.

"Should we tell someone? That he's there?" said Storm, peeling off her jeans as if it were the most natural thing in the world. Goosebumps showed on her legs.

"They would trace it."

Storm pulled her shirt over her head and Maria bent to untie her hiking boots.

"I still think we should tell someone."

"We can't risk it."

She placed her boots next to Storm's pile of clothes.

Storm paused, thin and exposed in her pale peach bra and underwear, a ghost in the fog. She was frowning and looking as if there was something she wanted to say.

"You're right. I just hate to think of him still there."

Even after everything they had done to her.

Storm added her bra and underwear to the pile and walked unflinching into the water. Maria barely noticed her nakedness after the countless immersions over the winter.

The vertebrae on Storm's spine stood out less than when they had first arrived at the cabin, and a small bit of roundness had added to her hips. Maria rolled her pants to above the knee.

Storm had already laid down in the shallows when Maria reached her. She had her eyes closed and the short strands of her red hair floated in the rhythm of the waves.

Needles of cold drove into Maria's feet. She waited, the fog beginning to shift and thin, as Storm's lips slowly turned blue.

A strand of seaweed tangled in her feet, and Maria pulled it off, tossing it back out to sea. A fleeting shape appeared on the slope above, only to disappear into the fog. Her heart rate spiked until the shape appeared again, resolving into Amanda making her way down the incline. There was a loosening inside her, of a worry that never truly went away.

Maria placed her hand behind Storm's shoulders and lifted her to sitting. Her lips were blue and her skin translucent. It was an insane practice, if it hadn't been for Storm's slow, steady progress to recovery. Maria threaded her arms beneath Storm's knees and lifted her out of the water. Storm had started to shiver by the time she set her down on the sand. There had been times when they had misjudged the time and Storm hadn't shivered, instead sliding into hypothermia.

Amanda arrived as Maria helped Storm dress.

"Where were you?"

Amanda picked up Storm's oilskin and helped thread Storm's arms into the sleeves while Maria tied her boots. The smell of cigarettes and excitement radiated off her. She pushed Storm's hair from her forehead and used the towel to dry it off.

"You said you wouldn't steal anything," said Maria.

They helped Storm to her feet.

"I didn't."

Amanda supported Storm as they crossed the beach, while Maria put on her socks and boots. When she caught up to them, Storm had let go of Amanda's arm and was making her way up the slope. It would be slow going at first, until the blood returned to Storm's limbs.

"Then where were you?"

"Be patient. All will be revealed."

"I'm not patient."

"I know."

The fog was breaking with flashes of the ocean appearing in the whiteness. Halfway up, they rose out of it and climbed the final distance in the first warmth of the rising sun.

Storm arrived at the clearing first, followed by Amanda. By the time Maria stood before them, Amanda had her arms stretched out, beaming as she presented a pile of metal and spokes on the ground.

"Bikes?" asked Maria.

They were small, more like trick bikes, with low seats and high handlebars.

"They're perfect," said Storm. She was circling the pile, cheeks flushed and fully re-invigorated after the climb. She lifted the top one and set it upright. The seat barely came up to her mid-thigh.

"They're for racing," said Maria.

Storm got on her bike. "It's a great idea. I don't know why I didn't think of a bike sooner."

Amanda beamed and lifted the second bike off the ground.

"Where did you get them?"

Amanda flipped up her hood as she sat on it, her hand resting on the high handlebars.

"You look like you're ten years old," laughed Storm.

"Even better," said Amanda, taking a few experimental loops around the clearing. "I figured they'd be good on the trail and when we got to the city."

It was a faster way to travel. With any luck they could be at Amanda's by nightfall.

"We'll still need to be careful," said Maria. "Keep our hoods up and try to look like young kids."

Storm flipped up her hood and followed Amanda in doing laps.

"You should save your strength," said Maria, though she felt lighter watching them circle happily. It was a brief glimpse of what their lives could be like if this burden ever lifted.

* * * *

They reached the outskirts of Rima in late morning, the single-track growing wider and more compacted the closer they approached. They pedaled down the quieter residential streets, the first small Gatherers appearing tucked beside garages or next to a shed. Seeing them brought a rush of anxiety, that they would still be here, drawing energy from the world and their owners. She wondered how many afflicted hid within the houses, unwilling to give up the wonder of the small devices.

Storm fixated on a larger version that looked newer and brighter than the others, so focused that she drifted towards the side of the road. She corrected in time but when she looked back again, she swerved into the curb and crash-landed on the grass.

Maria and Amanda braked hard, and Maria was about to get off her bike to help, when Amanda stopped her.

"You're a ten-year-old boy, remember?"

Maria exhaled and breathed against the spike of adrenaline, as Storm slowly stood and righted her bike. She looked paler inside her hood, her gaze darting back to the large device that stood in front of a three-storey modern home. Rows of windows provided a reflective backdrop.

"That's one of the ones from the test facility." Storm's hands shook when she reached for the handlebars.

"We can't pay too much attention," said Amanda. "This won't be new for them."

Maria snatched a glance at the smooth whiteness of the device and the upward hands of the Gatherer logo. It looked serene and benign, exactly the way it had been designed.

"It doesn't make sense that it's here," said Storm, a dangerous pitch to her voice.

Maria steered her bike close to her.

"That's not what we're here for."

"But those people—"

"We knew there would be more of them," said Amanda, coasting to Storm's other side.

"But those are—"

"Yes," said Maria. "Now get on your bike."

Storm whirled, ready to unleash her shock and anger. Maria held her gaze, waited as her emotions distorted her features, until she finally sagged. Maria had seen the process countless times, Storm taking on the responsibility of the Gatherer even when it had been a long time since she had been in control.

Storm climbed slowly onto her bike, and Maria and Amanda watched, unable to do anything except stay by her side.

"You go ahead," said Amanda, a gentleness in her voice she rarely let show. "We'll follow behind."

They passed hundreds of Gatherers on their ride through the city. Most were small, but occasionally they saw one of the larger versions, many of them with a ring of white grass or foliage around them. Few people were on the streets, the city strangely quiet, and there were still no signs of being followed. It made her nervous and agitated, every new cross street and opportunity for an ambush.

"Do you see that?" said Amanda to Maria when they passed by a park with a large Gatherer next to a row of vehicle chargers. There was a white band around the bottom edge and even the base of a nearby tree had lost its color.

"It's on all the big ones," said Maria.

Storm rode ahead and had noticed less and less the further they got into the city. At one point she swerved hard away from an electric vehicle, only to be forced back again by a Gatherer installed on the sidewalk. As the buildings became closer together and streets narrowed, more Gatherers showed on roofs and in alleyways, almost every flat surface put into service for the energy-gathering devices. The news had reported on the growing number of Gatherers being used in the cities, but Maria hadn't truly appreciated the scope.

"Are you okay?" she asked Storm when they stopped at a light. Her hood was pulled so far forward Maria couldn't see her face, but the bend of her shoulders and her strained movements spoke to her suffering. There was an almost imperceptible nod within the hood.

Storm's knuckles were white where she gripped the handlebar and she half stood to get enough force on her pedal to start forward when the light changed.

"We're almost there," said Amanda.

They took a roundabout route through a rougher section of town. Kids played on one of the streets, their calls and chatter an island of life amid the deadened silence. On the detour around them, they saw few Gatherers, with only the occasional flash of a small, older model in some of the back yards.

When they finally reached the park near Amanda's house, Amanda led them to an underused corner, sheltered by a sparse cluster of oak trees. Empty swings hung from the play equipment across the open field.

"This is a dead spot," said Amanda. "You're safe."

Storm dropped her bike in the grass and collapsed against a low brick wall. She sat with her knees bent and her face resting in her hands.

Maria placed her bike next to hers and opened the backpack. She handed Storm the water bottle and a granola bar.

Amanda had stayed on her bike.

"I'll be back in a couple of hours."

"They could be watching the house," said Maria.

"There haven't been any breaches to the security. I would know if anyone had been there."

Storm ate a piece of the bar slowly, focused on her task.

"And you'll get out right away?"

Amanda nodded. "Of course."

A long-discarded plastic water bottle was half buried at Maria's feet, beside a crumpled blanket she had been careful not to touch. She chewed a few pieces of beef jerky that didn't sit well in her stomach. She spit them out.

"We decided this before we left the cabin," said Storm, sounding tired as she scraped the last crumbs out of the wrapper. "We knew we would have to take this risk."

"We hadn't been seen when we were at the cabin."

"They wouldn't have expected us to come to Rima," said Amanda. "And we aren't going to have access to that kind of connectivity any-place else."

Amanda prided herself on the servers she had set up in her dining room and the bank of monitors that allowed her to view to the entire network of surveillance throughout Rima. They hoped her computing power would give them access back into the Gatherer Corporation's system.

Maria snapped a twig into tiny bits, letting the pieces fall back to the ground. She looked back towards the street, where the streetlights had just begun to come on.

"Can you feel the fields?" she asked Storm.

Storm crumpled up the wrapper as she shook her head.

"I'm fine here." The nearest house was on the far side of the park beside the parking lot with the few remaining vehicles. "But the sooner I can get to Amanda's and below ground, the better."

Amanda rocked the bike back and forth, hitting the crossbar against her legs.

"Can you get there without being seen?" asked Maria.

The freedom of the bike ride had invigorated Amanda; her restless energy having grown the farther they traveled into the city.

"I've gotten us this far."

"We don't know who might be watching," said Maria. "I should go."

Amanda waved her hand in dismissal. "They can watch all they want. It'll be dark. If I see anyone at all, I'll hike it. And you'll be able to check in on my tablet." Maria recognized the cockiness that went with the energy, felt the tremor of warning that came with it. "I'll be fine. This isn't my first rodeo."

"It's your first time at *this* rodeo."

The empty swings swung in the faint breeze, her view across the close-cut grass clear. Maria still didn't believe that whoever that man had contacted hadn't caught up to them. Stanton could be waiting for the right moment, and Amanda's house could be that moment.

She shook her head to stop the circling thoughts. Already her heart rate was elevated, and would stay that way until Amanda returned.

"You promise you'll be careful?"

Storm rose from the ground and came to join their small circle. She seemed steadier, if weak.

"The warehouse is in the center of the dark zone," said Storm. "It'll be the only one with people in it."

"With windows along the roof," said Amanda.

"Right."

If Amanda didn't return before dawn, Maria and Storm would wait for her in the dark zone, a relatively safe place for Storm to wait — provided they weren't seen.

"What if someone follows you?" asked Maria.

"I'll lose them."

"You might not know they're there."

"Or maybe I will."

The first cricket of the night chirped.

"Promise me you'll check it out before you go in."

Amanda drew the Glock from her pocket and turned it over.

"Let me see that."

The metal was cold when Amanda dropped the pistol into Maria's palm. She checked it was loaded. She wanted them to remain together; every division added more risk.

She handed it back and Amanda slid the pistol into her pocket before lifting her pedal, the hood and growing darkness not hiding her excitement. Maria's stomach clenched.

"Do you have the extra magazine?"

Amanda patted her pocket. Maria didn't even want to imagine the situation where she would need it. Amanda pushed back her hood, shook out her mane of hair before she pushed down to start forward.

"Turn on your tablet as soon as you're out of range."

Sticks cracked under the tires and with a final wave Amanda was bumping across the grass, the glint of the streetlight on the handlebars the final thing Maria saw before she turned the corner.

The silence of the park settled around them, only the crickets breaking through the night.

"She'll be fine," said Storm.

"She doesn't understand what she's up against."

She should run after her. Call for her to come back.

"Yes, she does." Storm sat against the wall, and pulled her coat around her, unidentifiable even up close.

EIGHT

ADAMS

Adams gripped Megan's hand, veering out of the way of a young reveler in camo pants and a tie-dye headband who was running at full speed. The dirt drive was filled with civilians, darting in and out between chaotically parked cars and small groups sitting cross-legged drinking cans of beer or sharing a vape. Music blared from the open door of one of the vehicles.

It seemed no one else had taken Stanton at his word that Storm hadn't been there, and several hundred people jostled against the wood barrier that had been placed across the drive to the Wellness Retreat. A young woman, so stoned she had to lean against a tree to stay upright, held a sign reading, *The World Needs More Storm*.

He drew Megan to the side and led her between two vehicles so that they followed a path of smashed ferns and grass along the edge of the driveway, away from the main line of movement. He hoped Megan at his side would make him out to be an odd suburban dad coming to gawk with all the others. He eased his shoulders, slouched, and let his abdominal muscles relax.

They stopped within view of the barricades, the ground uneven beneath their feet. Megan stood close to him, her blue eyes taking it all in.

Several of the afflicted he had seen on the video stood behind the wood barricades, each with an aged Winchester rifle across their chests. It was like watching an army of the living dead, something you expected to see in a movie rather than in real life.

The house lay a hundred meters from the blockade, the charred remnants of a barn further behind it, amid a sea of tents. The news report had listed it as a retreat, yet the stick-like guards and the charred half-walls of what was left of the barn made it feel more like a place of death than life.

The music surged louder, the intro notes of a song he recognized, not placing it until the revelers were on their feet swaying and sing-ing at the top of their voices. He pulled Megan closer, feeling the volatility of the crowd.

"Why are they here?" asked Megan. She watched the crowd as they belted out the second verse.

"Maybe they were hoping to see Storm."

Two young women swayed as they sang, their arms wrapped around each other. Their expressions were ecstatic, probably drunk or high, but underneath it, there was fear, their grip on each other a little too tight.

"Like us."

Megan was focused on the young woman with hair cropped short like her mother's, both ears pierced multiple times, as were her nose and eyebrow.

"Come on," he said, pulling her behind a brand-new electric vehicle and towards the gate. "Don't get distracted."

People from the road were being allowed entry, one at a time, and greeted warmly by the woman, Gwyneth, who had been on the news. She hugged each of them and they hugged her back. It reminded him of being in church, where the priest said a few words to his parish-ioners as they left.

The people that had been allowed entry held pamphlets in their hands, and walked around in small groups as if sightseeing. They were intensely interested in the plain white house, the weathered tents, and the burned-out shell of the barn. People in white tunics walked between them, the ones that could, talking with the groups and appearing to answer questions.

It looked more like a recruitment event; the white tunic converts waxing on about their life-changing experience to willing seekers. He wanted to straighten his shoulders and assume the precise efficiency of his military training, the shell that he'd always been able to hide within. He squeezed Megan's hand in reassurance, as much for him as her.

They took their place in line. The smell of charred wood filled the air. "Where was she?" a woman ahead of them in line asked when she reached Gwyneth.

"Around the barn," said Gwyneth. "When she set it on fire."

The woman exhaled in shocked awe, before she eagerly moved forward.

"Welcome!"

They had reached the front of the line and Gwyneth came forward; her arms outstretched. He drew back, dragging Megan with him.

He should have let her hug him, his resistance drawing too much attention.

"Sorry, I—" He let his shoulders roll inward and averted his gaze in an effort to look more like a civilian.

"It's okay," she said, directing her attention to Megan.

"What's your name?"

Gwyneth's voice was too high, and too friendly, and Megan looked past her, towards the barn.

"I know it's all a bit crazy," Gwyneth half-whispered while giving him a wink, "but you'll like it here. All the children love it."

"Was she living here?" asked Adams. He tried to sound awestruck, ecstatic that she had been there. "Is this where she got better?"

He saw a brief flicker of regret, perhaps at having missed that opportunity, before her expression returned to its welcome benevolence. She was all flushed red cheeks and glittering eyes, the picture of innocent health.

"She and Kowalski only came here to destroy our Gatherer. It was a hateful thing to do and only points to how troubled she has become."

Gwyneth looked to the couple behind them as she said this, nodding to confirm they understood this message.

"Storm isn't hateful."

Megan had her chin tilted up as fierce as any soldier. Gwyneth pressed her lips together, not quite quick enough to hide her irritation.

"Who knows what goes on in a mind that has lost its way. I only wish we could have helped her."

"Maybe she didn't want your help."

Adams blinked, not having to fake his surprise. Gwyneth gave him an irritated look. Megan's face was tight with fury, her face pinched in a frown.

"Did the police catch her?" he asked.

Gwyneth lifted her gaze away from Megan, her mouth still open with whatever she had wanted to say but held back.

"That isn't something they would share with me."

"But they were here?"

He made sure to sound excited, the presence of the police only adding to the thrill of Storm having been there.

Her expression settled into a crystalline hardness, frustration lying beneath it.

"Sorry, but there's a long line-up." She gestured behind them as she handed him a pamphlet. "I'm sure one of our helpers can answer any questions you have."

There was a twitch below her left eye. He was sure he had seen it. Yet she flicked her hair, blocked him from seeing her face, and turned to the next people in line, a group of teenagers hunched close together.

He moved several steps away before he paused, the clearing crowded with tourists and the ghost-like presence of the afflicted. He scanned for someone paying too-close attention or for the disciplined movement of a soldier amongst the crowd.

Megan let go of his hand and ran towards the barn, her thin arms pumping and her legs straining forward. The same way she had run towards her mother.

A boy in a yellow shirt ran briefly beside her but turned away when she ignored him.

Adams followed more slowly, feigning interest in the house and the entire retreat, seeing the clearing as Maria would have: the closeness of the trees to the tents, the open field behind the barn, and the easy access to all of it. There was no reason they should have been seen. It would have been an easy in-and-out.

Megan slowed between two rows of tents. They were white canvas, set up in lines around the barn. These people were sick and willingly lived next to a Gatherer. He pushed himself to keep going.

"What is it?" he asked when he caught up to Megan. She had stopped at the bottom of the ramp that led up to what would have been the barn's entrance. Tourists mingled in the charred remains, circling and touching the melted plastic husk of what had been the Gatherer like it was a sacred object.

Megan looked to the ground below her feet, lifted one foot and then the other. She walked a few steps up the ramp, and came back down, and then repeated the process. None of the afflicted in their white tunics were inside the structure, a group off to the left of the ramp were visibly agitated at the people who were inside. There seemed to be an argument as to whether or not to stop them.

"Did she really mean for them to touch it?"

The man who protested was stooped and used a cane yet showed no signs of aging on his face. "We were the ones to go next. Now, with all these people…"

The man scanned the clearing, his gaze briefly catching Adams' before it moved on, no recognition or interest in who he was. When he spoke next it was too low for Adams to hear.

Adams moved closer to Megan who had stopped a few paces from the base of the ramp. The smell of burning was everywhere. For the first time, she grabbed his hand, instead of him taking hers.

"I want to leave."

She spoke softly, yet not low enough to hide her fear.

"Is something wrong?"

He bent down so she could speak quietly. Her pupils were dilated, and her breathing fast and shallow. There was a sudden weakness in his legs, like at the start of a fever.

She backed away from the barn, pulling him with her.

The Gatherer he had installed at their home hadn't affected him, though it had stolen the life of his wife and daughter. Was that what he was feeling? He was almost grateful for it, at the idea of being able to go with them, for the choice having been made. He and Megan stood several rows from the ramp, a breeze cooling the sweat under his arms and slicking down his sides, and he had the sense that time had passed. The activity of the clearing continued as normal; people mingled; tourists gawked. The tent next to them had its door open, the flaps pulled back to show two cots, both empty.

The boy in the yellow shirt stood beside them.

"Hi! I'm Eli!" He had tight black curls and a wide smile. Healthy. Happy. "Do you want me to show you something?"

"Not really," said Megan, sounding impatient. She looked back towards the barn and the shell of the Gatherer.

"No one else has seen it." The boy's excitement rolled off him in waves.

"What is there to see?"

The boy looked up, as if Adams hadn't existed for him until he spoke.

"I can show you where she hid, before she set the barn on fire."

Adams looked for the adult who was setting them up. No one paid them any attention, all eyes focused on the barn.

"Is it far?"

Eli was restless, his energy a strange force in this place. He pointed to the trees that bordered the rows of tents. There might have been a slight opening, though it looked no different than any of the small spaces. Except this one was in a direct line to the ramp and would be the perfect place to keep watch.

"That would be great."

Adams gently turned Megan's shoulders, forcing her to look away from the barn. He tried to see what she was looking at but there were only the same loitering groups.

Eli skipped ahead of them.

"I heard them talking, you know. I didn't realize it was them. I thought it was somebody else. It wasn't until later that I figured it out."

There were fewer people in the outer rings, only a few slow-moving residents, none of the tourists interested in witnessing the sparse squalor where the afflicted lived. It was no different than the dark zones in the city where the afflicted had taken shelter and the healthy had never gone.

The boy stopped at a spot in the trees as uniform as all the others. Megan had fallen behind, her head bent as she walked.

"Didn't they come at night?" Adams asked.

Eli held back a branch and Megan walked through the opening without looking up. Gwyneth still welcomed a long line of people at the entrance and the residents that had been at the ramp had disappeared.

Adams ducked through the opening, bumping into Megan in the moment it took his eyes to adjust. Eli brushed past him and stood next to a large fir tree, his hand resting on its bark.

"They were right here." He pointed to a stand of ferns tangled with the low branches of a pine tree. He climbed between a branch and a fern and disappeared. Megan followed. "The three of them sat here, see? You can see the entire village from here."

From outside the glade, Adams heard each word, despite Eli's conspiratorial whisper. It was the perfect place to stake out the area. A faint trail led away from the hideout and the clearing, winding its way through trees and fallen trunks. It was an easy escape route and a clear view of the barn.

"—that's my tent right there and I heard them whispering when they arrived. But I'm not allowed to leave the tent at night, so I didn't see the other two leave, I only heard them."

Yet why come here at all?

"Are you sure there were three?"

Eli paused, annoyed by Adams' interruption.

"They had different voices, plus the one who stayed was smoking a cigarette."

It was even less likely Maria would have trusted someone who would smoke a cigarette on a stakeout, announcing their location to anyone with a sense of smell. A layer of moss grew on the side of the tree, coating the rough bark. Adams leaned against it. It hadn't been them. Maria didn't smoke and Storm couldn't. What had the third person even been doing?

Eli had lowered his voice further and he could hear Megan whispering back, having some kind of argument. They reached a decision, judging by the sudden quiet. Eli emerged first, pine needles caught in his hair and on the seat of his pants. Megan followed, looking more natural beside the boy, more like a child.

"There were three of them here. I heard them," said Eli.

Megan's attention had drifted to the path, following its route away from the tents.

Adams stuck his head into the small hideout, saw the scuffed layer of pine needles. It was impossible to tell how many people had sat and watched.

"Did you show this to the police?"

"They only cared about what Gwyneth said. About how she stopped Storm and Kowalski in the woods, but I could hear this woman swearing and talking to herself. She was mad."

"Did you see them?"

Eli shook his head.

It could be the nighttime imaginings of an excitable boy. He had done that enough times himself, trying to invent excitement and intrigue in his life where there wasn't. Or it could simply be a way to distract himself from whatever had happened here.

"Is that where they escaped?"

Adams indicated the path that disappeared into the uniform nothingness of the trees.

Eli kicked the base of the fir tree.

"There was a third person here. She's the one that set the fire."

The boy was determined that someone believe him, and Adams did believe that it hadn't been Maria or Storm that had set the fire.

"Show him," said Megan.

Eli glared at Megan, his face tight with betrayal.

Adams looked from Megan to Eli, the murmur of the visitors coming in through the trees.

Eli moved back so that he stood at the edge of the small shelter, the ferns and branches pushing around his face and shoulders.

"You promise you won't take it?"

"I promise."

Adams had expected a new path or a photo of Storm and Maria. Instead, Eli drew something from his pocket and stretched his arm forward carefully. The square, silver box of a Zippo lighter lay in his palm.

"Did you find that in there?" Adams nodded towards the shelter.

Eli curled his fingers around it.

"By the barn."

It would be covered with the boy's fingerprints.

"Can I see it?"

Eli held it close to his chest.

"He'll give it back," said Megan. She had moved to the edge of the forest, looking back towards the barn.

Eli turned it over and ran his thumb along what looked like an inscription before he dropped it into Adams' outstretched palm.

The lighter was well-worn, much of the texture that was carved into the silver metal worn off at the corners and on the front of the cap. The shape was outdated, boxier than the slick models produced now. One side held an inscription: *No looking back.*

This wasn't Maria's. He would have seen something this well-used, especially given the length of time it would take it to get this worn.

He flicked it on and watched the long cool flame for several seconds before he snapped shut the lid.

"When did you find it?"

"After the fire was out."

"And no one else saw it?"

Eli frowned.

"It was in the grass. I only saw it 'cause the silver is shiny."

"So you didn't show it to the police?"

The pine branches stopped Eli from moving back but Adams knew he wanted to. It wasn't so much the police Adams was worried about, but Stanton, who would gain access to whatever they had found.

"They didn't believe me. So, I didn't show them."

Adams nodded and wished he could help with the boy's loneliness.

"What else can you tell me? Were they all women?"

Megan stared through the trees to the barn. There was something wrong with her fixation. After the fire, there shouldn't be anything there.

"Yes. Two of them went down the ramp to the barn because one of them wanted to look. The other one kept whispering for her to hurry up. But they only got halfway before they stopped. Most of the patients can't go any closer."

"Because it hurts too much?" asked Adams.

He nodded. There was grief there, someone close to him having suffered.

"But they didn't start the fire?" Adams prompted.

Eli took a deep breath, looked back to the barn as if seeing the memory. "They ran away all of a sudden, once Sash started barking."

"But not the other one, who was smoking?"

"No." He pointed to the opposite side of the tents and a direction that would have provided a long straight route to the barn. "She went that way." It could have been Storm and Maria who had approached the barn. But it didn't make sense they'd taken on someone reckless enough to light the barn on fire. They wouldn't have wanted the attention. Unless it was a distraction.

"Can I keep this?"

He held up the lighter.

"You said you would give it back."

Adams crouched so he could look into his eyes. The sadness the boy was concealing was more visible up close.

"I know. But it will help us find out if Storm was here."

The boy's expression shifted, and he watched Adams differently. Adams had stopped being the bumbling father, had slipped into the comfortable place of taking charge. Eli looked to Megan who wasn't responding and to the brightness that came through the branches from the clearing. "She was."

"I believe you. But I need proof or no one will believe me. You understand that."

"Are you the police?"

"No. But I'm trying to find Storm so I can help her."

This only confused him and Adams' heart went out to him. He was trying so hard to make sense of it all. When there was no sense to be made.

Eli nodded, though his gaze didn't leave the lighter until Adams had slipped it in his pocket.

"Do you have people here that are sick?" Adams asked.

Eli's guardedness increased and his gaze darted towards the clearing.

"I came here with my Gran."

"Is she sick?"

His features seemed frozen, eyes dark globes inside.

"She was taken."

He had lifted his chin and chest, the movement doing nothing to hide his pain.

"Taken where?"

Eli's gaze flicked to the barn.

Both Eli and Megan now looked towards the barn, Megan vacant, and Eli with a look of resentful longing.

"I was too young to go with her."

Nausea rose like a black sickness. He understood now about the rows of tents and the celebration that had been scheduled. Gwyneth fed these people the lies that made them give themselves to this Gatherer, thinking that something else waited for them besides death. This was not a wellness retreat, but a retreat to death. Lambs taken to slaughter. He smelled the death that had been in the treatment facility, that same smell having followed him here. Like the whole world had been infected, the level of the disease only just beginning to show. It was a miracle Eli was still healthy.

"You should come with us," said Adams.

Megan looked at him, bleary-eyed as if just waking up. Eli looked between them with suspicion.

Gwyneth still greeted people, a line of tourists stretching out of sight down the drive.

"I'm helping Ms. Sween."

"She has lots of help now. With all these people. And this isn't really a place for kids. Is it?"

The struggle showed on Eli's face, between the loss he had experienced and the lies he was told to believe. It was another reason not to leave him here, another child's life taken by the Gatherer.

"You should come." Megan's voice was sleepy, distant.

Adams needed to get her away from there, whatever residue that Gatherer had left behind still drawing her.

Eli looked to the tents, fear and loneliness underlying the bright boy they had first been presented with. Megan moved beside him. Took his hand.

Eli still didn't move.

"Can I say goodbye?"

"You can get your things. But Ms. Sween can't know you've come with us."

Eli looked through a gap in the leaves towards the burnt husk of the Gatherer, perched on the small rise where the barn had been. His face was twisted in sorrow and rage. It hadn't been Gwyneth he had wanted to say good-bye to.

"You'll be safe with us," said Megan. She was leaning away from the clearing.

Adams bent down and put his hand over top of where Megan still held onto Eli.

"I know you don't know us, and you don't know who to trust, but this place is dangerous."

Eli blinked, as if Adams had finally confirmed what he had suspected.

The gaze he lifted to Adams was that of someone centuries old.

"Do you know where this path leads?" asked Adams.

Eli's response came slowly. "To the road." He was wiry and strong; this place had not yet ruined him.

"We're going to take this path. If you decide to come, we will wait for you just before the road. But don't take too long."

Adams turned towards the path leading away, afraid to let Eli go but knowing the choice had to be his.

Megan lingered a moment, whispering something before she released Eli's hand.

Megan shuffled in front of Adams, slow with fatigue. When Adams looked back, Eli no longer stood where they had left him, the woods dense and quiet. They drew away from the clearing and Megan's pace increased. Adams felt the change, his breath easier, the death of that clearing falling away. Further on, Megan lifted her head, once again taking in the world around her. He wondered if Maria had taken this path and he had finally found her trail.

Megan was scrambling over a fallen tree when the pound of small feet came from behind them. Eli wore a backpack and had a windbreaker tied around his waist, his limbs seeming to fly in all directions as he ran.

"This is where Gwyneth stopped Storm." Eli was out of breath as he scrambled over the log. Adams reached to steady him as he jumped to the ground.

Adams scanned the pine needles and moss, but the forest had absorbed whatever traces of them had been left behind.

"It was the guys who came later who asked more questions."

It took a moment for Adams to understand what Eli was saying.

"What guys?"

Eli looked incredibly young with his coat tied unevenly around his waist and his backpack slanted to one side. Younger than Megan, yet as good as her at adapting.

"Kind of like you." Eli paused, the stretch of forest on the side of the trail suddenly fascinating. "Pretending to be all relaxed – but not really."

Adams swore to himself. If Eli could see through him, he had to assume others had, like Gwyneth.

"How many were there?"

"Just two."

"And when did they come?"

He shrugged and tightened the coat tied around his waist.

"This morning."

Which meant they had acted on the news of Storm's appearance with a speed that only came with resources. And they could already be on Maria and Storm's trail. He almost regretted bringing Eli, yet what had been the alternative?

"Can you run?"

Adams picked up Megan and she crawled onto his back. Eli nodded solemnly, all business.

"Okay. Let's move."

NINE

STORM

S TORM SAT WITH HER back against the stone wall, the deepening darkness dropping her and Maria into shadow. The air felt as cold as the stone. She tucked her hands further inside her sleeves and rested her arms across her knees.

The lights around the parking lot shone bright in the deepening dark, far enough away that she was out of danger. The houses beyond the play equipment were also too far to cause her harm and she couldn't feel the bursts from any nearby cell phone towers.

She drew a long slow breath, savoring the inertness of the cool spring air.

That steadiness always gave her hope. That regardless of what humanity threw at the world, the earth would endure and close over any evidence that humans had existed long after we were gone. It was a kind of safety net that no matter how badly humans screwed up, they couldn't cause any lasting damage.

That naivete had vanished with the touch of the despair in the test facility, an unseen, unrecognized by-product of the corrupted Gatherers Stanton had created. The absence, she had called it instinctively, for the depletion of a fundamental energy that we hadn't known existed. It had been there again among those tents. A horrible growing absence that those desperate people had mistaken for the divine. She had understood their desire to go with it, to follow the flow of energy wherever it went, only the deepest part of her reptilian brain keeping her from letting it take her.

The park lay in a precarious quiet, an island amidst a world that was crumbling around them. How long would it be until they were pulled under or ceased to exist at all?

She ran her hand over her forearms, seeking the reassurance of the warmth of her skin.

Maria stirred beside her, caught in a moment of calm before awareness dawned and she sat up.

"Is she back?"

"Not yet."

The hands of Storm's watch showed just past 2:00 a.m., more than four hours since Amanda left. The time had passed slowly, the empty park unchanging but for the shift of the swings at the end of the chains.

"She should be here by now."

Three streetlights marked the section of road they could see, their distribution patterns leaving stretches of shadows between them.

"Things always take longer than you think."

"It shouldn't have taken more than an hour."

The spill-off from the streetlights illuminated the frown on Maria's still features as she absorbed every detail of the park and road.

"Maybe she's doing what you asked and staking it out first to see if it's being watched."

"Not likely."

Maria stood and moved towards where Amanda had disappeared. She drew her tablet out as she walked, waiting until she was at the far edge of the street before the light of the screen flashed across her face. Storm felt the signal of it, a faint energized streak across her skin.

She breathed, knew the duration would be finite, the signals from the device weak. Except Maria was staring at the screen too long, utterly still as she gripped the tablet. She tapped the screen and waited, and Maria's worry added to the tension across Storm's skin.

After what had to be at least ten minutes, the screen flashed off, and Maria strode back across the grass. She was walking too fast, her eyes wide when she stood above Storm.

"There's no signal."

Maria was out of breath, her gaze jumping from the swings to the road, and to the distant houses.

"No signal from your tablet or from hers."

"It can't find her location."

Maria lifted her bike up, had her foot on the pedal.

Storm stepped in front of her, one leg on either side of her front wheel.

"Slow down. There are lots of possible explanations."

"She said she would turn it on."

Anger overrode Maria's distress.

"Maybe she forgot."

"*Forgot?*"

Storm laid her hands on the cool metal handlebars.

"She could be in the basement. You said it was fortified."

Maria's body was taut and she was pulling the bike against Storm's hands.

"She's too used to being the smartest person in the room. She doesn't understand this is a different game."

"Give her some time. Anything could have happened."

It was the wrong thing to say. Stanton could be waiting for her. Or her old boyfriend.

"Going after her won't help," said Storm.

She could see the effort it took for Maria to release her hands and step off the bike. Storm laid the bike carefully back in the grass as Maria paced to the stone wall and back, her attention jumping around the park as if her diligence would force Amanda to appear.

She had returned for the fifth time when voices floated to them from one of the adjacent streets. After an endless moment, when neither she nor Storm breathed, three teenagers appeared, strolling towards the park. One was taller than the others; all of them unhurried and unaware, totally consumed by the small world of their trio.

When they reached the edge of the park, the shortest one broke from the other two and ran towards the swings. She had already started swinging when the others reached her. One took the second swing, and the other climbed the support structure to hang from the top bar. Storm longed for that sense of invincibility, the belief that no matter what the world threw at her, she was ready for it.

Storm retreated into the shadow of the wall, and sat down, her head against the hard stone as the first teen pumped high into the sky on the swing, never flying up and over the bar no matter how hard she tried.

Maria sat beside her, shifting and fidgeting, no position allowing her to relax.

"What happened at the barn?" she said, her voice abrupt and rushed.

The stand of oaks was more than enough to keep them hidden, yet Storm's mind had returned to the exposure she had felt among the tents.

One minute walking in the cool night, the next a tension across the surface of her cells caused by something critically unbalanced. It had been like seeing the world from the outside, the ground and the tents and even Maria beside her, all the shape and structure they were intended to be except they had become untethered from the energy that grounded them to the earth. She had felt the pull of it in her gut, of energy being drawn away, like a rug sliding out from beneath you except you didn't fall, instead stayed where you were, unaware of the gap that left you caught in a web in mid-air.

"I don't know."

Maria shifted again; this time frustration added to the impatience.

"I don't believe that."

Storm pulled her hood up, wanting the illusion of protection it provided.

"The first thing I felt was the despair flowing over me. Except it was stronger this time. More of a torrent of energy being drawn away."

There had been the power of it and the desire to let herself be caught up and pulled downstream. It was what Gwyneth had mistaken for the draw of a higher power. Even though there was the darkness, there had also been a promise: that if she let it take her, she would understand it, the instant before she was snuffed out.

"And Gwyneth says it will heal them?"

"She called them her congregation."

Maria swore as she rubbed the top of her thighs. A heavy dew was creeping in, making everything damp to the touch.

"And she thought you had been sent to them."

Storm puffed out her cheeks as she exhaled. There was no end to how the Gatherer had been twisted and convoluted. It was a force so agile and insidious; she often didn't think it would ever be contained. The Gatherer she had created had caused harm, but the corrupted Gatherers had the potential to destabilize the world.

"I'm glad Amanda destroyed it," said Storm.

Maria's face was too shadowed to see her expression.

"So am I."

The mention of Amanda's name brought their fear rushing back, the street where she should be appearing still empty.

The teen swung back high and fast, and with a single push forward of her legs, launched herself off the swing at its highest vertical point. She soared briefly, seemed to hang in mid-air until she dropped hard to the ground. She landed in a spray of sand, couldn't hold it, and rolled in a tumble of legs and open coat until she came to rest on the grass. She lay still for a moment as if wounded and Storm couldn't take her eyes off her until there was a slow movement of a roll onto her back, her gaze fixed to the stars that had once again proven beyond her reach.

"Do you still think we can stop it?"

Storm felt the enormity of it again, but also an absence, as if it were trying to fill a hole that had no bottom, and something essential was out of balance.

The firmware update they had planned wouldn't overcome that level of force. In theory, it should work, but since she had felt the touch of that growing absence, she couldn't help but think of it as a band aid on a gushing wound.

She opened her mouth to speak but Maria spoke for her.

"You don't know."

Storm rose and moved towards the edge of the trees that sheltered them. Branches hung low over the corner of the stone wall where Amanda had disappeared, the streetlight beyond shining on bare pavement, like a video on a loop that never arrives at the image you desperately need to see.

The teen who had swung from the top rail came to help the one who had taken flight. Storm watched with a longing that caught her off guard as the three linked together and meandered away from the equipment towards the street on the far side.

She stepped into the open area and felt the pull of Maria's hand on her arm.

"Don't," said Maria.

The swing shifted with the momentum of the teen, the last bit of movement in the park.

"Amanda said the park was clear."

Their small oasis felt smaller now, surrounded by a world they couldn't navigate as well as Amanda.

Maria's grip loosened until her hand fell away. The gesture was so defeated that Storm sought to reassure her but had no words that would overcome Amanda's absence.

Storm crossed the open area with Maria close behind. The park felt quieter in the open, and more abandoned.

The swing was an old style, a single strap of canvas hung between two chains, a divot dug in the dirt below it where riders had dragged their feet. The chains were cold on her hands, the canvas snug around her hips.

Maria leaned against the support pole, scanning for movement or surprises, yet she didn't interfere.

Storm's legs were thin, her thighs pressed close together as she pumped her legs, her toes tucked close beneath to avoid the dirt. Her muscles strained with the effort and soon she was breathing hard, leaning back with her arms straight. She pumped harder, a long push forward then back, the breeze pushing her hood off so that she swung with the air through her hair.

She wasn't as high as the teen, didn't have the raw energy to reach her peak yet she pushed just the same, Maria watching the long swing as Storm rose higher and higher. She pointed her toes to the stars above her, felt the seat drop before the chains caught her and returned her along the same path, up and back.

She could feel the weakness in her hands where they gripped the chain. She pulled her legs back one last time, hoping for the strength to reach the peak and to finally let go.

Maria turned her head to follow her path, stepped behind the swing as she passed as if she too needed to follow it. Storm leaned back a final time, and let her toes point to the sky.

T E N

A D A M S

A DAMS GRIPPED THE HANDLE above the door as Hamel steered them down the off-ramp.

"Did she ever mention anyone like that?" Adams braced his hand on the dashboard against the force of the turn. "Someone she would trust that much?"

"Kowalski?" said Hamel. "The only reason she trusted us was because she had no other choice."

Adams nodded. It had taken Kowalski a long time to trust any of them, and even then, she had sometimes been over-diligent in checking everything they had done.

"They must have had some place to hide over the winter." Maria had grown up on the west coast of Canada, but that was all he knew. She had never told stories about growing up or what she had done before she signed up, and he had never asked. She had been a competitor, the two of them rivals at first sight, recognizing in each other that drive to succeed. No wonder she had never trusted him.

"They could have been anywhere."

They waited at a red light to turn onto a stretch of malls and fast-food chains, less than half the parking spots filled. "But some place Stanton couldn't find them."

If Stanton was claiming publicly that Storm had been with him all along, then he would have been looking. Hard.

"If anyone can stay ahead of Stanton, it's her," said Hamel.

It didn't seem possible. Adams had been on the other end of military searches and there had always been the understanding that they *would* find what they were after. They had the technology and the resources.

He turned his head to check on Megan and Eli, who rode in the back seats. They had slept through the night and currently had their heads close together in consultation.

Adams dug the lighter from his pocket and handed it to Hamel.

"Do you recognize this?"

Hamel didn't, the wear-and-tear marks telling them nothing except that it had been well-used and well-loved.

"*No looking back*," read Hamel as he looked back to the road. "Not a bad philosophy. That's what they used to light the fire?"

Adams nodded and explained where Eli had found it.

"So, if we find this person, we find Freeman and Kowalski?"

"Maybe."

Adams ran his hands over his face, his eyes burning. Eli claimed to have heard three women talking, and Adams was making decisions on intelligence from a boy he barely knew.

They had stopped at a second light. Eli's father's place was two blocks ahead according to the blue path of the GPS.

They drove slowly down the quiet street. Tidy houses sat back from the road behind mowed lawns, the occasional basketball hoop mounted above a garage, or a hockey net on the drive. There was no one on the street, the windows were blank, as if the world had withdrawn and held its breath. They rolled to a stop at the intersection. Adams felt like an intruder, their stealth and intent intrusive in this frightened neighborhood.

The street to the right led up an incline, the houses on either side further back from the road. A large group of people — the first they had seen — had gathered further up, some standing in the center of the road, others closer together on an expanse of grass. They stood with arms crossed and leaned in over something, like they wanted to get a better look but not get burned.

"What's up there?" asked Hamel.

Eli lifted his head from whatever he and Megan were looking at.

"A bunch of houses and a park. I don't go up there much."

Megan met Adams' gaze before turning to look at the crowd. His apprehension rose when she leaned forward.

"We should check it out," she said.

"Not sure we should engage," said Hamel.

Adams looked at Megan, who watched the milling crowd with a perplexed frown, the same way she had looked back towards the barn.

"It'll only take a second," said Adams.

Hamel took a second look towards the crowd. He would be assessing it the same way Adams had, checking for signs of weapons or organized behavior among the bystanders. Adams didn't see any aggression, but there was definitely agitation. And fear.

Hamel turned the vehicle towards the crowd. They approached slowly and parked a good distance away. There were maybe three dozen people.

"Do you recognize anyone?" said Adams.

Eli had crawled between the seats and crouched between him and Hamel. You didn't see gatherings like this anymore. There were no beverages or food, and a couple people had dogs on leashes as if they had been out for a walk when they had been drawn over.

"That guy with the big dog is my dad's neighbor. And the boy who's hanging at the edge of the crowd is my half-brother." Eli hadn't mentioned siblings before now.

There was a sound of a muffled shout and the tall, wiry boy with curly hair like Eli's waved someone over.

Hamel turned off the engine and caught Adams' attention, a question unspoken between them. Adams nodded. They would go armed.

Adams got out first, and Megan crawled over the seat after him. Eli came slower and stood in the open door next to Megan as Hamel joined them.

They looked drawn and worried, and Adams couldn't tell if they were just tired and hungry or if it had been a bad decision to stop.

They walked slowly towards the crowd, Megan out in front and Eli hanging back. Adams tried to relax his stride and make his surveillance discreet.

The grass was brown with the first green shoots of spring growth poking through. It was more of a field than a park, which accounted for the half-dozen dogs. A few people looked their way when they approached, but with only passing glances.

Eli didn't go to his half-brother; instead, squirmed his way into the crowd. Hamel moved around to the other side of the group. Adams and Megan walked together into the loose crowd, people stepping aside to let them pass.

The focus of the group's attention was a long streak that extended half the width of the field and a meter wide. Every blade of grass in the streak had been turned white, as if God had come down and painted a single stroke. The ends were frayed, the brown and green of the grass pushing into the white.

He snapped one of the brittle blades. It came off in his hand and disintegrated into small pieces, like dust. Megan knelt beside him and hovered her hand over the middle of the streak, the way she had hovered over the web at the hospital.

"It's a message," said a man across from Adams. He was bald, with the round softness of middle-age.

"You think everything's from aliens," said a broad woman with unkempt gray hair. "It's a chemical spill."

"What? That dropped from the sky?"

The streak was over thirty meters long and Adams almost thought he could see a faint continuation of it further down, the way a water line breaks through and dips along the surface.

"How long has it been here?" asked Adams.

The three looked at him in unison, he the obvious outsider.

"It showed up yesterday," said the aliens guy. "But it's bigger this morning. They've called the city's landscaper to come and have a look."

Eli was suddenly beside him, breathing heavily as if he'd been running.

"Have you seen this before?" Adams asked quietly as someone proposed that it was a practical joke with someone using a can of paint, despite there being no evidence of paint.

Eli nodded.

He, Eli and Hamel congregated several paces back from the crowd.

"Is it the same as the barn?"

Eli looked to the far end of the crowd where his half-brother stood with two other teenagers. "It was all white along the bottom of the walls. The same as that."

"Brittle too?" asked Hamel.

The boy nodded, distracted as he watched the group.

"But there's no Gatherer here," said Adams.

Megan crouched beside the streak, holding her palm open as if above a fire.

Some of the crowd had started to disperse. Others walked parallel to the streak for the entire length. No one touched it or stepped over.

It was possible a Gatherer lay underground, but not likely. There were no signs of a bunker or entrances for anything other than a park.

"What's over there?"

Adams nodded towards one end of the streak and the houses that backed onto the park.

"More houses," said Eli. "And the road we came in on."

"And there?" Adams pointed past the opposite end of the streak.

"Same. More houses and then the swimming pool."

The alien guy was watching Megan, frowning with suspicion. Eli noticed too and he moved beside her, pulling her hand back surprisingly gently and getting her to stand. It made Megan look simple or confused, which wasn't a bad thing.

"What do you feel?" Adams asked when Megan stood beside him.

She was rubbing her hand, the skin a bright red.

"Is your hand okay?" asked Eli.

She looked surprised, like she hadn't been aware she was rubbing it.

"I think so." She wiped it on her thigh.

"We should get going," said Hamel, nodding to an official-looking guy getting out of a pick-up emblazoned with the City's logo. "That's probably the landscaper."

Most of the crowd had turned towards the new arrival, clustering closer together as he approached.

Their small group moved casually back towards the minivan. They had arrived back at the van and opened the doors when Adams realized Eli wasn't with them.

He looked back to the crowd and saw Eli, standing in the group with his half-brother, their resemblance unmistakable. He was happy he'd brought him back here, despite his protests. He would be better off with his family.

The older boy shoved Eli, and one of his friends caught him, pushing Eli back towards his brother. Eli tried to step away and one of the older boys blocked his path.

"Shit," said Adams, he and Hamel in stride back towards Eli.

One of the friends, who towered over Eli, held his arms behind his back while his half-brother poked his chest. Eli squirmed but couldn't get free.

"That's enough," said Hamel when they were several strides away.

Eli's half-brother barely looked up and continued to poke at Eli.

"Whoa, whoa, whoa," said Hamel, holding up his hands in supplication.

Adams wouldn't have been so nice.

"What's going on?"

The boy didn't let Eli go, the presence of adults doing nothing to curb their actions. The brother sneered down at Eli.

"He's contaminated."

Hamel and Adams had stopped one step from the small group, though Adams wanted nothing more than to pull Eli free.

"How do you know?" asked Hamel.

Eli wouldn't look at them, his face flushed as he struggled to get free.

"Hold still, you little runt," said Eli's captor.

"Let him go," said Hamel.

The boy pulled Eli's arms tighter so that he winced in pain.

"He said that's enough," said Adams, stepping forward.

"He's a freak. Just like his Gran," said the brother.

Hamel had moved closer to the brother; Adams stood within reach of Eli. The brother couldn't be more than fourteen, wielding his finger with the pure viciousness of a child.

"I'm going to need you to stop that," said Adams.

Something in his voice finally penetrated the boy's brain and he registered the threat in his stance and Hamel's.

"He doesn't belong here," said the brother.

"Neither do you," said Eli, though he grimaced as the boy pulled his arms.

"Either you let him go, or I make you," said Adams.

There was a moment of stillness, while the boy's gaze met Adams'. He looked young and confused as his certainty faltered. Adams wanted to meet whoever had told him this was acceptable and led him down this path of violence.

Eli stumbled forward when the boy released his arms.

"You're coming with us," said Adams to the brother. "Your parents need to know about this."

The brother smirked.

"Go ahead."

"Come on, let's go," said Eli, pulling on Adams' hand.

"Running scared, little brother?"

"Not until—" said Adams.

Hamel crowded Adams, forcing him to move away.

"We can't just let them get away with it!"

Hamel jerked his head, indicating the exercise was over.

"You okay?" Hamel asked Eli. He walked in front of them, rubbing his arms and ignoring them. "Why didn't you tell us?"

Megan waited at the side of the van, looking beyond the end of the streak in the direction of the pool.

"It's why my Gran and I left. Once she got sick, they were——"

Adams didn't need to know the details. There had been countless stories of families abandoning their loved ones when they showed symptoms. The same way Megan's father had left her and her mother; their mistreatment by their families connected them.

"I'm so sorry," said Adams.

Eli looked away, his face set in stone.

When they reached the van, Megan opened the door for Eli and they climbed inside. She slid it shut behind them.

"Who does that to their own kid?" said Adams.

"Lots of people."

Eli's half-brother and his friends lingered on the field, and Adams wanted more than anything to go over there.

"So, he's coming with us?" said Hamel.

The landscaper had reached the streak and knelt, ready to pronounce a verdict. It would be a guess – nothing could explain that slash except a Gatherer that wasn't there.

"We can't exactly take him home."

"We'll need to find a place for them. Once we find Storm."

Adams climbed into the passenger's seat and heard the low hush of their whispers. He marveled at their adaptability. Both orphaned and abandoned, and now living out of the back of a van with two soldiers like it was the most natural thing in the world.

"I'd like to go to the swimming pool," said Megan.

"It won't be open," said Adams. "It's too early in the season."

She pointed in a direct line from the end of the slash.

"I don't want to swim."

"I can show you where it is," said Eli, as if the incident with his brother had never happened. "Turn right up there, by the fire hydrant."

Hamel started the engine and pulled away from the curb, steering around the landscaper's truck, the emblem of the City of Rima plastered on its side. The landscaper stood over the streak, his head turning as he traced its path back and forth.

ELEVEN

AMANDA

Amanda rose up on her pedals as she jumped the curb, absorbing the landing in her knees. The chain clanked before she returned to her smooth, silent ride, the hum of the wheels vibrating beneath her. She did a quick wheelie, to see if she still could, but she only managed to lift the wheel briefly off the ground. She pedaled for a dozen meters hands-free, feeling as if the quiet, empty night was hers alone.

Halfway down the block she turned, crossing over onto the rougher gravel of the lane way. It was darker in the lane and she passed the sagging roof line of an old garage next to the gleam of a newly installed gate. Garbage cans against the fence marked most of the lots and the sweet, rancid stench of garbage underlay the freshness of the breeze.

Where the lane reached the pavement again, she braked and planted her feet on either side of the bike. The sidewalks were empty, as was the road. The vehicles parked along the street were connected to charging stations, two vehicles for every plug. She looked for the Gatherer that fed the stations, knowing it would need to be a larger version to provide that kind of power.

When she didn't see it, she pushed forward, crossing the road quickly into the adjacent lane. Long, narrow yards backed onto the rough lane way. She was three blocks from her house and knew to avoid the camera that was mounted on the top corner of the red brick house, and to ride close and duck beneath the range of one that was poorly placed on the roof of a garage. The feed didn't provide anything except a view of rats scrounging for garbage and the lower half of people's legs as they walked by. She had had access to all the cameras from her house, the network she had created extending far beyond her actual physical building. It would be good to sit at her terminals again, her fingers flying over the keyboard as she moved through her networks, altering feeds and being the ruler of her environment.

Not that she would go back to hiding out once this was over; it felt too good to be riding free again, and to be back alongside Maria. She smiled at how annoyed Maria had been when she hadn't been able to stop Amanda from leaving. It had always been one of her greatest pleasures to tease Maria, her relentless need to protect others making her an easy target. She tried not to think about how good it felt to be inside Maria's protective shell again.

She crossed the street her house lay on, two blocks away, and took the lane that ran parallel behind the houses. She hid the bike amidst the trees behind a dumpster. If she had access to the network, she would have known if anyone was watching. With the blanket coverage she had it was impossible to move within three blocks of her house without her knowing.

She strolled casually down the lane, keeping to the shadows. She was surprised she didn't feel more afraid. There was a time that stepping out of the house had terrified her too much to move. Trust Maria, always wanting the best for everyone, to be the one to drag her out and face her fears.

At the end of the lane, she slipped between a fence and an enclosed garbage box, the plastic walls doing nothing to mask the smell of rotting waste. The space was just wide enough for her shoulders and she crouched down, her back against the container, the tangle of last year's dead leaves catching at her feet.

She could see the upper floor of her house and the top of the fence on this side of the backyard. The windows were dark, the light over the back porch unlit. Had her neighbors even noticed that she had been gone? She had rarely interacted, believing, in her trauma, that Simon's eyes were everywhere.

She settled in, longing for the drone that she had left in its case in the kitchen. It had been her eyes in the neighborhood. She checked her tablet, made sure she was still broadcasting her location, and slid it back inside her coat.

The windows of the house directly behind her were dark, the light on the back porch shining on a yard strewn with children's toys. Beside that, a single lighted window on the second floor showed no movement. As she watched the empty windows of her house, she felt an ache to be home. She checked down the lane, the darkened garbage cans providing a million places for someone to hide. If anyone was even watching. There had been no alerts on her alarm system, the access detection on the windows unbreeched. She had had it built as a fortress and that integrity still held. She slid a fresh pack of cigarettes from her pocket and turned it in her hands, the cellophane glinting.

She was pissed at herself for leaving her lighter in the truck. It had been a touchstone in the years since Maria had gone and even with Maria returned, she had become used to the weight of it in her hand.

Tires squealed several blocks away. She cocked her head, listening, but there was no follow-up noise to hint at anything larger. The night was as dead as an Atari gaming console with about the same chance of revival.

Taking a long sniff of the cigarette pack before she slipped it back in her pocket, she started down the lane. It was strange to be walking the path she had spent so much time watching on video, waiting for one of Simon's men or even the police to come and find her. There was no one here now, any more than there had been back then, her fear generated entirely from within.

She slowed as she approached the gate and stood for several seconds listening. A chain-link fence blocked the yard directly behind hers, the same incessant blue flicker of a television screen flashing in the downstairs window.

She pressed the code into the lock on the gate and slipped through, comforted by the click of it shutting behind her. Grass had begun to push up in the crevasses of the stone path and her steps were uneven as she felt her way towards the house. Even among the other dark facades, her house looked abandoned, the absence of occupants showing in the wilted plants in the garden boxes and the too-dark reflections in the windows.

She climbed the three wood steps to the small deck. Her Muskoka chair had been knocked over; it must have been a hell of a wind to accomplish that. She stood close to the entry panel and waited for the facial recognition, struck by her degree of relief when the display turned on. She stayed still as it scanned her face and only breathed at the dull clunk when multiple locks disengaged.

The kitchen was stale and cold and for a moment felt so wrong she had the thought that she had gotten the wrong place. She closed the door, the stagnant air catching in her throat as the locks ground into place behind her. She turned on the light, though she didn't need it, the layout of the house ingrained on her skin. She had walked these rooms for months, the only sound the brush of her feet on carpet. That stillness had once been soothing, a balm to her agitated nerves. Now, the isolation was cloying and close.

She ran her finger along the stove top she had never used. She left a cleared streak in the layer of dust. It would be better once Maria and Storm arrived. Their presence would be enough to banish the loneliness of that time.

The light from the kitchen spilled into the formal dining room, the table still gleaming beneath the same layer of dust. It had come with the house, part of the model home, and it had served its purpose as a façade for her lonely existence. The bank of computer monitors in the next room and the servers that fed them had been her sole connection to the outside world.

A section of blue cable lay curled at the open door. She ran forward, heart in her throat as the silence of the house transformed into something darker. Her nine monitors, and the servers that fed them, had disappeared. Discarded cables curled on the ground, her keyboard tossed to one side, the modem crushed to pieces. The chair that was imprinted with the shape of her body lay tilted on its side.

She ran back past the securely bolted door in the kitchen, down the long hall to the front corridor – the bolts and security on the front door were as securely in place as at the back. Strangers had walked these corridors and hallways that had once been solely hers. Her chest shook with her heartbeat. Were they still here? This had happened months ago, the dust that had settled on the table and carpets was undisturbed. But how had they gotten in?

She sprinted into the dining room and let out a long moan. The door to her underground apartment hung open, held only by the bottom hinge. The panel that had controlled entry was dark and void. She paused at the top of the steps leading down. A pile of papers lay spread on the stairs beside a discarded shirt and a coffee mug she hadn't put away before she left. A circle of mold lay in the bottom. She couldn't move, certain the intruders waited for her downstairs, a horrible treasure waiting at the end of the maze. She took out her tablet, punched the screen to call Maria, only remembering when it didn't connect that it would be off. Only used for Maria to see her.

She breathed through her nose, pressed the palm of her hand against the coolness of the walls. She should leave, like she had promised. Yet… no one had been here for a long time.

She took a step down. The light switch, when she turned it on, didn't illuminate the lower level. Her neighbors could have discon-nected her from the micro-grid, except the kitchen light had turned on. She took another step. There could be no one down there, yet it was more frightening knowing they'd been in her space. They would have found the security module she had used to control all her systems. It was probably how they had prevented her from seeing any alarms. She listened. Wished Maria was there. For all her bravado, Amanda didn't really know what to do.

She descended three more steps, the dimness thicker, and still no noise from the dark basement. In a quick jump, she landed on the basement floor and flicked the light switch around the corner.

The place was in chaos. Couch cushions torn open. Drawers dumped out and cupboards left open. The monitor she had had mounted to the wall was intact but the router and the modem along with the security control module were gone from the rack on the wall. Her empty drone case had been turned on its side, the drone nowhere to be seen.

She tried to think of the information they had found; what secrets had sat on the hard drives. She had been careful. Someone cleverer and with more resources had been here, swept in like her fortifications had meant nothing.

She hurried to her bedroom, to the panel beneath her bedside table. It was open, cleared out, her passport and back-up storage drive gone. She stumbled to the bathroom, where four months ago she had cut Maria's hair, her hands shaking as she pried open the tile behind the sink, an empty concrete inlay where she had once kept her secondary passport and identity. Panic spread into her chest and mind. She ground her teeth, turned her fear to fury. How dare they make her afraid.

She let the tile drop, pivoted on the door frame and launched herself through the room, past clothes dumped on the floor, books splayed face down, and the coffee beans she had used before she left, strangely undisturbed on the counter.

She was at the bottom of the steps, her foot on the first step when she froze. There was something changed in the dimness of the dining room above her. She lifted her foot off the stair, her mind racing for another way out. It had been so reassuring when she had been hiding out. Only one way in to watch. Now it meant only one way out.

She felt, more than heard, the shift of weight. She knew every bone of this house, every sound. She fled back to the bathroom, playing a game of hide-and-seek she couldn't win. She stood paralyzed, listening to the full sound of footsteps now. Her white, terrified face looked back from the wall of mirrors. She'd been stupid. And cocky. And had not heeded Maria's warning.

Something clicked. They weren't even trying to be quiet.

She stepped into the shower. The tiles were bone dry and a rim of minerals had built-up around the drain. She pressed herself against the cold ceramics and had the irrational thought she should turn on the heat lamp, as a shadow fell across the door. Her heartbeat echoed against the sheer walls. She pushed back into the corner and gripped the Glock in both hands.

She heard the tread of boots on the carpet, felt the disturbance in the air. Her reflection looked back at her from the mirror: tangled hair, too-wide eyes. A trapped animal.

"Amanda?"

It was a woman's voice, familiar but the name out of reach. Like a teacher or something. Or her doctor. But that didn't make sense.

The mirror showed the straight line of the door frame and the dimmer space of her bedroom beyond. The woman stayed out of view, which also meant they couldn't see her.

"We aren't going to hurt you."

Amanda's anger burst through her fear. Of course, they would. Why else were they here?

They talked in low voices. Amanda barely recognized herself in the mirror. Her face was too white, too narrow, too terrified.

There was a crackle of a radio, and more quiet words.

She met her own gaze. Stared at the terror that matched the frantic signals along her nerves. She wasn't a hero. Didn't know how to get out of this.

"This is my house."

She sounded like a petulant child, her self-assurance and the woman who had craved excitement gone.

They had made it past her defenses as if they didn't exist. So, who was the laughingstock now?

"How did you get in?"

Amanda listened to her heartbeat, the yellow walls of the bathroom too bright and the wrong shade.

"It wasn't hard once we found you."

"How did you?" Her voice cracked on the last word.

There was a low murmur, the woman the sole female voice.

"We need you to come out."

"Come into the bathroom. So I can see you."

"Once you put the weapon down."

She scanned the roof and walls for technology, anything that would have given them a view.

"You come in and then I'll put it down."

She had just confirmed she had the gun.

There was further muttering, more urgent.

"Okay. I'm coming in."

She recognized the voice at the same moment that Alicia Freeman stepped into her view of the mirror, the rigid bob of auburn hair around a pale face, and the vivid blue eyes.

"Not what I was expecting."

Alicia wore a casual blue blazer that must have hung beautifully once and now looked oversized. She had her hands out in front of her, facing Amanda's reflection, and Amanda admired her bravery. She held no weapon and appeared to be unarmed.

"Is Storm with you?" asked Alicia.

The question confused Amanda. Alicia could see there was no one with her. They'd cased the whole house.

"There are three heavily armed and well-trained individuals in the other room," said Alicia. "It would be best for all of us if you came quietly."

Amanda felt the old stirring of rebelliousness and was inordinately pleased at her rallying spirit.

"Why are you even here?"

Alicia sighed, slid her thin hands into the elegantly tailored pockets of her blazer.

"We found your malware in our network."

Amanda waited. That wasn't the full explanation. The malware was untraceable. Nothing that could lead to her in the physical world.

"And you left traces of yourself when you altered the video network for Ms. Kowalski."

That part at least made sense. She hadn't really understood the danger then, or who might be looking for Maria. She had been careless.

"If you already found the malware, you don't need me anymore."

Her grip on the Glock was hot and sweaty, the gun weighing more than it should.

Alicia stepped further into the room, her runners leaving no marks on the tiles. She turned from the reflection to face Amanda. Her freckles were dark smudges on colorless skin and there was a peaked weariness around her eyes.

"The weapon. Please. I don't want you to get hurt."

Amanda pushed back harder into the tiles.

"Can't you stop them?"

Alicia's gaze didn't waver, and Amanda had a sudden view of Alicia's inability to act, the diplomat sent in where there was no hope of ceasefire. Storm had said Alicia was trying to do the right thing yet "heavily armed and well-trained" sounded like a threat. Either way, she was trapped in a bathroom, with no way out but through.

She lowered the pistol. It clunked dully on the tiles.

"Thank you."

Alicia seemed to deflate as three men came in behind her. They had wide shoulders and thick necks and enough gear for a battle zone. They flowed around Alicia, powerful and fluid next to her pained stillness. Amanda had a moment of pride that they had put this on for her.

She held up her hands, a rifle pointed at her chest. She didn't resist, calmed the part of herself that wanted to fight like a feral cat. Her hands were cuffed behind her back, swift and competent, and surprisingly painless.

They had the same precise movements as Maria. These were the units Maria and Storm had talked about, specially assigned to Stanton and the corporation. Maria knew this opponent, and Amanda had purposely ignored her.

She had one last glance of Alicia staring at her reflection, before she was rushed into her overturned bedroom and up the stairs.

TWELVE

ADAMS

ADAMS CURLED HIS FINGERS around the chain-link fence, the metal rough and cool. Hamel stood beside him, the two of them peering at the black rubber sheet covering the community swimming pool, not yet opened after the winter. Dead leaves floated in the stagnant water on top of the tarp, the bright yellow of a plastic bag caught among them. A second chain-link enclosure lay behind it, enclosing the neighborhood substation, a large white Gatherer wedged in between the switch gear. The outer shell of it was gray with dirt and some of the corners had been cracked by the elements.

"They've set up a micro-grid," said Hamel, "using the wires from the old distribution system to deliver the electricity to the houses."

"How many does it feed?"

Hamel shook his head. "It's impossible to tell without something to measure it."

It looked the same as any old piece of infrastructure, grass growing up between the gravel around it, the plastic shell unseen as part of the landscape except by those who looked after it.

Adams looked back to the vehicle. The white streak had pointed them towards this Gatherer but now that they were closer there was no sign of the blank slashes along the earth.

The pool sat on the knoll of a hill, above the city of Rima, and beyond the Gatherer the grid of streets spread until it reached the ocean. At the edge, just before the shoreline, the headquarters of the

Gatherer Corporation rose into the sky, the glowing upward hands of the Gatherer symbol just visible.

Adams circled the perimeter fence, moving in the direction of where they had seen the first streak. Hamel investigated in the opposite direction. A cluster of trees grew further downhill, forming a thin border before the line of backyard fences that marked the edge of the public land. His boots crunched over the dead blades of last year's grass and the green shoots of the new growth. There wasn't a single blade of white among them.

He looked up towards the Gatherer inside its fence and back towards the original streak, searching for the trace of white forming into a line. The place was dormant, only just starting to wake from winter.

The edge dropped off steeper on this side, a rocky cliff dropping down onto another suburban street. He saw no outlines of white Gatherers among the houses, all of them presumably fed from this larger, central device.

He walked back up towards the pool, disappointed at the lack of connection between the streak and the Gatherer. He had been sure the absence of color had been caused by the device. Yet perhaps the woman had been right: it had been a chemical spill of some kind. Though that didn't explain Megan's reaction.

He walked faster in frustration, the increased movement returning him to focus. They had let the streak distract them when there were a hundred other explanations. Or at least one.

Hamel met him at the top of the hill, shaking his head in answer to Adams' unspoken question. They briefly looked over the expanse of the city, and Adams' gaze sought out the dark zone along the river where he had first met Megan. It was indistinguishable from the rest of the industrial park in daylight, yet he still felt the shameful guilt. Were its depowered streets empty now? Or had more afflicted come to fill the spot of the ones they had carted away?

"Do you think they're down there?" asked Hamel.

Adams stopped in the middle of turning away. He scanned the tops of buildings, the white outline of a Gatherer visible on the rooftops of some. There would be nowhere for Storm to take shelter in the city.

"They'd be mad to go back in."

They circled back around the swimming pool. The orange life ring which hung on the wall of the change rooms had been whitewashed by the elements. A growing wind blew up from the ocean, damp and cutting.

Eli waited inside the minivan, his face a round oval behind the reflection. He hadn't wanted to get out of the van and Adams couldn't blame him. He got out as Adams and Hamel approached.

"Where's Megan?" asked Adams.

"I thought she was with you."

Adams scanned the empty knoll and the enclosed pool. Eli looked in all directions.

"She followed you, right after you left."

Cold rushed across Adams shoulders, flooding into his hands in a painful rush.

They all faced the knoll, the cluster of firs beside the pool swaying in the growing wind.

"Hamel, check the far side. Eli, you're with me."

Adams started walking and switched immediately into a jog. Eli kept pace at his side.

"She wouldn't let me come," said Eli. "She said she wanted to go alone."

"It's not your fault," said Adams. "But we need to listen now for even the smallest sound."

The boy nodded; his mouth set in concentration.

They had skirted around the base of the hill in the direction of Adams' previous route. The wind obscured most sound and their view was of an unbroken area of muted brown and struggling green below a gray sky.

She wouldn't just wander off. She wasn't that kind of kid.

They reached the bottom of the hill, ran along the border of trees, searching for a flash of blonde hair or the light blue of her jacket. The back windows of the houses were blank. Megan could have been hidden behind any of them. A fallen branch half covered in pine needles took on the shape of Megan's running shoe before it reshaped into the splintered stump. He kept running, part of him tracking Eli's raised breathing behind him as he tried to keep up.

They reached a particularly neglected yard, the grasses tall and matted, a broken lawn chair discarded in the corner beside a rusted barbecue. The windows were murky with years of dirt and the broken screen door leaned against the wall. Had there been movement behind the windows? Neglect didn't mean threat, often the opposite, yet Megan had to have gone somewhere.

He was about to open the gate, the latch broken, when Eli stopped him. "Someone shouted."

Adams heard only the rustle of wind in the trees.

"Was it Hamel?" asked Adams.

"From over there." Eli pointed towards the fenced pool.

He and Eli met each other's eyes, the boy's pupils wide, and then they were running towards the sound around the bottom of the knoll. Hamel's shoulders and torso appeared first and then the bright spot of Megan's hair. She had her palms over the ground, moving them back and forth in a wide arc, a small, rounded ball in the expanse of grass.

He ran directly to her, stopping behind her several steps at Hamel's signal. She stood and moved away from him. After several steps, she crouched again, moving her hands in the same sweeping motion, like the guys at the beach with the metal detectors over the sand.

He knelt beside her.

"What is it?" She seemed not to hear him; consumed by whatever information she was receiving. "Is there something there?"

She stood again, and moved further away, continuing along a straight line. She was moving downhill, following a line in the direction of the cliff that separated them from the city.

He stayed close behind her, the wind buffeting around them so that she seemed even more fragile.

"Can you tell me anything?"

She shuddered, and her fingers curled in towards her palms.

"It's like the wind."

Her arms dropped and she slumped against him. He held her tight to his side. He was out of breath, the air itself feeling like a threat. There was no place to run, no place to hide from this thing, its reach insidious and omnipotent.

In a single motion, he picked her up and carried her in his arms. The trees swayed, the wind raced through the grasses, and he tasted salt on his lips. He spun in a circle, Megan tight against him. He felt surrounded, the sights of shooters trained on him, yet there was only the field and the sky and the indifference of the city.

He shouted in frustration. Megan squirmed against the tightness of his grip yet if he let go, she would be gone, just like Valerie and Camille.

"Adams."

Hamel stood beside him, looking out over the view that should have been hopeful, the vital, invigorating arrival of spring and Eli a boy playing in the grass. Except the Gatherer hung over all of it, whatever Storm had unleashed having turned to a force they could not see.

"We're done here," said Hamel.

Adams was unable to move. Any step forward was rife with danger.

"It's alright," said Hamel.

Megan linked her arms around his neck and leaned her head against his heart.

It gave him the strength to step back. He turned his face into the breeze, Hamel and Eli fell into step beside him.

"Do you know what it is?" asked Eli.

At one time Adams believed he could know everything, be so prepared and informed that no situation would ever best him. Now, with Megan's weight in his arms, it felt as if he knew nothing at all.

THIRTEEN

ADAMS

ADAMS USED THE TIP of his pocketknife to carve a long line in the wood on top of the picnic table. He blew into the crevasse, and shavings tumbled across the tabletop. He hadn't decided what to carve yet, knew only the satisfaction of pushing the blade into the weathered wood and uncovering the lighter wood beneath.

Hamel tapped on the keyboard of his laptop in intense bursts followed by stretches where he frowned and his eyes scanned the screen. Adams brushed shavings from the end of the line and lifted his gaze to where Megan and Eli played at the water's edge.

"Don't get your shoes wet!" he called across the beach.

Only Eli looked up before following Megan. Their small bodies were in constant motion, bending, throwing, and celebrating when a stone skipped across the waves. Megan was hardly recognizable from the girl he had carried away from the swimming pool, her cheeks flushed, her hair pushed back in the wind; a few hours of sleep and Eli's attention enough to leave the trauma of the streaks behind. Eli had barely missed a step when they'd driven away from his father's house, not even lifting his head. When he had finally looked up, he'd watched the passing houses for a long moment before his gaze flicked to Adams, the sadness in his eyes too deep to bear.

Eli handed a stone to Megan and bent his arm to demonstrate how to get the right trajectory.

Hamel swore at the screen.

There were a few more strokes of the keys. At the water, Eli jumped for joy, as Megan intently searched for a stone beside him.

"Look at that."

Adams leaned over.

"Wait," said Hamel. He clicked a final time on the track pad and swung the screen to show Adams.

It was a satellite image, zoomed in too close, with fuzzy outlines of rooftops filling the spaces between the ribbons of roads.

"What am I looking at?" asked Adams.

Hamel pointed to a section of solid green, a park in the center of a neighborhood. He moved his finger along a lighter strip of ground, like a slightly faded section of grass. He zoomed out and navigated to another green space, several streets from the first. Under magnification there was another pale line. He repeated the process and showed Adams three other possible white slashes before he zoomed out to a view of several blocks. The black rectangle of the swimming pool, surrounded by lighter concrete, lay at the center. Hamel pointed to each of the green spaces he had already shown him, his hand moving in a circle over the screen.

"The streaks—" Hamel traced the short length of each as he talked. "—point back towards the Gatherer."

They were spokes on a wheel, all radiating out from the central hub of the Gatherer.

"It's like at the hospital," said Hamel.

It had the same spokes, the Gatherer in the middle.

"And the warehouse," said Adams, remembering Megan walking ahead of him, a wire running along the concrete beside her. "But there's no wires."

Hamel was moving the satellite image again, showing the overview of Rima, the streets lost in the sea of buildings.

A gull cried, swirling above Megan and Eli, mistaking their stones for food or perhaps hoping for something else. Megan had pulled off her shoes and was rolling up her pants.

"The same thing happens here." Hamel pointed to the north-east corner of the city. "And here." He showed a similar pattern of green spaces with lighter streaks. "This has the Gatherer at City Hall at its center, these ones all point to the Gatherer at the arena. And these are the ones we can see, because of the green spaces; there could be more under the buildings, or showing up in basements where no one sees them."

"So doing what? Turning the concrete white?"

Hamel shrugged.

Megan had stepped into the water, the waves crashing around her feet. Eli was tearing off his socks, in a hurry to follow. He flinched as his toes touched the waves. Megan was already calf-deep. Eli hopped out of the water, attempted to run in again, but never got more than a step from the beach.

"So that's how it draws energy towards it?" said Adams. "Along these spokes?" There could be hundreds of these wheels around the city. "It can't just draw energy through the earth."

"Who's to say what it can and can't do," said Hamel "Before Storm invented it, we wouldn't have believed the Gatherer was possible."

Adams snapped the blade of the pocketknife back into place and returned it to the pouch on his belt. He hated the stealth of this thing, spreading its tentacles, and taking more than intended, its disease, and now this, all happening out of sight.

"Has anyone else noticed yet?"

Megan had gone as deep as her knees and bent to let the tops of the waves run through her fingers.

"There have been reports online, a few people discussing them. But no one has seen the pattern yet. Or if they have, they're not saying."

The spokes of the north-east wheels extended further than the others, some of them hard to distinguish where they meshed with other wheels.

"—Anywhere there is a large Gatherer. I've identified at least four in the foreign capitals where the Corporation gifted the new Gatherers."

The gray sky was high above them, the gray of the ocean equally immense. The top of the weathered table was indistinguishable but for the single line he had carved in the wood. He focused on the line, and the roughness of it under his finger. He saw again the body bags where he had found Valerie and Camille. Instead of falling into the horror of their still faces, he looked further, saw the dozens of other bags in the room. Civilians who had come for help and hadn't received the care they needed.

"Is it intentional?"

There had been an announcement, that the Corporation was gifting the new, larger Gatherers to governments around the world. It had looked like an extensive PR campaign, a way to wipe away any final resistance to the energy-giving devices. But this felt too right, that Stanton would use this to deliver a weapon capable of killing and inciting chaos. He could almost feel the tendrils of the device wriggling out into the world. A streak could be underneath them right now, expanding and sucking the life out of everything around it. He wanted to pick up his feet, lift all of them away from its seeking, sucking lines.

Eli shouted. He was hopping and waving his arm in the air, pulling on something in the water. There was a flash of Megan's curls in the waves, rising and falling.

He ran, all adrenaline, splashing into the waves in his boots, and lifted Megan up and out. She was cold and wet, and he almost dropped her, having a hard time keeping her close. It took a second to recognize that she was struggling, trying to get out of his arms.

"Leave me!"

She was ice-cold, her skin the temperature of the water. He barely got her to the stones before she twisted free, landed on two feet on the beach.

She made to go back in.

"Megan. Stop!"

It was an order meant to penetrate whatever fog had hold of her.

She kept going, and he held her back, not expecting the strength in her small frame.

"Megan!" He struggled to keep hold of her, hated having to fight against her.

She twisted her arm out of his grasp and he grabbed her around the waist. She strained against him.

Eli was yelling, dancing around them, adding to the confusion.

Adams scooped her up, holding the squirming mass of arms and legs against his chest, and walked back to the table.

Hamel's lips quirked up in amusement, as the three of them approached, Eli close enough to trip on.

"Put. Me. Down."

Megan's fury was equal to his own, and in a surge of frustration he set her down.

She shook out her wet hair and glared up at him, a formidable ball of defiance.

"I like the water."

Her lips were blue. She turned to go back in.

"Megan. Hold on a second."

Hamel spoke the words casually, as a question, not a command. Adams' irritation at the lot of them grew, especially when Megan paused to look back at Hamel.

"I want to show you something. See what you think."

She navigated around Adams without looking at him, her jeans dark with water and her sweatshirt clinging to her torso. She settled in beside Hamel, her attention on the screen.

Adams was suddenly depleted, his frustration turned to sorrow in an instant. What he wouldn't give to be struggling with Camille again, to be a better parent. He trudged back to the van to get Megan dry clothes and a towel, as Hamel explained the spokes to Megan and Eli.

As he grabbed a pair of track pants and a hoodie out of the back, he had a moment of complete absurdity. You didn't stop a threat to humanity by hauling two kids around the country. He had gotten completely off-track.

He leaned against the rear bumper, the dry clothes in his hands.

Megan and Eli sat beside Hamel, and he could imagine their faces pinched in concentration. Maybe you did save the world by taking care of two children; his fate was woven so tightly with theirs that it wasn't an option to not have them with him.

He dug out a mostly clean towel and considered changing his shirt that had absorbed much of the water when he had carried her. He closed the trunk, the wind colder on his wet torso as he squelched back across the stones.

"This is the one you saw today," said Hamel, pointing at the screen. "These other ones point to the same Gatherer."

"Can you show me the first one?"

Hamel zoomed out as Adams gave Megan the towel. She held it in her lap.

"Here."

Hamel pointed to a green area further out from the swimming pool. He let his hand drop, frowning in consternation.

The first streak they had seen was too far out to be part of the spokes that spread out from the pool. It ran in the same direction but was off on its own, in a separate area. More like a stem than an actual part of the wheel.

"Can you move that way?" said Eli.

Adams took back the towel and started to dry Megan's hair. "Put these on." He dropped the clothes in her lap.

She ignored them and it was only when Hamel turned the laptop away and nodded at the clothes that she actually paid them any attention. With a huff, she stripped off the wet shirt and pulled on the dry hoodie, dropping the discarded shirt in a pile on the stones. She did the same with the pants, wriggling out of her jeans and underwear without so much as a pause of self-consciousness. Hamel and Eli looked away.

As she tied up the drawstrings, Adams picked up the wet clothes, wrung out the water and draped them over the end of the table to dry.

Hamel had pulled the view farther out and had drawn lines over the top of the image to highlight the locations of the spokes. There were a half-dozen wheels spread across the city, each centered around a larger Gatherer. The park near where they had intended to drop off Eli wasn't part of any wheel.

"Did the first streak feel different than the second?" asked Adams.

Megan used two fingers on the track pad to enlarge the image of the first streak. There wasn't much to see but blurry pixels.

"They feel like dominoes falling over."

"In both directions?" asked Hamel.

Megan shook her head, pulled out on the image.

"One direction."

"Was the second streak different?" asked Adams.

It *should* be stronger, since it was closer to a Gatherer, yet he was aware of the assumptions he was making, trying to fit it into the laws of the world he knew.

"It looked farther than the first."

She sounded distracted, the memory enough to pull her back.

"You mean stronger? Or bigger?" asked Hamel.

She shook her head. "It wanted me to go with it."

"Did it come from far away? Like from space?" asked Eli.

Adams didn't laugh. Because what the hell did they know? They had no idea what this thing was. Maybe Storm hadn't discovered it, but it had been given to her as a means to get it spread throughout the world, some kind of subversive strategy. Far-fetched, but no more so than the reality.

Hamel switched to another image, showing the entire region. Small dots showed the known locations of the spokes.

"It's not an alien. It's part of the earth," said Megan.

"The earth doesn't want you to be part of it," said Hamel.

Megan shook her head in frustration, even as a look of longing overtook her. "It's not like that. It was…It wasn't like that." He had to remember she was a child whose mother had just died. Even though she was gifted and precocious, she was ill-prepared for any of this.

"Eli, can you go grab Megan's shoes and socks?" said Hamel.

They had left them by the water, the socks pushed into the tops of their runners.

Adams sat where Eli had been, sheltering Megan from the wind and putting her between his and Hamel's warmth.

"Did it hurt?" Adams asked.

She took a deep breath and pushed the laptop away.

"The first one was like the hospital. Only stronger."

Eli sat at the water's edge pulling on his shoes. From their viewpoint, it looked as if he sat directly in the waves.

"The second one was different, it tried to pull me. All of me, not just my body."

They watched Eli clamber over the stones towards them.

"It made me sad." Megan started to shiver.

Hamel closed the laptop. "That's enough for now." He caught Adams' eye. "It's time to get going."

Adams collected Megan's wet clothes as she and Eli walked carefully over the stones towards the vehicle.

Hamel hung back, waiting until they were out of earshot.

"Is she making it up?"

They had reached the vehicle and Eli had opened the door for her. Megan crawled into the back seats, and Eli followed, as tired as after any day at the beach.

"She has no reason to."

"Attention, maybe?" said Hamel.

A washroom lay at the far end of the beach, its shutters closed, and a red tag of graffiti scrawled across the concrete wall.

"She felt them at the hospital when her mother was still alive. It's not new."

The children's silhouettes were visible in the back seat.

"It seems too sophisticated for Stanton," said Hamel. "These lines or connections or whatever they are, they're subtle. It's out of character."

"Maybe he doesn't know."

The gull alighted on the peak of the washroom roof, its chest a thick white. It cocked its head and ruffled its wings, the whole world waiting to see what he would do.

"And if he does?"

Then they needed more people, more resources, and an entire team of exceptional people.

FOURTEEN

AMANDA

AMANDA OPENED THE TOP drawer of the desk, the same paper clip crammed in its corner. It had lain in the same spot each time she had opened the empty drawer, yet every time she circled the desk, she opened it again hoping that something – anything – would have changed.

She picked up the paper clip and bumped the drawer shut with her hip. Standing at the wall of windows, she pushed out the center piece of the paper clip and extended it into a crooked wire.

There was nothing it could do for her. There was a guard stationed outside the door even if she did manage to pick the lock. The windows offered fewer options, the ground at least a dozen storeys below. She longed for a cigarette; her hands had reached a hundred times for the pocket of her jacket which they had taken from her.

The darkness outside the window had turned to a heavy dusk and the time when Storm and Maria would have left the park had long passed. She tried not to think of them leaving the city without her.

As the sky lightened, the pathways below her clarified into gravel tracks bordered by manicured gardens and the line of the horizon changed into the restless expanse of the ocean.

Before they had taken off her blindfold, she had been expecting seeping dungeon cells and torture devices in her growing terror. Instead, she had gotten the endless drabness of an office, only the desk and an infuriating computer to distract her.

She had been gleeful when they had left her alone with an access point to the network and had silently depressed the keys as she navigated past the password. Yet every time she tried to connect; the computer crashed. Sometime in the middle of the night, she had let her hands fall from the keyboard and understood why it had been left in the room.

She leaned close against the windowpane, trying to see down the wall of the building to the ground level and the back entrance. Only a single person had hurried from the manufacturing center to the office tower, flashing in and out of the pools of light along the path. Otherwise, the compound of the Gatherer Corporation had stayed a perfect tableau of stillness as the night disappeared.

She had a view of only the corner of the manufacturing center, yet she knew what it was. Knew the layout of the compound and its security systems intimately, after having roamed freely through them. What she wouldn't do to have that access now, and to the entire city network. To see who stood outside her door, know where all the people were, and with a click of a mouse make sure that Storm and Maria were safe. She ached for that connection.

The world turned a shade lighter, the perimeter fence and the soldiers stationed along it taking shape. Storm couldn't have imagined the compound she had founded on transparency and the miracle of limitless energy would become a militarized zone. She couldn't have imagined the suffering it would bring, either.

Amanda pushed the paper clip back into shape and bent it out again, feeling the pivot point growing weaker. She looked to the black dome that hid the camera lens in the corner of the room and wondered what she would have to do to get anyone's attention.

The sun wasn't high yet and the open area lay in varying shades of gray. She moved until her nose almost touched the window, trying to refocus her vision. The shadows made it look as if swaths of white cut across the grassy area, on diagonals towards the office tower. She tilted her head and tried to change the angle of the light, but the white bands still blazed across the lawn.

The door clicked and she turned.

She had never seen Stanton in person, her only contact through his abundant press conferences and interviews, yet there was no mistaking who it was.

He wore a full khaki uniform, his pants tucked into his boots, and his mane of white hair reached his collar. It was all the same parts of him, yet he looked smaller in person, the chest not as broad, the white hair yellow and lank, and a discoloring of age spots across his high forehead.

This was the person who had been hunting Maria, the one who kept her ever-vigilant, sure that he would arrive at any time.

"Ms. Delaney." There was stiffness in his movements, the briefest moment of hesitation. He had always exuded power and a raw physical strength, yet his movements looked like effort.

"I'm General Stanton, the commander of the military unit protecting the Gatherer Corporation."

It was the same deep and vibrant voice, sounding like a voice-over from someone else. She moved away from him, along the wall. His chest was still massive, the underlying structure intact, yet he had collapsed somehow.

"That sounds important."

"It is. Since the Gatherers are now the engine of the world."

She searched the grim lines of his face for sarcasm. Her palms were sweaty, her sides slick. People without senses of humor always frightened her.

She reached the corner of the room, one edge glass, the other solid wall. It had been a mistake to walk away from the door, but she had needed so strongly to get away.

"You are a friend of Maria Kowalski."

His directness was disconcerting. There was no preparation or easing into the conversation. No attempt to make her feel comfortable.

"I was."

He ran a finger along the top of the defunct monitor.

"Do you know where she is?"

The day outside the window grew brighter, the crests of the rolling waves and the swaying tops of the fir trees taking shape.

"No."

He lifted an apple that lay on the breakfast tray the guard had brought earlier. He absently turned it before putting it down.

"With all your skills and your connectivity, you have no idea where they are?"

"There's not much connectivity in here."

He straightened the white plastic spoon along the edge of the tray.

"You realize she is wanted for murder and terrorism. Not a person you should be aligning yourself with."

She waited for the threat or the violence, whatever he would bring to force her to tell him what she knew. High white clouds stretched above the ocean.

"I knew Maria when she first enlisted," he said. "She was determined to prove to the world how good she was. I like that in a soldier. That need to compete. It was a mistake to put her under Havernal's leadership. I believe all of this could have been avoided if he hadn't corrupted her."

Havernal had been the one to first ask Maria to leave her unit to find Storm and a cure. Maria was still trying to complete that mission.

"She makes her own decisions."

"Yes, you knew Ms. Kowalski before she came to us. Two hell raisers intent on giving the world a royal fuck-you."

Amanda breathed. "I wouldn't put it that way."

He watched her from sunken eyes, like his body was sliding off him, leaving only the ferocity of his will.

"I don't believe that people are capable of change. It's why the Gatherer is so important. People will never stop consuming, will always need something new to power their wants. You and Maria are both criminals. You have been since the beginning. But you are in over your heads. This isn't a game, or a dare to see how wild you can be. Your irresponsibility is threatening the very future of our world."

She wondered if in his weakened state, she could overpower him.

"That's why you've developed the larger models? To provide more energy?" she said.

She kept her gaze on the grounds and the gently curving path towards the ocean.

"We've been open about that. There have been press releases—" He opened his arms, palms up, like he had nothing to hide. His wrists were thin, swimming in the buttoned cuffs of his uniform. "The transparency of the organization was something Ms. Freeman established before she left."

Even she could see all the things that could go wrong if she tried to overpower him, including one of the guard's bullets in her head. The tops of the fir trees swayed below her. If she were a flying squirrel, it would only take a single leap to get there.

"But not so open about the afflicted. Or those that are dying."

She had a memory of the clearing with its rows of tents. The sick and dying giving their lives up to a device as if it were some kind of God. The fury of it was so strong she pushed away from the corner, paced along the front of the window.

"Your hostility is misdirected," he said.

"And you're here to tell me where to direct it?"

She was trapped between moving in front of him or behind. Both felt dangerous.

"I'm here for you to tell me what their plan is."

"There is no plan."

She didn't need to lie; their plan had been gone the moment the malware in the Corporation's system was discovered.

He moved away from the desk, towards the window, and she stayed opposite him, unable to stop herself from maintaining whatever distance she could.

"Then why did she come back?"

"I don't know."

He sighed, and she had never known how frightening a breath of air could be. He rubbed the window with his thumb, as if wiping off a smudge.

"You were inside the compound's network when you helped them escape. Yet somehow you have no idea why you have all chosen to return at this moment."

"I haven't seen them since they escaped. I don't know what they have planned."

"Then where have you been the last five months?"

She should know better than to try to lie. They had been watching the house, knew she hadn't been there.

He turned his back to the window, his hair a helmet of white around his face.

"There are rules of engagement in the military, did you know that? Of when to leave someone behind. It's not personal. It's about cutting losses and completing the mission." He formed a silhouette in front of the window, blocking the reflected light of the ocean. "Ms. Kowalski will already have left you behind."

She bit down on her response and the knee-jerk desire to strike back.

"I don't know what you mean."

She ached for a cigarette, needed the long, slow draw of smoke into her lungs to think clearly.

"Let me clarify for you." He circled the desk and she moved with him, opposite points on a circle. "There's no one coming to rescue you. You are here as long as I choose to keep you."

"I've been in worse places."

He smirked, low and cruel, and she wished she had kept her mouth shut.

"I'm sure you have."

He knew about Simon, her life before, and what had finally driven her away from it. She stayed still, had the irrational thought that if she stayed in one place, he would go away. Like the rabbit that freezes, believing its camouflage is enough to save it from the coyote. Could he hear the hammering of her heart?

He picked up the apple again and unclipped a pen knife from his belt. He cut off a chunk and let it fall to the tray.

Her feet felt numb, disconnected.

"We found them; you know. Not far from your house. Riding a pair of stolen bikes." Another chunk dropped onto the empty shininess of the desk. "Embarrassing, really. Ms. Kowalski was a great soldier once. Now——" He shook his head as he laid the cut core beside the chunks. "——she's lost her way."

She couldn't believe anything that came out of his mouth. It didn't stop the images in her head of Maria and Storm being hauled away, or of Storm writhing from the burn of a field, all their bravado and plans gone up in smoke before they had even started. She could imagine the media frenzy when Storm and Maria were apprehended. The inventor-turned-terrorist, finally brought to justice.

She smiled. For at the center of that frenzy would be Stanton, claiming justice and self-righteousness as if he had created them.

"Then why are you here?"

His jaw tightened, and she saw the smallest reflection of his struggle. She reveled in that moment of victory. From the moment Maria had shown up on her doorstep in the middle of the night, Amanda had understood her own role. Storm and Maria would always be more important in the story, and she would be the supporting cast. Stanton wouldn't be here if he had found them. He wouldn't even care that she existed. He wanted her to be afraid, and all she felt was victory.

"I was just giving you a chance to save yourself."

He returned the knife to his belt.

"Bullshit."

The looseness along his jaw hardened and he walked stiffly around the desk. She could see the illness now, the effort of each step.

"You're sick." The shock of it stunned her. She backed away.

His face flushed purple as he bore down on her. "You think you can get away from me?" She had a memory of the man Simon had killed, struggling forward without knowing he was finished. "No one knows you are here. So you can hold out, and protect them. But eventually you will tell me, and I will find them. And at that point, I won't need you anymore."

The veins on his forehead bulged, and the skin around one eye was raw.

"Sergeant!"

She flinched at the force of the command, so at odds with this struggling, old man. The door opened.

"Sir?"

She inched towards the window.

"I need you in here."

The soldier slipped in and stood at attention next to the door. He stared straight ahead, his arms behind his back, as if he were on inspection rather than in this bare office. Her heart beat so loudly she barely heard Stanton speak.

"You're a smart woman." Her hands started to shake. "You would have been an asset to the development team, if you weren't so—"

There wasn't enough air to breathe.

"Misdirected?" she said, hating the shake in her voice. She had worked too hard to feel this helpless, hated herself for her fear.

He pushed the tray out of the way and sat on the desk, his movements suddenly looser, and more relaxed. The casualness of it terrified her. His bony knees poked through his uniform.

"Now," said Stanton, and he clasped his hands in front of him, like a teacher about to tell a story. "Where should we start?"

The glass was cool against her shoulder, the arriving spring day distant and unfocused compared to the sharpness of the room. The cut edges of the apple had started to turn brown.

"First I'd like to know the plan," said Stanton. "There's a reason Ms. Freeman and Ms. Kowalski are back in the city, and I'd like to know what it is."

She could feel her breath move in and out, her heart slamming against her ribs. She had survived horrible things before, had made it through.

She looked to the outline of the door, couldn't stop herself. The soldier's head almost reached the upper frame.

She saw Stanton nod, out of the corner of her eye, and she scrambled back into the corner. The young soldier moved in one fluid motion, as if he were the air itself. There was a terrifying beauty to its fluidity and strength. She pressed back further, wishing the glass would break and set her free.

FIFTEEN

MARIA

ARIA RODE CLOSE BESIDE Storm, part of her attention on her and part on what had happened to Amanda, whose absence had intensified in the light of day.

Storm was bent low over the handlebars and wavered on the bike, her face hidden within the confines of her hood. She wasn't taking much in, her entire focus on moving forward, and Maria had wondered more than once if they were on the right path. Maria had had to grab her handlebars to keep her upright when they had made a bad detour and passed beneath the tracks of the high-speed train at the wrong moment.

They followed the murky waters of a canal, the pavement of the narrow utility road cracked and broken, the stench of the stagnant water undeterred by the freshness of the morning air. She longed to return to where they had seen Amanda pedaling away and follow wherever she had gone.

She swerved to avoid a large pothole and Storm rode right through it, leaning hard to one side before emerging. Maria reached to steady her, until Storm righted herself, the effort it took showing in each pained push on the pedals.

Storm lifted her head as they rounded a curve and braked hard. A three-meter-high, chain-link fence blocked the road and Maria swerved to avoid hitting it. The fence reached beyond the edges of the road, cutting between the sides of two warehouses and extending to the edge of the canal so that anyone wanting to pass would have to enter the fetid water.

Storm got stiffly from the bike and stared down the fence with the recognition of a known enemy. Several thin wires ran in parallel above the barbed wire.

"They put an electric fence around the dark zone?" Maria asked.

She had seen the reports of teen gangs tormenting the afflicted, or of the plague-deniers following the afflicted in the streets, yet she had seen less formidable barriers in war zones.

"They couldn't have the afflicted just wandering around."

Maria had no recollection of the dark zone, the area that had once been free of electricity, where the afflicted had sought shelter. The last time she had been near it, she had been too delirious with infection and fever to know where she was.

"They were keeping the afflicted in?"

Storm walked towards the fence and Maria hurried to follow. Storm flinched where she grabbed her arm, but her eyes were clear, if pained, her expression of sorrow, not reverence.

"It's not live," said Storm.

Even without the electrification, the fence was a formidable barrier with thick, rough steel links, the top stretching a good meter above Maria's head. Storm walked parallel to it, turning sideways to squeeze through where it ran between the warehouses.

"Wait."

Storm stood in the shadows of the buildings as Maria moved the bikes behind a stack of skids that were piled next to the canal. She checked the opposite shore, yet the emptiness on this side was reflected in the bolted doors and shaded windows of the shuttered businesses on the other side.

The smell of dirt and damp caught in her throat as they moved into the alley. The fence was unbroken, a marvel of flexibility the way it wove between buildings and across roads, forming a meandering perimeter for what as far as Maria could tell was a warehouse area identical to where they stood. Service roads ran between steel Quonset huts, well-kept warehouses, and boxier, rundown buildings.

"There's no people," said Maria.

Storm had paused where the fence blocked the road, looking through to the street that ran straight and empty, a larger, barn-like structure at its end.

"They stay away from the perimeter."

They walked for several minutes before Storm stopped in a section where the fence ran through a bedraggled, stringy bush with a water utility building blocking the view on the other side. With her hand resting on one of the support poles, she peeled away a corner of the fence.

Maria had an image in her mind of Amanda running along the fence, not knowing this was here, and unable to get through. She shook her head, couldn't let her thoughts follow that trail.

"How did you know this was here?"

Storm's time in the dark zone had been brief, long enough to witness the suffering of the afflicted and add that guilt to her burden.

Maria checked over her shoulder, yet there had been no one all morning on either side, vehicle traffic and the underlying hum of the city only a few streets away.

"Megan showed me."

The girl who had known the tunnels in the city well enough to guide Storm through them, and who Storm had left behind.

She followed Storm through and stood within the shelter of the bush, the small buds on the branches catching in her hair. The utility building sat a few paces away, its unmarred, brick exterior solid among the decline. Windows had been broken in the surrounding buildings and doors pried open, the marks of forced entry on the door frames. Grass grew tall in the cracks in the asphalt and a layer of dirt covered the shattered glass on the ground.

Storm wove carefully through it, intent on finding the warehouse and the afflicted hiding there. Maria almost stopped her. In areas where people were hiding out, there were footprints in the dirt, or the occasional piece of fabric or a personal item dropped. Here, there were only wind-swept streets and blank windows opaque with dirt. There was no movement, no unexplained shift of light. All was still and long abandoned.

Storm walked ahead with a confidence at each turn that spoke to her memory. Her pace quickened the further they wove past gaping doors and the shells of old vehicles. She slowed as they approached a warehouse like many of the others, a single steel door providing access on one end. Outside the entrance, a glass bottle balanced on a wooden bench and a deck of playing cards lay scattered in the dirt. The upturned faces were faded and warped enough that it must have been weeks, if not months, that they had lain there. Dirt had collected in front of the door, small waves across its surface, the tracks left by the most recent wind.

Storm looked from the cards to the door, the evidence finally accumulating enough to penetrate her excitement. A blanket with a yellow duck embroidered on the corner had been trampled by wind and rain against the wall.

Storm moved abruptly to the door. Maria checked behind them before she followed, the emptiness of the street unchanged.

The warehouse felt colder than outside, and Maria stopped on the threshold. The windows along the top of the wall provided a dim light, and the faintest scent of candles lingered in the air. Several hundred cots lined the cavernous space; many were bunks, their metal frames thin vertical lines that cut the space. Photos had been taped to the frames, blankets left on beds, a discarded magazine spread on the closest cot and a pair of worn running shoes tucked beneath it. A desk and a children's play area lay close to the door, the red of a toy barn and the yellow of a plastic table covered in a layer of dust.

Storm pushed back her hood, and Maria saw the moment she understood. She caved a little, resting her hand on the back of a plastic lawn chair. She had wanted to see these people, to have whatever comfort they could give her. And they had both hoped Amanda would be there.

Maria started at a sound above them, moving in front of Storm when she saw the bird, a pigeon or maybe a dove, flying away from the ragged edges of a nest in the rafters. It circled a few times, flew to the far corner, and escaped through a broken window.

Storm crossed to the desk and lifted the top sheet from a stack of papers. She read it and put it down, lifting the next. She had read through half a dozen when Maria moved closer and looked over her shoulder.

They looked like patient files, a name written across the top, a brief physical description with a list of symptoms. Some included one or two, others over a dozen.

David Anthony. 5'4" Fits of anger interspersed with long periods of inattention. No physical symptoms.

Storm laid down the one she had been reading.

"How long do we wait?"

As long as it takes is, what Maria wanted to say, but part of her, the part that was a soldier, knew that they shouldn't wait at all.

"Until dark."

Or morning, or however long it took for Amanda to arrive.

"We can check for a boat in the canal," said Storm.

It was their plan B. Or what they had come up with at the cabin. If they couldn't get to Amanda's they would go to the dark zone and leave the city by boat. The same way Storm and Maria had arrived five months ago, except the plan had been for the three of them to leave together.

Storm wandered past the toy area, spinning the wheels of a yellow school bus, the unblinking stares of the passengers looking out at them. Maria's foot nudged a metal water bottle, and it rattled across the floor, stopping at the leg of the desk, the noise echoing between rafters.

They moved together into the higher space of the main warehouse. A wide aisle continued to the end of the building, cots lined on either side, the air so still their movement broke it open.

"Were these full?" asked Maria.

Storm stood next to one of the bunks, her hand resting on the upper bed. It was neatly made with a quilt of dark green, the only bed that didn't look like it had been left in a hurry.

"There wasn't enough room for all of them."

A blanket hung off the side of the next bed, and a stuffed donkey had been left in the center of the aisle, one of its eyes missing. A wire ran beside it, down the center of the aisle.

Maria climbed onto an overturned bunk, balancing on the metal frame so she had a view of the entire warehouse. There were hundreds of bunks, and it was only from this perspective that she saw the pattern, like a labyrinth laid out from above.

"The bunks are arranged in arcs," said Maria, as she caught up to Storm as she followed the path of the wire.

Storm steered around a plastic crate that had been used as a bedside table, now toppled on its side, a box of tissue crushed beneath it.

"They curve around a central point."

She ran her fingers along the metal bar of a bunk with a gentle touch. She stepped over a tricycle, the smallest running shoe lying beside it.

"And what's it supposed to do?"

Maria ducked to see the adjacent rows as Storm continued to follow the wire. The pattern was clear now, all the rows spiraling out from a central point.

She caught up to Storm as she crouched next to a rough opening that had been chipped out of the concrete floor. The wires ran into it, from all directions, but whatever they had connected to was gone. Storm looked down the path of each wire as if she might see its end.

"Is that where the Gatherer was?"

The hole was small, no larger than two of Maria's palms.

"They thought it would heal by creating some kind of energy. But I think it had more to do with the people. Everyone being together."

Storm touched the end of a wire, the outer sheath stretched where it had been torn away. She lifted her head.

One of the bunks had been pushed aside, its placement out of line with the pattern.

"Why would they leave?"

Storm's gaze fell to the skewed position of the bed frame, rested on a pair of pale pink slippers.

"They were forced."

"By who?"

The paint had chipped on the pillar behind Storm, leaving the orange rust exposed. It would have been chaos with so many people leaving. Whether they had fled or been herded. The floor was at least clear of blood stains and bullet holes.

"It takes a lot of logistics to move this many people," said Maria.

"How would they move them? They were all afflicted. The vehicles—"

Their voices would have echoed. Their fear amplified the same way Storm's echoed now. Maria wanted to believe the move had been orderly and benevolent, yet a planned sortie didn't leave this much behind.

Storm dropped the severed wire and crossed to the middle of the aisle, a clear line extending from one end to the other.

"They would have been a constant reminder of everything that had gone wrong with the Gatherer," said Maria.

"They were trapped. Even without the fence."

Storm's voice had risen, her distress bouncing back to them from the rafters.

"There were hundreds of people hiding here," said Maria. "That kind of crowd draws attention."

They would have been evidence to get rid of, an inconvenient truth that needed to be out of sight. There would have been a child attached to the stuffed donkey, and she felt ill at the thought of Stanton taking them from this place of shelter to a place far away, or to kill them. The silence suddenly felt like the ghosts of those people, the only voice they had left.

Amanda.

Nausea rose in her gut, her fear bursting through the barricades she had tried to set up.

Stanton would do whatever it took to get what he wanted. To find out what Amanda knew.

"We can't be here."

She stood, scanned the full warehouse, from one door to the other.

Why had she not seen it?

"What is it?"

The danger Amanda was in, extended to them. For whatever Amanda knew, Stanton would — no matter how brave Amanda tried to be. She hadn't wanted to believe it, thinking Amanda hadn't been caught. But there was no other explanation.

She helped Storm to her feet and strained to hear. For the troops that would come, on his orders.

"This way."

They ran back the way they had come, the cots a hindrance now, veering them away from the exit.

"Did you hear something?"

"Shhh."

They stopped behind a bunk within sight of the door. She was completely blind here, the windows too high to offer anything but sky.

The water bottle lay where they had left it, now feeling like a trap they had fallen into.

"Stay behind me," Maria said as they stood inside the outer door. She depressed the emergency bar ever so slowly, wincing at the dull thunk.

The sun was just above the horizon, highlighting the plastic crates in a circle around the discolored playing cards, and the exposed openness of the street. It was still the same solid quiet, yet fragile at the edges.

They ran past the overturned crates, to a narrow alley across from the warehouse. It smelled of old fish, the smell rancid near the covered buckets along one side. It was dusk between the high walls. Their running footsteps reverberated back to them.

The openness of the gray concrete along the canal showed at the end of the alley. She turned away from it, running parallel to the main road, considering whether she should offer to carry Storm, when she heard a sound that stopped her heart.

She pushed Storm into an alcove barely big enough for one. Storm opened her mouth to speak, and Maria held up her hand. She couldn't be sure she'd heard it, but it had felt so familiar, so natural. The feel of troops moving silently towards a target. Footsteps silenced, breathing slow, all of it combining into a disturbance that she recognized in her bones.

They backtracked and took the alley towards the canal. The movement had been towards the warehouse, a targeted flow. It would spread out, eventually overtaking the entire dark zone.

She pulled Storm along, forced herself to move as silently as their assailants, and to not think about what had happened to Amanda. Storm's breathing was too loud, her footfalls like thunder.

They reached the end of the alley and Maria pushed them both against the wall. The leaden water of the canal took shape, the concrete banks extending towards the density of the city in one direction and back towards the wider river. Old skids were stacked along the edge and cracked barrels that wafted the smell of fish stood further back.

She strained to hear the smallest disturbance. They were either too far away or she had imagined it. Yet she had smelled the adrenaline and sweat, her body's response unmistakable.

"What now?" whispered Storm.

Maria touched a finger to her lips. The right equipment would hear everything. They may already know where they were.

There was a whir above them and Maria pulled them even tighter below the eave. She saw only the briefest glimpse as the drone buzzed overhead. She had used the same devices herself; the power of the technology was awesome when it wasn't you that was being tracked.

They were pinned in place, by the drone and the troops. She pointed to the canal. It was maybe ten meters across. The water would be frigid, too early in spring for it to have warmed.

Storm shook her head.

Maria pointed back down the alley and to the sky before gesturing that they needed to move.

Storm shook her head again, pointed along the canal, towards the city.

A shadow flickered at the end of the alley. A body passing by the entrance. So *not* her imagination.

A pier jutted into the canal with a rusted ladder down its side. They would be able to slide into the water, no splashing, or frantic strokes.

"We'll have to swim across," she whispered. Her body was settling in, the racing heart, the adrenaline, the danger, all aligning into a precise focus.

She grabbed hold of Storm's hand, but she pulled it free and shook her head fiercely.

"I know where we can get out."

"The soldiers are already there. This is our only way out."

"They will see us."

Their shoulders were pressed together against the wall. Storm's heartbeat pulsed below the skin of her neck. As wired and focused as Maria.

"Where?"

"The same way I got out before."

"Do you remember?"

Storm checked overhead for drones before she leaned out carefully.

"Past the bend there's an old car dealership. The old subway connects to there."

Around the bend was at least a hundred meters and the water as icy as the stream Storm had lain in.

"Can you do it?" Maria asked.

There was a fleck of yellow in the blue of Storm's eyes, and several strands of gray at her temple.

"Can you?"

They ran together, hunching low though it would make no difference. If the drone was in range, it would see them. Maria expected the high-pitched buzz with every step, or the running steps of the troops.

Storm descended first, the ladder creaking under her weight. Maria followed, one side of the ladder pulling away from the pier. Flakes of rust came off in her hands.

A road ran perpendicular to the canal, straight and long to the gate at its end. There was a troop hauler parked at its end. Maria ducked low and moved faster down the ladder.

The water was ice on Maria's skin, piercing painful stabs as she lowered into its depths. She couldn't breathe, the muscles in her chest refusing to release.

Storm was already at the end of the pier, pulling herself around the corner. Maria followed as the buzz of the drone returned. The pier blocked her line of sight. She pushed herself close to the brown slime on the concrete and kept pulling herself after Storm, praying, to whoever would listen, that this was not where this would end.

SIXTEEN

ADAMS WATCHED THE ENTRANCE to the grocery store, where Megan and Eli had disappeared. He drummed his thumb on the steering wheel and turned the radio on, searching for a radio station until Hamel told him to shut it off. There was an un-shielded wire in the radio, and it interfered with the connection Hamel had set up on his laptop.

An elderly woman pushed a cart into the store, holding tight to the handle. He peered through the small sections of open window between the advertisements, trying to catch a glimpse of Eli and Megan at the checkout.

"I'm going in."

He unbuckled his seat belt.

"Give them a minute."

Hamel was immersed in his laptop, the click of the keyboard the only sound other than the worry of Adams' heart. How the hell was he supposed to do what they needed if his heart was being ripped out at every moment?

A pregnant woman loaded her groceries into the trunk of her car, looking up at the sky as if she expected the collecting clouds to rain down on her. When she dropped a box of cookies onto the ground, it was Valerie he saw picking them up. He reached for the door.

"Shit."

Hamel's voice snapped him back. He clicked on the track pad repeatedly, his expression taut.

"They've been seen."

He turned the laptop towards Adams. The headline read, *Storm Freeman Back With A Vengeance.*

Adams pulled the computer closer and scrolled through the article, scanning the blurry photos.

"What does it say?" asked Adams.

"She's been seen multiple times but none of the sightings are confirmed."

The photos could be any slim woman or even adolescent boy, the photos all taken far enough away to be unidentifiable.

"These aren't her."

"I know," said Hamel. "But look at this."

He navigated to a different website where the headline read *Is There a Storm on the Horizon?*

Adams checked the url. It wasn't a news site he recognized.

There were more blurry images and inconclusive videos. Hamel scrolled to the bottom of the screen. It was a clip of two cyclists, in the early dawn, riding small BMX bikes. They wore hoods, no helmets, and Adams was about to dismiss them when they cycled beneath a bridge at the same time as a high-speed train flashed across it. The rider on the right collapsed, like they had been struck, swerving dangerously towards the wall of the underpass. It wasn't particularly noteworthy; the kid could have been drunk or high. It was the response of the second rider that gave it away. Her head had lifted at the approach of the train, and she had pushed down hard on the pedals, coming parallel to the first rider in two powerful strokes. She had reached out as the full impact of the train arrived, holding the handlebars as the rider collapsed, and coasting both of them out from under the bridge, and beyond the camera's view. There was no reason it should have been included in the article, nothing to indicate it was Storm. But every single reaction by the second rider had been Maria. He had seen her move a thousand times in training, felt her respond when they had been on a mission. It was what made her so good. When something happened, she responded almost before it started.

"Do you know where that is?"

Hamel brought up a map of the city.

"The track comes lower to the ground here and here." He indicated a spot in the north end, near the terminal, and one closer to where the river entered town.

"How long ago was it taken?"

"There's no time stamp but it looks like early morning."

Adams followed the route they had been taking. As time had progressed Valerie had only gone into town at night, when businesses were closed and buildings quiet, and then not at all. Where would Storm and Maria be going at the start of a new day? Their route led to the river, to the neighborhood of large mansions that edged the water. Storm could have a contact there. His gaze went further to where the houses got smaller and turned into older style businesses, then changed to warehouses beyond the canal.

He paused, fixed on a nondescript grid of streets, white roofs and odd-shaped buildings in the satellite view. Those alleys still returned to him at night. The afflicted like ghosts haunting the alleys, the smell of sickness and death in the warehouse where there should have been protection. He felt the lightness of the old man as he had lain him in the transport vehicle.

"They're going to the dark zone."

His voice was raw, hard to get out.

Megan and Eli clambered into the back seat, all crinkling plastic bags and accompanied by the intoxicating smell of roast chicken. Each held a half-eaten ice cream bar.

"—My Gran wasn't as sick as your mom. She was just ready."

They dumped the bags behind the seats.

"We got one of those roast chickens 'cause they smelled really good," said Eli. "Plus some chips and other stuff."

Hamel looked back to the screen, and Adams knew he was testing Adams' theory, fitting in the pieces. He nodded once, closed the laptop, and said over his shoulder.

"Put on your seat belts."

"Don't you want chicken?" Eli was pulling out the plastic dome, trying to hand it between the two front seats.

"Not yet."

"Where are we going?"

Adams drove carefully, though every nerve wanted to push the vehicle faster. It was almost noon; they would have been at the dark zone since that morning. Had anyone else figured out who the pair was and where they were going? Stanton could have recognized Maria, would have seen the quick reaction and known it was more than a helpful friend.

"What's the fastest way to get there?"

Hamel used his tablet to guide them, calling out commands so they moved effortlessly through the streets, never fast enough to draw attention. He'd been in the back of the transport vehicle when they had come for the afflicted so he didn't recognize how close they were until the perimeter fence was visible at the far end of the street.

"Pull in here." Hamel's voice was clipped.

Adams steered into an adjacent street.

"Go to the end of this street and turn back the way we came."

The gate in the fence had been wide open; a transport vehicle was parked across the entrance and several armed soldiers were standing around.

"Why are we here?"

Megan's wide eyes looked back at him in the rear-view mirror.

"Down here," said Hamel.

Adams turned into a smaller street beside a yard full of obsolete cars. Some had frames crushed, others remained whole.

"In there."

Adams pulled into a lane behind a dumpster. The walls pushed close to the vehicle, only inches between the mirrors and the brick.

"Is someone chasing us?"

Eli leaned forward between the seats. In the mirror, Megan looked pale and frightened, her gaze fixed back towards the dark zone.

"Hold on, bud," said Hamel.

Eli didn't move back but stayed quiet.

Adams shifted into park and shut off the engine. The quiet vibrated inside the cab, the air too thick with the smell of roasted chicken.

"Do you think they saw us?" said Adams.

"We'll find out soon enough."

The alley was cramped, their visibility restricted. At the far end, in the brightness of the street, a person walked past the entrance, their head bent to their tablet.

Behind them, the dumpster blocked most of the view, an uneven layer of gray clouds above it.

Megan un-clicked her seat belt and climbed from the back to the middle seat. They waited five more minutes. Every second, Adams expected an ambush from above or behind, one they wouldn't be able to defend.

Hamel gently eased open his door and slipped out. Adams nodded in acknowledgement, watched as he squeezed past the mini-van and disappeared around the dumpster. Adams hated being the one waiting, always aware of Stanton's target on his back.

Eli climbed between the seats. His face was drawn, his hands in tight fists as he scanned the same way Hamel had. "It's scary being a soldier."

"It isn't usually like this."

Soldiers were usually part of a larger force, rarely with an emotional component. It was about the mission, completing the task. Adams was more concerned about this resilient, damaged pair than he should be.

"Why did we come here?" asked Megan. The oversized sweatshirt and track pants made her look too young and fragile.

"We think Storm and Maria are here."

Megan lifted her head. She climbed forward, squeezing into the seat next to Eli.

"Are there soldiers looking for her too?"

"We have to assume that's why they're here."

Megan added her scrutiny to the narrow alley and the patch of brightness at its end.

Time stopped. Attenuated. The rustle of their clothes and shift of their feet were the only sounds.

When Hamel appeared at the passenger's door, Eli cried out. Hamel was breathing hard, his energy bursting into the silence.

"There are three guys at the gate," said Hamel, as he climbed in and Megan and Eli scrambled into the back. "And at least a dozen inside the fence. All FFO."

Troops in full fighting order meant someone wasn't messing around.

Adams started the vehicle, the whir of the electric drive feeling as loud as a shout. The alley walls were high like a maze, and he could imagine Stanton the scientist peering down at them waiting to see what they would do next.

"Did you get inside?"

"The fence is six-gauge steel with three strands of barbed wire and an electrified wire on top."

"Was it powered on?" Megan had pushed herself back into the corner. "Sometimes they turn it off."

Hamel shook his head. "I wasn't close enough to see."

"Did you see Storm and Maria?" asked Eli.

Adams approached the end of the alley, poking the hood of the vehicle into the more open roadway. It wasn't much more than a strip of asphalt between secondary buildings.

Hamel pointed. "Turn here."

"Did you see them?" The pitch of Megan's voice hinted at panic.

Adams turned into the road, driving slowly, most of his attention behind them.

"No," said Hamel, and as an aside to Adams added, "These guys aren't regular soldiers."

"Stanton's?" asked Adams.

He could feel Eli and Megan listening, learning, and seeing the world in a way most people were protected from.

"That's my guess."

Stanton had more resources than they ever would and the futility of it threatened to overwhelm him.

Megan was suddenly at his shoulder, her small chin close to his ear. "They might be hiding."

"These guys always get their target," said Adams.

Hamel gave him a quick warning glance. He had a map on the screen again, zoomed in to the area of the dark zone. It showed the inky blue of the canal, the roofs of warehouses along the edge. Hamel traced a finger along a route between buildings, running from a point on the canal and going north, before turning east and running straight to the edge of the river. It was an easy area to defend, two sides protected by water.

"They wouldn't find me," said Megan.

"Why not?" Eli laughed. "Are you a superhero or something?"

Megan regarded him coolly. She looked so much older than Eli. "I used to live here."

Eli flushed, looked away from her. "I didn't know that."

"Were the troops searching?" asked Adams.

"They had secured the perimeter. Beyond that I couldn't see." Eventually they would find them.

"We have to go get them," said Megan. "Those men are—" Megan looked at Adams. For he had been one of those men. Had taken her and her mother to the remote hospital.

"—Are following orders," finished Hamel.

Were they though? How far did you have to be pushed before you questioned the instruction? These were men Stanton had selected. They would have bought in, believed in whatever Stanton told them. And why not? They were an elite force, removed from the norms of morality. Or so he had once thought.

"Where would you hide?" asked Adams.

She leaned between the seats. Fine blonde hairs dusted her cheeks. "In the tunnels."

Hamel looked ahead of them, then at his map.

"It's too close to the water. There can't be tunnels."

"It's only one. It comes to here."

She pointed to the west side of the dark zone on the tablet, the point closest to the downtown.

"And that's how we would get in?" asked Adams.

"It's where Storm and I got out."

SEVENTEEN

STORM

A SET OF STAIRS HAD been cut out of the concrete bank of the canal, the bottom step ending flush with the water. Storm's legs were numb, her hands useless clubs and her chest so constricted she fought to breathe.

There was nothing to hold onto, an ancient slime covering the cracked and crumbled steps, and her hands kept sliding off, like they wanted to be in the water. But that made sense because the water was good for her. It would make her feel better, so maybe that was why her hands refused to close and the water seemed to pull her back in. She should stop fighting it, let the water do its work of healing and repairing the damage of the fields.

For a moment, she couldn't hear the stream running past her, the water hurting everywhere she touched. She choked on a mouthful that tasted of dirt and oil, almost not alive at all. When she came up for air, her eyes were below the level of the bottom step, the five steps like a mountain to climb.

She lifted her arm, and it came slowly. She was sinking, her face tilted to the sky, her chin lifted above the surface. The sun shone through a gap in the clouds, and she realized that was what she must be feeling, the warmth of the sun on her back, and creeping up her toes. It was so far away.

Something in the water pulled at her. She fought against it, yet her responses were too slow. Her arms and legs were busy with something else and would be there in just a minute. Even her fear was slow to come, like a train whistle far off. The creature that lived in this toxic canal had come to take her as its own.

She tried again to push off, but it had her around the waist, squeezing her and slamming her up against the steps. Then it was pushing her, forcing her onto the bottom step so that she was lying half on and half off, and Maria's face was close above her, her blond hair plastered against her head.

The cold returned then, the air on her skin like ice. Maria crouched beside her, dripping water. Storm tried to rise and Maria held her down. For a second, Storm thought it was the creature again, but Maria was looking over the side of the steps, and Storm remembered that they were still running. Endlessly running. There had been troops and the empty space where Megan's Gatherer had been. The empty bunks.

Maria lifted her, the pain exquisite where she touched her. They were moving; Storm seeing the ground as she jostled on Maria's shoulders. There had been other times when she had been carried by the strength in Maria's shoulders. A power line. An ocean. The sun touched the back of her neck and she shivered, a violent, full-body convulsion.

Maria set her down behind a lidded box, grains of spilled sand around their feet. Storm sat with her back against it.

"Storm."

Maria had shaken her. Storm looked up.

"Good. You're still with me."

Water ran down Maria's cheeks and neck. They had left a trail of water on the concrete and turned the sand wet that overflowed from the box.

The wall of the warehouse closest to them was a dirty white. It had a high peaked roof, a single door and an off-set window. When she and Megan had come at night, it had been more about shadows and staying far away from the glow of the city. She crawled to her knees, looked around the box towards the outer perimeter of the dark zone. She shook with cold.

The last time, the lights of the Ferris wheel had been off in the distance, the blaze of headlights streaking across a bridge. In the daylight, the Ferris wheel was too far away, yet there was a distant bridge that spanned the canal.

"We're not far enough," said Storm.

Maria swore and scanned the sky.

"Can you run?"

She was hauling Storm to her feet. Storm stumbled against her. Maria righted her, half-carrying her as they ran along the front of the warehouse, targets in front of a blank screen.

They stopped at the edge of a building before crossing over to the next. The morning was quiet, the sun having disappeared. On the other side of the canal the racket of a garage door rolling open broke the quiet. A man had his back to them, never looking towards what would be an abandoned space for him.

The angle of the bridge was changing, starting to fit more with the vision from that night. Yet perspectives changed in the daytime, things closer than in the dark. The next building had once been a plumbing supply store, the block letter sign still bolted above the door. None of what she was seeing fit in place.

"Are we close?" asked Maria.

Storm looked behind them, to where the canal disappeared around a curve. A tingling whisked across her cheek, the trace of a current as it passed by, irritation but no pain. And the pieces fit into place. The overpass, the curve of the canal, and the faintest steel peak of the Ferris wheel in the distance.

"It's up here."

They passed another building, that looked too new and well maintained to belong in the dark zone. With each step her certainty grew. They passed the wood crates that had provided their protection and even the smell of the canal was right, a cool draft delivering its acrid pungency in a steady stream. The door was as she remembered, the paint along the edge chipped where it had been pried open more than once. She tried to remember where Megan had hidden the crowbar.

Maria pushed her against the wall, then forced her to crouch. There were no sounds, the light dull. In the corner of her eye, two soldiers slipped around the corner and stopped in front of the door.

EIGHTEEN

ADAMS

"IS THAT IT?" ASKED Adams

They were parked on a side street, the entrance to the old subway stop just visible around the corner. The commuter lot was empty and the entrance barricaded with yellow tape.

"There are staircases before you get to the tunnels," said Megan.

The entrance was a single set of double doors and the building little more than a header for the staircase. This section of the subway had been plagued with flooding and had been closed for years. It didn't look like it had seen much traffic even before it was shut down.

"Everyone ready?" said Hamel.

Megan was first out the door, followed by Eli, and Adams wondered what the hell he was thinking. They whispered to each other in the dusk of the lane and Adams couldn't lift his hand to the door or do anything to put this mission in motion.

He was going to be that fool who didn't learn from his mistakes. He'd taken Camille to the treatment center, exposing her to a danger that he hadn't suspected. Now, how could he know what waited for them in those tunnels?

"We need to move," said Hamel. He stood in the open door, fully outfitted in his combat gear. Megan and Eli stood behind him in jeans and hoodies and equipped with flashlights.

"This is wrong," said Adams.

Hamel tucked an extra magazine onto his belt.

"Yes," said Hamel. He stepped out of the door and closed it almost completely. "Now let's go."

Adams followed him into the morning cold, the gray light not reaching their parking spot. He and Hamel wore mariner's ball caps in an effort to slow down the facial recognition. The kids had their hoods pulled up. As they walked into the commuter lot, they did their best to look like a family on an outing in the middle of an industrial zone.

Eli didn't even have to try. He ran straight to the double doors and rattled the chain holding them shut. Megan followed more slowly, stepping around the yellow tape, and Hamel and Adams pretended to wave Eli away. Old parking meters edged the side of the parking lot closest to the entrance, and a digital ticket kiosk was still mounted to the wall. Megan pushed a few buttons and pressed the touch screen.

Hamel joined Eli and tested the doors. Adams still pretended to wave them away. Megan pushed Eli out of the way and he pushed back, possibly not hard enough, and then the two of them were doing a good job of looking like a brother and sister scrapping over nothing at all.

While Hamel pretended to discipline them, Adams made a quick cut to the chain with the bolt cutters. In less than three seconds they were inside, with the door chained shut on the inside. Megan and Eli were already halfway down the first flight of stairs, with Hamel close behind. A white wrapper reflected light in the parking lot, caught in a tuft of grass pushing up through a crack.

He had expected soldiers. With the number of troops they had seen at the dark zone entrance, they should have been swarming the area. Except the units wouldn't be concerned with people getting in, only those getting out. He turned from the brightness of the lot and followed them down the stairs.

After two flights, they reached a small subway station. The bars of three turnstiles glinted in the beams of their flashlights. The ticket booth reflected their distorted images, and Adams recognized the unlikelihood of their band of four being successful.

Megan and Eli climbed over the turnstiles, undaunted by the blackness of the space above the tracks. Even if Storm and Maria did reach these tunnels, how would they ever find their way out? Hamel climbed over the turnstile. Adams shone his light back up the stairwell and strained to hear any sounds. There was rustling behind him and he spun, his pistol drawn. A rat skittered around the corner, disappearing into the dark. He let out a slow breath. He needed to calm himself, assess the danger instead of reacting.

He leapt over the barrier and arrived at the edge as Megan dropped down onto the track.

"Wait," said Adams.

She walked along the bottom of the track, her hood pulled back.

"It's not live," she said, without looking back.

She had used the tunnels when she had lived in the dark zone, but until now he hadn't fully understood what that had meant. She would have traveled in this darkness with nothing more than her wits and a flashlight.

Hamel walked ahead with the kids and Adams kept a lookout on the black void behind them. They followed the line of the track silently, each of them lost in whatever thoughts this darkness brought. He couldn't shake the feeling that a train would overtake them, even though the subway hadn't operated for years.

He imagined finding Maria and Storm huddled in the dark, wide-eyed, and grateful that they had arrived. Except not once had he seen Maria helpless or without some way to get herself out of a situation – she might have met her match now, with the number of elite troops currently swarming the dark zone. He took a few quick steps, and Megan and Eli sped up to stay ahead so they moved through the tunnel at a faster, more urgent, pace.

"Do you hear that?" said Eli, after what could have been twenty minutes or five. He reached out for Megan to stop.

"Turn off your lights," said Adams.

The blackness was complete, their only frame of reference the sound of dripping water. He drew Megan close to him and heard the shuffling as Hamel did the same with Eli.

He felt the pressure of the concrete and earth above them. Cool, pungent air blew on his face.

"What is it?" whispered Megan.

"Can't you hear it?" said Eli.

Adams heard the water dripping, his own breathing, and if he stretched, the low whistle of air through the tunnel.

"There's water ahead of us."

Megan pulled away from him and Adams squinted against the sudden brightness of her flashlight.

"There's always been water here," she said, already moving down the tunnel.

Eli hurried to catch up to her. "It's more than the drips, there's water running. I think the tunnel is flooding."

"Slow down," said Adams, and Megan ignored him. They weren't that far from the canal, there could have been a breach.

"Megan!"

She and Eli stopped. Eli's eyes were wide, and Adams could see his fear. Megan faced down the tunnel, only her head turned towards him.

"The tunnels have always been flooded," she said, "It's why no one uses them anymore."

She flashed her light ahead of them, illuminating the edge of an expanse of water. The slick blackness pushed up against either side of the tunnel, its oily surface extending into the dark. He could just make out the outline of a platform on the far side of the water.

"At least we know why there aren't any troops," said Hamel.

"How deep is it?" asked Adams.

"We have to find a different route." Eli stood ten paces back from the water. There was a high pitch to his voice, on its way to hysterical, and Hamel moved back beside him.

Megan walked to the water's edge and he thought she meant to go in, except before she reached it, she turned sharply towards the wall.

"Megan?" The concrete dampened Adams voice so it didn't travel far.

"The bottom collapsed but I know the way across." Her light arched over the black water and the crumbling concrete on the far side.

Adams exchanged a glance with Hamel. There were soldiers who would balk at that water.

"As long as you go where I tell you, it doesn't go above your knees."

"And if we don't?" said Eli.

Adams joined Megan. The water's surface was black and smooth, and he tried not to think of what might lie beneath.

"You just have to follow me."

Adams imagined her alone in the dark feeling her way across.

She bent to take off her shoes.

"Keep your socks on for the glass."

"I'll wait for you here." The desperation in Eli's voice pierced through the tunnel.

Hamel crouched in front of him while Eli vehemently shook his head.

"It starts here and goes across." She gestured to the center of the stagnant water.

"When was the last time you were here?" asked Adams.

She shrugged and picked up her shoes.

The afflicted had been relocated from the dark zone months ago, leaving plenty of time for erosion to do its work.

"It could be different."

She stepped into the water. "I check before I step. He doesn't need to be afraid."

Hamel left Eli where he was and joined them at the water.

"Eli can't swim."

The boy had moved further away, his back against the side of the tunnel, and gripping his flashlight in both hands. The darkness loomed behind him, brightening his small circle of light. Megan might have traveled these tunnels alone, but Eli was not her.

"We don't have time for this," said Adams.

"So one of us goes back with him to the vehicle?"

Adams shook his head and walked carefully back to Eli.

"Hey, bud."

"I know how to get back to the station. I'll wait for you there."

Adams sighed and calmed the anxiety that reared its head at the idea.

"We need to stay together."

"I can't swim."

Eli twisted and untwisted the head of the flashlight.

"Hamel and I can help you. It's not going to be deep."

Eli shook his head. "You don't know that."

"I can carry you."

"I'm not a baby."

Eli's face was twisted with fear and embarrassment and Adams wished they could be anywhere else.

"Then you'll have to walk."

Eli looked towards the water, as if he were looking death in the face.

"Hamel and I will be with you, and Megan knows the way. We won't let you go."

Megan was already feeling for the next step in front of her.

"But it has to be *now*."

The cool air was on Adams' back, like a promise of whatever waited for them.

Eli's grip was tight as they walked to the water's edge. They removed their boots and rolled up their pants.

Without a word, Megan came out of the water and took Eli's hand.

The water bit with cold and was oily on Adams' skin. Megan checked each step and Adams didn't dare move his feet beyond where she told them to stand. There was broken concrete beneath their feet and the bottom slanted downward in several sections. He held tight to Eli's hand and tried not to look too closely at the blackness that swirled around their legs.

"Well done," said Hamel when they reached the other side. Megan had guided them on a winding path where the water had not once reached above his shins.

Eli was pale and shaking but he managed a weak smile as they climbed onto the platform and put on their shoes.

They faced an escalator that led up, natural light from above providing the shape of the platform and the two tracks below it. Old ads were mounted on the half-dozen pillars that separated the two tracks; the glass too dirty to reflect more than a dull glow. The tunnel they had come out of continued past the platform as if going to the next stop.

"Are we within the perimeter?" asked Hamel. He stood close to the jagged edge of the stopped escalator, his face lifted to the light at the top.

"We passed under the fence back there." Megan pointed behind them. "Near the water. This is the last subway stop."

"And Storm knows it's here?" asked Adams.

"It's where she and I accessed the tunnels," said Megan.

"I'll go check it out." Hamel held his Glock and had one foot on the escalator. "Stay out of sight until I get back."

Adams started to go with him and stopped. Megan and Eli still held hands, flanked by the six pillars.

"I'll go on my own," said Hamel.

"It's safer with two."

Hamel glanced at the two children. "Not anymore."

Eli let go of Megan's hand and came to stand by Hamel, looking up at the light the way Hamel had.

"There are people up there. I can hear them moving around."

Adams heard the drip of water, the whoosh of air moving through.

"Are you sure?"

Eli's mouth was set in a grim line.

"One of them is laughing."

Hamel hadn't moved, his face tilted to the level above and the wash of light. It shifted as if a shadow moved across it.

"There's also—" Eli pointed to the tunnel that continued past the platform. There was the distant trudge of footsteps.

Adams grabbed Megan and Eli and hustled them behind one of the narrow pillars. Hamel took the next pillar, both with weapons drawn.

A flicker of light appeared in the tunnel, swinging back and forth as it came forward, the outline of a figure visible behind it. An oil lamp, judging by the glow, the figure like some ancient lighthouse keeper coming out of the mist. Adams had a momentary chill, that this was what he was seeing, a ghost brought in by the water to haunt these tunnels instead of the open shore. The ghost's feet slapped in water and he muttered, his voice a stream of senseless words.

The man arrived in the station, unaware of them, his long shaggy hair hanging around his face and his clothes near black with dirt and grime.

A metal contraption extended down from his head, like a dozen spider legs curved around him in a cocoon. It was made of metal, and from the sound of its creaking it was less ghost than horrific steam punk contraption gone wrong.

"That's Lucifer," said Megan, not particularly quietly.

Adams held a finger to his lips, but Megan stepped out from behind the column and waved at him.

Lucifer walked on the parallel track, oblivious to them, or anything outside of his own world. It frightened Adams to see it, for he had been close to that kind of madness in his grief, knew how close it could be for anyone.

"What's he wearing?" asked Eli when the apparition had disappeared into the parallel tunnel.

"It's a homemade Faraday's cage," said Hamel. A device that directed electric fields and currents away from an area.

"Is he afflicted?" said Adams. One of the few who had escaped the military when they had come to round them up.

"Or crazy?" said Hamel.

"Both," said Megan.

Hamel moved across the platform to the edge of the tracks. Adams followed, still haunted by the strange vision.

"Is that really his name?" asked Eli, as he and Megan joined them.

"It's what he wanted to be called."

Megan's voice faded at the end, overtaken by whatever memory Lucifer had triggered.

"What's down there?" asked Hamel. He was looking towards where Lucifer had appeared.

"There's a room with pipes and stuff. Where the water comes in."

They stood in disappointed silence, none of them wanting to test what waited for them at the top of the escalator.

"Deeper than back there?" asked Eli.

Megan jumped down onto the track. "No. In the pipes. It's where the tap water comes into the dark zone."

A utility room. Less obvious, the kind of place no one paid attention to.

"Can you get us there?" asked Adams.

Eli sighed behind them. Megan took his hand.

The natural light from the escalator faded as they moved into the tunnel. It was the same width and height of the earlier tunnel, except the rail didn't continue here, the concrete bare but for the accumulated dirt and trapped garbage.

They had barely gone twenty paces when a collapsed pile of earth and rubble blocked their path. The dirt was packed between stones and in some places had been pushed aside.

A worn path led up one side to an opening large enough to crawl through. A rope had been tied between rocks as a makeshift railing and he tried to imagine those that had come before them, scrambling through this hole in the dark.

Megan disappeared through the opening followed by Eli. Adams bent to follow, trying to keep them in sight but they were too fast, their outlines already blended into the dark. He squirmed through on his elbows, panicked when the passage was longer than he expected, his worry a hard ball in his chest when he crawled out the other side.

Megan and Eli waited in front of a concrete wall. They stood so still and watched him so calmly that they could have been ghosts, about to disappear. As Hamel crawled out behind Adams, wiping the dirt from his clothes, Megan stepped to a gray metal door he hadn't seen, held open by a rock wedged at the bottom.

"I'll go first."

Adams rushed down the bottom of the collapse and stepped between Megan and whatever was on the other side of the door.

"It isn't far now," she said.

He eased it open and got the first glance at a high cavernous space filled with long runs of pipes and conduits overhead. The light of an LCD screen shone in the distance.

"Eli and Megan can wait here," said Hamel.

Eli pressed close against Adams's side while Megan crouched next to the wall, scraping dirt away from the base.

"What is that?" Hamel leaned closer to see the marks scraped into the concrete.

"We used it to keep track of who had come through." She brushed dirt away from a long list of scratches, which could have been initials.

"Is someone here now?" asked Eli, sounding frightened.

Megan rested her finger on one of the scratches in the list. "No one but Lucifer. For a long time."

NINETEEN

MARIA

MARIA PULLED STORM INTO the alley hoping the soldiers stationed at the door hadn't seen them. The alley ran beside a plumbing warehouse and pieces of PVC and large empty spools blocked their way. Water from the canal flowed over her ribs and into her shoes, her wet clothes making every movement harder. She checked over her shoulder, the band of light at the end of the alley unbroken. Storm stepped over an old toilet, its tank rusted and orange, and Maria climbed over a stained tub lying on its side.

At the end of the alley, they bolted across a wide street, stopping inside an alley of warped asphalt and sheer walls. They stood shoulder to shoulder, straining to hear. The sound wasn't definite, but she could feel the troops spreading out around them, their silent footsteps resonating through the ground, their breath disturbing the air.

"Can you get us back to where we came in?" said Maria, hoping the soldiers hadn't already closed the break in the fence.

Storm looked back the way they had come and checked the sky, before moving into the alley. They ran parallel to a main road and at each intersection, they glimpsed the brightness of it. Once they saw troops jogging past, at another break a black SUV. Their pace got slower as they checked each cross-street. At one point, the whir of a drone passed overhead, and they dove into an entryway. Maria's heart was beating in her throat as they waited for it to pass.

They moved faster, Storm's labored breathing echoing back from the walls, the alleys growing wider as their options narrowed. They were circling back to where they had come in, yet each abandoned building looked the same as the last.

"Are we close?" asked Maria as they crossed a paved area large enough for several vehicles.

"A couple blocks," said Storm, between pants. "At most."

They jogged down yet another alley that smelled like fish, Maria matching Storm's stride.

The two soldiers came out of nowhere, the four of them face-to-face in the tight space. They all froze and in that brief instance, Maria had the advantage. She shoved Storm aside and kicked one in the chest sending him back into the wall and broke the other's wrist as he reached for his holster. The soldier yelled, and then she and Storm were running, the alert sounded so that they heard feet pounding and the jangle of weapons on belts.

There was no place to hide, the road wider as they drew closer to the perimeter. A single building with a smashed window offered shelter but would be too easy a place to find. Up ahead, she recognized the utility building they had passed on the way in, could see the perimeter fence beyond it.

There was no time to look behind them, no time to hide. They rounded the corner of the neat utility building, saw the bushes that protected the opening, and Maria ran into the back of Storm. She had stopped ten meters from the fence.

"What are you doing?" hissed Maria. She tried to drag Storm forward. There were several troops further down the road, clustered around a vehicle, less than a parking lot away.

Storm shook her head, her gaze fixed on the fence.

"It's live."

Maria heard the click she had been ignoring, the sound live electrical fences were required to make.

"We can't stay here," said Maria.

Storm's face was lax, beaten. The fence stretched in both directions. The soldiers down the road stopped examining whatever had caught their attention. They would turn at any second. The pound of feet came behind them.

Arms wrapped around Maria from behind. Pinned her arms to her sides. Someone had Storm and was dragging them both backwards. Maria struggled, kicked, used every move she knew to get free and the person holding her stopped them all. They were dragged through an open door and she heard Storm gasp in pain.

Maria thrashed and twisted, funneling her fear and anger into the kick of her legs and the strike of an elbow. As the door closed, she finally landed a boot on his foot, and was gratified by the sharp intake of breath.

She stopped.

"Shit, Kowalski, we're trying to help you."

They stood in a narrow space, trapped between gray metal cabinets on one side and water meters on the other. The light came only from a single opaque window, but the dimness was enough to recognize Adams's restless energy and Hamel's cool competence beside him. The shock of seeing them froze time for a blink until Storm stumbled into her, frantic as she pushed past her on the way to the door.

"She can't be here," said Maria.

The fields from the cabinets would be strong enough to burn Storm's skin.

Hamel waved them towards the back of the space. "This way."

Storm struggled to go back to the door they had come in. Maria held it shut.

In a single fluid motion, Adams lifted Storm and slung her over his shoulder. Maria bolted the outer door and caught up as Adams descended four narrow steps. Hamel stood at the bottom, holding open a second utility door, the space beyond it pure black. Maria hurried after them.

TWENTY

AMANDA

MANDA HELD HER WRIST against her ribs and cradled her palm with the other hand. Her thumb throbbed, the pain radiating up her forearm and into her shoulder.

Stanton had said her hands were her greatest weapon. She adjusted her elbow, tried to support the hand a different way.

Bastard, she thought, holding onto her anger, for without it she would have curled into a ball in the corner.

The sun dropped towards the horizon, its rays slanting in the office window. She licked her lips. Ached for a cigarette.

She remembered a long stream of words as the guard had hovered over her, waiting for the permission to inflict more pain. She had told Stanton of their plan to use her house and of their meeting in the dark zone and she thought the shame would eat her alive.

She pressed her good hand against the glass and leaned into it. Her skin itched and ants crawled in her hair, her need for a cigarette almost equal to the pain. There wasn't even a chair to try to throw at the glass, the twelve-storey drop to the ground now looking preferable to Stanton's return.

She lowered herself to the floor, her back against the side of the desk, her dread pounding in time with her thumb. Dust had collected along the carpet, and a spider had spun a web in the corner. The network portal set in the floor had gathered the same dust, turning the beige carpet dark around its edges. The latch on the door clicked.

There was an intake of breath, then Alicia's voice.

"Where is she?"

Amanda popped her head up, not wanting to give the guard any excuse to re-enter the office.

"I'm here."

The guard, who stopped half-way into the room, was different than the one who had come with Stanton. Alicia stood just inside the entrance, a water bottle in her hand. She said a quiet word to the guard and closed the door behind her.

Alicia's gaze dropped to where Amanda pressed her hand to her ribs.

"How are you?"

Alicia wore a pant suit that hung loose on her gaunt frame, the dark blue a perfect contrast to her now dull auburn hair. Her make-up was done but it only accentuated her sunken cheeks and thin lips, her attempt to stand tall and proud falling short.

"What was it you said?" said Amanda. "It would be best for all of us if I came quietly." She cradled her thumb in her uninjured hand, trying to remove the pressure, any pressure from the swollen skin. "I guess you meant best for you."

Amanda's voice cracked and she cursed herself.

"No. I meant best for everyone."

She said it as a matter of fact, a more uncompromising version of Storm's directness.

Alicia reached in her pocket and pulled out a small bottle. She laid it and the water beside each other on the desk.

"These will help with the pain."

Amanda laughed, short and bitter.

"You expect me to trust you?"

Alicia's gaze fell again to Amanda's swollen thumb.

"They *will* help."

The setting sun highlighted the lines beneath Alicia's make-up and the hint of gray at her roots.

Amanda snatched the bottle of pills off the desk. The movement shot agony into her thumb. She gasped and lifted her face to the ceiling, the throbbing unbearable.

Alicia took the bottle and struggled with the child-proof cap before shaking two capsules into her palm.

"Make it three," said Amanda.

Amanda swallowed the three capsules as pain radiated into her elbow. She didn't know where it or her arm began.

"It'll be a few minutes before they kick in."

Amanda turned her back to the black dome mounted on the ceiling, hating whoever watched at the other end of the camera. Had they watched while he had twisted her thumb, heard her cry of pain?

"Can you get me some cigarettes?"

Alicia sat on the edge of the desk, visibly relieved at sitting down. A red blotch of a rash showed below her cuff.

Amanda stopped with the bottle half-way to her lips.

"You're sick."

Alicia looked at where the red poked out beneath her sleeve. She pulled the cuff down her wrist and smoothed it over the rash, as if it wasn't there.

"That's not why I'm here."

Amanda couldn't speak, her anger flaring red and hot as she remembered the afflicted at the wellness retreat who had refused to see what was happening, as if it could be ignored.

Alicia looked towards the ocean and the blurred outline of a container ship that floated on the horizon.

It made Amanda ill to see her lank hair and the frailness that consumed her.

"I need to know how she is," said Alicia.

Storm had said her mother had stayed to do what she could. Is that what this was? Alicia trying to hang on and stop the worst of the damage? Amanda should have felt compassion for her, yet something was off.

"I would imagine pretty shitty, considering I told Stanton where they were." She lifted her swollen hand as if anything could justify betraying them.

Alicia had her brows pinched and seemed more perplexed than concerned.

"Don't feel bad about that. We were always going to find them." Alicia plucked at the seam of her pants. "But how is she? Has she regained her strength?" Her eyes were bright, the steel that had once been there replaced by something wanting. "She must be strong if she was able to return to the city."

Amanda held her thumb close to her chest. This wasn't the Alicia the world knew but something altered, changed.

"What does he plan to do with them?" asked Amanda. She felt the shame of her complicity in whatever they suffered. She looked to the black dome of the camera, wondering who the voyeur was behind the lens.

Alicia raised her eyebrows as she followed Amanda's gaze.

"There's no one watching."

"Why would I believe that?"

Alicia shrugged in a truncated movement, as if it caused her pain. She watched the black lens for several seconds, considering.

"The networks don't work anymore."

The comment was off-hand, so little of her indomitable self in it that Amanda questioned what to believe.

"All of them?"

There had been her failed attempts to connect to the network. Whatever the computer had tapped into enough to cause it to crash.

Alicia clenched and unclenched her hand, a tick she seemed unaware of.

"Is she strong enough? To be in the city?"

There was a flash of the old Alicia in her impatience, the person who had headed the Gatherer Corporation at its zenith.

"She wouldn't have come back if she wasn't," said Amanda.

Alicia nodded, satisfied and Amanda's unease grew.

"What is it he plans to do with them?"

Alicia rose stiffly and crossed to the window. She was trying to stand at her full height yet couldn't achieve it.

"Do you know? What he plans to do?"

A golf cart with the uplifted hands of the Corporation's logo on its side drove along one of the manicured paths. Alicia watched it until it disappeared behind the test facility.

"The military woman is of no interest to us. It's Storm who can help us."

She had a flash of relief for Maria before she understood what Alicia had said.

"Storm isn't going to help you."

The sun's beam shone directly into the office, bathing Alicia's haggard face in a searing light.

Alicia waved Amanda towards the window as if they were old friends. Amanda approached carefully, avoiding getting too close. The smell of sickness and perfume coming off Alicia caught in her throat.

Soldiers still lined the perimeter fence and at first Amanda thought Alicia was indicating their force as the reason Storm would comply.

"Do you see where the garden path turns towards the manufacturing center?"

It turned in a long arc, passing through the area that had appeared blurry that morning.

"Do you see the whiteness?"

Amanda refocused. What she thought had been a trick of the light that morning wasn't a trick at all. The same whiteness that had been at the base of the barn and had surrounded the smaller Gatherers encompassed the entire lawn, consuming grass and shrubs and pathways with equal ease. It flowed up the trunk of a tree and whitewashed the soil in the flower beds.

"How is that possible?"

Alicia ran her finger along the glass as if tracing the outline of the white. She seemed mesmerized, her longing too much like what Amanda had seen at the retreat.

"Storm's the only one who ever understood it," said Alicia.

The fear in Amanda's chest deepened, the rays of the sun suddenly too hot, their beams too bright.

"What is it you expect her to do?" said Amanda.

Alicia shrugged, wincing halfway through, her gaze sliding to where the test facility rose behind the manufacturing center. What once had been matte black now shone with a white luminescence.

Amanda looked to the soldiers guarding the perimeter, facing outward as they stood on a white expanse of grass. It felt as if the floor beneath her had fallen away.

"The soldiers aren't protecting the Gatherer; they're protecting the people who are trying to get in."

Alicia sighed. "We lost five techs this week. Three the week before."

A man hurried along one of the paths, his shoulders bent, before he slipped into the side door of the manufacturing center.

"Why haven't you evacuated?"

Alicia had to drag her gaze away from the test facility, her attention slow to follow.

She laughed quietly, a terrifying sound.

"We can't leave." Her indignation was fierce. "The original device must be saved."

The sun dropped below the horizon, the absence of its light making the white swaths brighter. It covered most of the grounds and parts of the buildings, its deadness everywhere she looked.

"And Storm is going to do that for you?"

Amanda thought of the small protections she had made to help Storm navigate the city. The path she had mapped to avoid the worst of the electromagnetic fields.

"She's the only one who can."

"It will kill her."

Alicia shook her head, a quick jerk.

"Nonsense. I know what she is capable of, more than anyone else."

The first edge came off the pain in Amanda's thumb, replaced by a strangling fear.

"You would sacrifice her to this?"

Alicia waved angrily at the white expanse.

"It won't be a sacrifice. She'll know what to do."

The hollows below Alicia's eyes had deepened now that the sun had set, her distance from death so much less than it had been.

"It will destroy her."

Alicia stepped back from the window and eased onto the desk, her shoulder next to the useless monitor.

"I know what my daughter is capable of."

Amanda was aware of their distance above the ground, and the empty floors separating them from the whiteness, as if they could stay out of its reach.

"Can you get me out of here?"

Alicia laughed, a bitter tinkling sound.

"Why would I do that?"

Dusk crept across the compound, absorbing details as it went, the whiteness the last to succumb.

"So I can help her."

Alicia shook her head. "Storm will come to us."

"She said you would help."

"Did she?"

There was a knock at the door and the guard poked his head in. Alicia was suddenly in motion, moving faster than she had since she arrived. She stopped at the door.

"You'll need to be ready. For when she comes."

The door closed behind her and fear cut like a knife across Amanda's chest, yet it was a brief sharp pain, her body already turning it to a red-hot fury that colored her vision.

She vibrated with it as she faced the closed door. She had always been at her best when in the thrall of her white fury. Reckless, yes, but more effective. The handle did not move when she tried to turn it. She kicked at it and succeeded in shooting pain into her leg and thumb. She grabbed the pills off the desk, shoved them in her pocket and took two long draws of water. Her hand shook. It could be nicotine withdrawal. Could be anger.

She needed to be out of these four walls, to warn Storm and Maria, and do whatever she could to stop this from happening. She ran to the desk and crawled underneath, able to put pressure on her injured hand for the first time. She exhaled slowly and ran her hand along the seam of the floor tiles, confirming the trace of cold air that was slipping through the crack.

It was faint but would have to be enough. She sat back, and checked the darkening blue of the sky, calculating the time until it would be fully dark.

TWENTY-ONE

MARIA

MARIA HELD TIGHT TO the railing as she peered into the blackness, her other arm tight around Storm's waist. They stood at the top of a metal staircase, only a few steps visible below them.

"What is this?" asked Maria. It smelled dank and wet, like air that has been too long shut in with the earth.

Hamel's flashlight was the sole point of light in a vast darkness.

"It's a water plant." His voice was close at her ear, the pressure of his shoulder at her back. "The mains are below us."

Storm's breathing was labored, as if she were still exposed to the fields. Maria took a step down, the staircase creaking beneath them.

"Did they follow us into the utility room?"

"Not yet."

There were only so many places she and Storm could have disappeared to, and a couple bolted doors wouldn't stop them for long.

"Where are they?" Adams' voice was low and urgent, the fear in it uncontained and rare enough that Maria stopped mid-step.

A light flared, illuminating two figures crouched on the landing below them. She gripped Storm tighter, already turning back towards the door when the figures clarified into two small bodies, like children playing at marbles. She recognized them as actual children at the same time as Adams pushed past her, the entire staircase shaking as he rushed down to them.

"You were supposed to wait at the bottom," said Adams as he reached them. He had a hand on each of their shoulders and drew them into him, as Maria tried to get her head around two kids in this darkness.

The children were around ten, a dark-haired boy with brown skin and a blonde girl, wearing what looked like identical hoodies and jeans. Adams rested his hand easily on their shoulders, like a father – except he couldn't be: Adams' wife and child were dead, and he didn't have a son.

"I'll explain later," said Hamel. He nudged her to keep moving. "Storm?"

The blonde girl was thin as a whip, tangled curls hanging into her eyes. She broke free of Adams and started up towards them. Storm let out the smallest gasp and drew away from Maria. The force of the two colliding shook the staircase, as the girl's arms wrapped tightly around Storm's legs.

Megan. The name came to Maria as Storm stroked the girl's hair. Storm's hand rested on her head, the gesture so tender the world paused. She had her faced lifted to Storm and the light of the flashlight made her curls glow, so she looked ethereal, like she'd come out of the darkness of a fairy tale.

"My mom died," said the girl.

"I'm so sorry." Storm held Megan close then gently pulled her back to look at her face. "How did you get here?"

"Through the tunnels. Same as before."

What Storm had really asked was how Megan was hiding out with two soldiers in the darkness of this underground realm. Yet the girl seemed unperturbed, her composure unsettling.

"There's someone coming."

It was the boy who spoke and Maria only had a quick glimpse of an anxious, upturned face and a tight hold on Adams' hand before the flashlight went out.

No one moved.

It was barely a sound at all, more of an awareness of bodies moving through space somewhere below them. The same way she had known there were troops tracking them through the alleyways, there were soldiers below them in the darkness.

Hamel tapped her shoulder and gave the slightest pull back up the stairs. Maria turned both Storm and Megan and faced them up the stairs, urging them upwards with a push on their lower backs. She followed close behind, the stairs making too much racket beneath their feet.

At the top, they crowded on the small landing, cramped together between the utility door and the troops below them.

"There's an opening in the fence outside the utility room," whispered Maria. "It may be our only chance."

"It's live," said Storm, speaking too loud.

"There's a breaker in the utility room," said Hamel. "I can trip it before you get there."

"We'll need a distraction. It's twenty meters from the door to the fence."

"I'll do it," said Adams.

"Me too," said the boy.

The inanity of it stopped her. Children strategizing a mission. Whatever grief Adams was trying to appease with this new family, this was not the place for it.

"Maria, you can take Storm, Megan, and Eli," said Hamel. "Adams does the distraction. I'll flip the breaker."

Maria stopped on the idea of Adams with a new family. One he had already gathered around him. She shook her head before realizing no one would see it.

"Storm and I will be recognized."

There was a clang far below, of something striking metal, the echo in the underground chamber distorting her perception of distance.

"The fence is our only option," whispered Adams. "Megan and Eli, you stay close to Maria and do what she says."

She felt Hamel turn towards the utility door. Storm recoiled against Maria, bracing for the touch of the fields.

"Wait," said Maria. "Adams can take Storm and the kids. They'll look like a traditional nuclear family, all afflicted, taking refuge in the dark zone."

"And make for the fence?" said Hamel, his voice higher with disbelief.

"I will be the distraction," said Maria.

"No," said Storm.

Maria felt for Storm's hand, wished she could see her face.

"You can trust Adams."

Storm gripped her arm.

"What if they recognize you?"

Maria could feel Storm shake her head, the pressure of her hand increasing.

"That's the idea."

"They'll—"

Maria cut her off.

"There's no other way."

A quietness slipped in. A pause that Maria recognized. The moment before the world would change.

"Okay," said Hamel. "Adams, you and Storm are the happy parents."

"Hamel and I will draw them away from you," said Maria.

There was the sound of Hamel turning the knob, the faintest slide of metal out of the latch. Below them there was only silence and darkness.

"We'll meet you at the cabin," said Adams.

Storm straightened, her weight against Maria lighter, though she was still hunched as if warding off pain. Maria let go of her waist.

"It will take me five seconds to get through the door and to the breaker," said Hamel. There was the sound of the suction breaking and a sudden draft of warmer, fresher air as Hamel left.

"If we don't—" said Storm.

"We will," said Maria. She wasn't ready yet to let that idea into her head. She took a deep breath, felt herself switch into being part of a unit again.

"You'll take the side entrance; we'll go out the main door."

She opened the door to the smell of burnt wires and a layer of smoke hovering in the utility room. The meter cabinets had gone blank, a red LED on the panel by the outer door the only indicator the power had gone out.

"You destroyed it?"

The flashlight gleamed on Hamel's cheek bone and made his eyes into dark holes.

"Makes it harder to reconnect." Hamel waved the four towards the side door. "It won't take long for them to notice."

Maria stepped aside to let Storm and Megan pass. Adams came with them, the flashlight in Megan's hand guiding them. He nodded to Storm as he stood beside her, holding the hands of Megan and Eli on either side. Storm dipped her head in acknowledgement.

Adams slipped on a high-visibility, fluorescent hydro-worker coat he found beside the door and handed one to Storm. It added bulk at the same time as it diminished her, making her look like every one of the afflicted.

"Be careful."

"You too."

They made their way back to the second utility door that was partially blocked by a spool of wire. Adams had one hand on the door, the other holding the boy's who looked proud and terrified.

Adams sloped his shoulders and his whole military countenance slid off him, replaced by the posture of the afflicted, a tortured position he would know all too well from Valerie and Camille. Storm stood close behind him, holding Megan close to her, the girl still with that same bizarre calmness.

"Wait until we're out the door," said Maria.

They nodded as if they were a family unit and Maria wanted desperately to change the plan.

"We'll give you ten," said Adams.

The gray cabinets loomed above them as she and Hamel moved to the main door, the water meters indistinct shapes against the wall. They paused at the entrance, both taking a final glance back at the small group that was little more than four outlines in the dark.

"We'll see you on the other side," said Adams, and Maria took solace in the familiarity of it, these men and the adrenaline a place she had been before.

"Count on it," said Hamel.

Hamel slid back the bolt and checked it was clear before they stepped out into the blinding light. She squinted to see the soldiers across the parking lot at the gate. There were a half-dozen, two posted on each side of the gate, two interrogating the driver of a personnel carrier that blocked the opening.

The break in the fence where she and Storm had entered had already been discovered. Soldiers searched in the bushes and others checked the abandoned buildings with boarded-up windows.

She and Hamel walked forward, their strides strong and purposeful. She held her head high, waiting for that moment of recognition when she would draw the attention away from the small family that would even now be slipping out the other side of the building.

She felt the moment of recognition on the back of her neck before she found it. A young man who stood beside the bush, frozen mid-gesture as he reached to push a branch aside. He frowned before his eyes widened, and even as his mouth opened to shout a warning, she was turning, pulling Hamel with her.

The soldier's shout filled the air. It was the alert of any predator that has spotted its prey, a rallying call to the rest of the pack.

She sprinted back to the utility room, arriving before Hamel, and yanked open the door. Pounding feet shook the ground.

She launched through the opening, whirling to close it as Hamel pushed through. She cranked the bolt shut as something heavy slammed against the other side.

They ran through darkness, her hand reaching for the railing that led down the three steps, the taste of smoke still hanging in the air.

She half expected to see the family where they had left them, but the darkness was unbroken, the place they had been empty.

She paused at the door that led onto the staircase, straining to hear sounds on the other side but the hammering from their pursuers overrode all else.

"I'll lead," said Hamel. In a single fluid movement, he opened the door and slipped through, moving from one darkness to the other.

Their feet clanged on the metal stairs as gunfire sounded at the first door.

Her adrenaline spiked as she held on to Hamel's shoulder, her focus on moving in sync as they raced down the steps.

At the solidity of the concrete floor, a light shone in the distance, far enough away it felt as if the space was impossibly big. There were others with it, the directed beams those mounted to the tops of rifles. Gunfire sounded at the second door above them.

Hamel stepped away from the lights, plunging them into complete blackness. They passed large undefined equipment, the occasional glow of an LED tiny beacons that guided them. Her hand never left Hamel's shoulder and her grip tightened when there was a surge of shouting behind them.

It was the call and response of the two groups following them.

Hamel flashed his light on and off. Her eyes burned, and the image of Hamel's drawn determined face lingered in her vision when they returned to dark. The brief light had done its job, the voices rising and turning in their direction.

"Keep moving," said Hamel.

She gathered herself around the calmness in his voice and his certainty. They moved faster, the air growing thicker and danker, and she imagined she pulled the weight of the soldiers behind them, a long, strong rope attaching them to her.

TWENTY-TWO

AMANDA

AMANDA LISTENED FOR SOUNDS of the guard resettling outside the office door. It had to be boring as hell standing there for hours on end, with nothing but the forgotten remnants of cubicles and computer networks to stare at. It would be brightly lit now, thanks to her frantic midnight trip to the bathroom, where her motion had activated the banks of lights. By the time she returned to the office, the entire floor had blazed with light, the windows reflecting the empty space.

Her office, or cell as she had come to call it, was illuminated only by the light seeping beneath the door. She moved to the window, the view unchanged from the hours she had spent choosing her path: out the side entrance, a quick dash to the section of gardens with the high grass and then – hopefully – a seamless, undetected blending into shadows as she made for the grove of fir trees. Maria had used the fir trees as cover when she had hidden within the compound. It made her braver to think that Maria had been there before her and made it through. She couldn't see any soldiers, though she had to assume they were there. The only visible feature was the swath of white that seemed bigger every time she looked.

She flexed her thumb. The final three painkillers had taken the edge off the worst of the pain. She took a deep breath and didn't even get half-way through the exhale before she was kneeling below the desk.

The sub-floor was made of steel-clad particleboard, and she caught the edge near the receptacle. She tilted it up and she rested it carefully along the newly opened hole in the floor.

She dunked her head into the opening and looked through the plenum towards the area beyond her office. The walls didn't extend below the sub-floor and enough light filtered through the joints in the floor to illuminate the space. It was half a meter high, with supports at the corner of each tile. It would have once housed the cables, wires and electrical supply that fed the Corporation's computer network, and the air flow that cooled that significant data power.

It had been that cool draft of air that had tipped her off that this space existed. These empty floors didn't need the cooling now, but it didn't stop the air from flowing through the abandoned space.

With a final look around the office, for no other reason than to check that she was really doing this, she grabbed the empty water bottle and slid ever so slowly and carefully into the plenum, the concrete of the floor cool beneath her hips. The need to stay quiet as she slid the tile back into place left her sweaty and her thumb pounded by the time it dropped into place. She rolled onto her stomach and released a cloud of dust. She breathed into her shoulder as she noted the distance to where the wall of her office would be, the point where the guard likely stood, the bulkhead of the bathroom in the distance, and further down in the opposite direction, the larger, though dimmer, mass of the elevator shaft. She placed the empty water bottle next to a support, as a marker if she had to return.

The space was too low to allow her to crawl and she squirmed along on her stomach, using her elbows to pull herself forward. Every swish of her forearm on the concrete floor echoed around her so that she was sure the guard would hear her, probably watching her from above as he marked her progress. She moved parallel to the outer wall, away from his position. At one point, there was a thump as he shifted his weight. She waited, listening for footsteps overhead, only moving again when her heartbeat receded to a dull pound.

The distance was further than she had calculated. Several times she had to circle around piles of discarded cables, whoever had cleared out the plenum having done a lousy job of it. She took extra care to maintain her direction, all too aware of how hard it would be to gain her bearings if she lost them. Peeking her head up through one of the tiles was a sure way to get the attention of a bored sentry, especially given the level of blinding light. Which was another reason to move faster. She had triggered the lights when she had gone to the bathroom. When no more movement was detected, the lights would sequentially shut down, leaving only the bank above the guard, which might be enough to keep him awake but not for her to navigate through this narrow space.

The pull of the cool air grew stronger as she squirmed closer to the bulk of the elevator shaft, whatever pressure differences had been set up drawing the air towards the shaft. It flowed as strong as a breeze now, the layer of dust she crawled through getting thinner the closer she got to the shaft. There were more cables, the few remaining connections all running in the same direction. She couldn't help but think of them as dead without the data running through them.

She reached the elevator shaft where the remaining electrical wires were bundled together, critical enough to be left behind for future tenants.

The vertical riser had to be close now. It was where the coax cables would run down or up, connecting to the other floors and ultimately to the server housed in the basement. She had seen it on schematics when she had been trying to access the test facility. She just didn't know exactly what it would look like in real life.

She followed a bundle of wires around the corner and stopped. She had hoped for a service door, maybe some kind of grate to remove. In her imagination, it had been plenty large for her to crawl through. Except three wire bundles disappeared into an opening no bigger than a notebook. She put her hand on the cold metal, had to swallow her dismay as her head bumped against the plenum tiles. She couldn't fit through this opening, no matter how far she exhaled her breath or sucked in her gut. She pulled on the cables as if that would magically change the opening to the door she needed.

She thought of how far back it was to the water bottle. She wouldn't make it before the lights shut off. She would be stuck in the plenum until daylight and by then she would be missed.

The plenum sub-floor was too low over her head, the space too small. It took a few moments to recognize her body's response: panic at the certainty of being caught and the foolishness of trying to escape. As usual she had upped the ante and made things worse than they needed. Yet what was the alternative? Stay in that room and wait for Stanton to return?

A draft cooled her flushed cheeks. It blew across her face, not into it, and there was a definite pull to the air over her hand. Ignoring her self-pity, she followed the breeze along the base of the shaft. At the corner she heard the faintest whistle of air moving through cracks.

In three pulls of her elbows, she lay in front of the vent she had imagined and knew must be there. It wasn't for the cables, but for air, that had cooled the countless workstations and now simply flowed through the empty floors.

Through the slats she saw the vertical riser, a shaft that would connect to each floor as part of the cooling system. Four screws attached each corner, holding the metal vent too tight to the bulkhead to allow her to squeeze her fingers under the edge. The slats were also too narrow, only her fingertips making it through.

She crawled back around the corner and retrieved a cut piece of wire that lay beneath the cables. About half the width of a cigarette, it was pliable enough that it held its shape, and she threaded it around two slats in the vent, pulling the end through so she held both ends in one hand. She pulled but was unable to get leverage in the cramped space and the screws remained as solidly attached as ever.

There was a hum, the floor and walls vibrating around her. She skittered away, imagining she would escape whatever catastrophe had arrived, only to realize the elevator had begun to move, and was rising up the shaft.

She rushed back to the wall, curled herself into a convoluted pretzel, so that her feet pushed against either side of the vent, and pulled. At first it didn't move, but in her panic she wiggled it back and forth, the growing hum of the elevator enough to cover the noise, and when the elevator thudded to a stop, the vent thudded with it. Amanda caught it before it hit the floor.

There was the heavy slide of the elevator doors opening above her and the quick, abrupt footsteps walking back the way she had come. Stanton? The steps sounded too fast. A change of guard? Or more food?

With only the briefest check of the air shaft, to confirm it continued between floors, she slid feet first into the cramped riser. It was a tight fit on her hips and she scraped a good chunk of flesh off each side as she forced her way in. She listened before she pulled her shoulders through and heard muffled male voices. It could be anyone, for any reason.

She held tight to the lip of the opening with one hand as she lowered herself carefully down.

The sides of the tunnel brushed her shoulders, the space more of a rectangle than a square, and she braced her thighs against the sides. She paused at the full length of her arm, her fingertips still clinging to the edge of the opening. She wasn't really holding herself; it was more of a controlled wiggle down the shaft, but it took a effort of will to peel her finger tips away from the lip.

The light of the opening faded above her as she descended. She had to hope there was another opening below her and she wouldn't be found dead at the bottom of the shaft weeks from now, like a mouse at the bottom of a bucket.

The sides of the riser flexed and bent as she moved and it felt like she was ringing a church bell to broadcast her location. She took frequent glances at the last piece of light above her and ignored the growing strain in her legs. Had they discovered she was gone?

She almost cried out when her foot kicked against a more solid metal. The opening into the plenum on the floor below. She kicked the vent several times, to hell with the noise, and took more skin off her hips and shoulders as she scrambled out into full darkness. She lay there for several seconds, listening but mostly breathing, clinging to the solidity of the floor beneath her. She jumped when the elevator clanged and began its descent from the floor above.

She expected it to stop on the floor where she lay, their footsteps as they disembarked directly above her head. It slid past, humming as it lowered past the floor below her. The sound slowly faded, though her fear did not.

She pushed on the tile directly above her, tried not to panic when it didn't move. The sub-floor couldn't be different from the one above. She pushed harder but the floor was a solid mass.

She felt for the opening of the shaft. Made sure it was where she thought it was. She tasted dust and had the irrational thought that she was underground. She touched her hands to her face, the feel of her fingertips on her skin reassuring and real enough to give her room to think.

The tiles closest to the elevator bulkhead wouldn't be movable. She squirmed further away, aware of the impossibility of keeping her bearings in the dark, and breathed again when the third tile she tried gave way and tilted up into the darkness — or, more accurately, dimness.

She scrambled out into what felt like the brightness of day. The space was identical to the one above, disassembled cubicles leaning against the bulkhead with a few outlets visible in the floor, the light coming from the glow of the city outside the windows. She went directly to the stairwell and depressed the release bar carefully, and slipped into the quiet bareness of the stairs. She made quick, silent progress, moving past the exits at each floor, counting the flights until she reached the door that read *Lobby*. She paused, staying out of sight as she peered into the cavernous space. It had a tall glass front, windows reaching two storeys high, a long semi-circular desk with a scrolling monitor mounted behind it, and the empty chair at what must be the security desk. The far side showed a burned area from the explosion that was barricaded off and under construction.

At the center, on its own separate raised island, sat a rough device with wires hanging from the bottom. She'd seen photos of the original Gatherer countless times, its primitiveness out of sync with what it had delivered to the world. In real life, it looked threatening without its gleaming white case, the inner crystals exposed. She was about to keep going down when a change in the moonlight stopped her. It shone through the glass and spotlighted the area, turning the floor and platform strangely white. As if the moonlight itself were being drawn into it. The hairs on her arm rose.

She continued with a new urgency. There had to be an exit to outside. It was required by law, yet her anxiety grew as the air grew damper and the staircase became less traveled.

It ended at a long corridor with several closed doors running off it. Supply rooms, maybe the server room. She considered going there, to see if there was a terminal she could access or verify what Alicia had said was true.

A red exit sign at the end indicated an exterior door. It had no window and a heaviness to it that spoke of strength. Mounted above it was the lens of a camera.

If she tried to disable it, she would be seen. She had to hope that the empty desk at the security desk meant that no one was watching or that Alicia had been telling the truth.

She would walk. Calmly.

The hall smelled of cleaners and must. She walked quickly, head down, her gaze locked on the red exit sign. The rows of white tiles stretched ahead of her. She expected the sound of running feet. The crash of a door.

She ran the last few steps before she stopped and carefully opened the door. A trace of fresh air streamed in, then rushed and she was gulping the damp, salty air. She would have a cigarette. Could almost taste it.

She slipped through the door and stood close against the wall. The shadow of the building sheltered her, the stage-like brightness of the gate visible through the trees that lined the drive.

There was something happening and it took her several seconds to figure out what she was seeing. The entrance was flooded with light, so bright that the protesters outside the gate looked sun-spotted as if bleached white by the brightness. The soldiers within all looked washed out, only occasional bits of gray indicating any color at all.

She pushed closer to the wall, paralyzed by the cries of fear coming from the gate, like a feral animal in pain. She looked for a soldier subduing a protester, or having resorted to violence, yet the protesters stood in an eerily quiet semi-circle, witnesses to the frenzy that was happening inside the gate. A single soldier gripped the metal bars as if he would shake it loose. He was stripped to the waist, and had no weapon, other than the agony of his voice that cut into every person there.

She should run, take this moment of distraction, but she couldn't look away, the suffering of the soldier visible in every shake of the bars, and the arch of his back and neck to the sky, like a captured wolf howling at the moon.

Two guards grabbed him, and despite their size struggled to keep his frenzy contained. The gate slowly slid open, the only movement the thrashing of the one soldier between the two, his cries ringing through the night. The gate opened just enough to let them pass, the protesters parting to let them through to the waiting school bus. It was a stark yellow in the whiteness.

The iciness of terror flushed through her as she finally recognized what she was seeing. She looked to her feet. Even in the dimness she could see the white of the grass, the flush that spread over the concrete in the front of the headquarters and raced towards the entrance. The open hand sculpture of the Gatherer logo in the front circle looked ancient, as if it had been crumbling for centuries.

She lifted one foot ever so carefully, afraid she would be fused to the whiteness, as helpless to escape it as the blades of grass. She lifted the other foot. At the feeling of that opening between her feet and the earth, she ran, not caring if she were seen or heard, her only awareness her footsteps pounding the earth and the growing distance behind her.

TWENTY-THREE

STORM

STORM CURLED HER TOES against the worn boards of the porch, pressing her feet into the inertness of the wood. The moon hung above the dense conifers that lined the opposite shore of the lake, its brightness casting a beam across the water. There were a dozen other cabins at the resort, each of them dark, only the rustling of the squirrels and the other nighttime animals causing any kind of noise. The quiet was unnerving after the adrenaline of the day, and part of her didn't trust it enough to let her sleep.

Adams kept watch on a bench at the far end of the porch. There had been little conversation since they had arrived at the cabin. His attention had been on feeding Megan and Eli and getting them calmed down enough to sleep, while Storm had sat on the porch regaining enough strength to move.

"Anything?" she asked.

"No."

His voice was deep, his French-Canadian accent having grown stronger as his fatigue and the day progressed.

"I thought they would be here by now."

"Me too."

They had arrived in the late afternoon when the sun was already halfway to the horizon. Their escape from the dark zone had drained her, yet with Megan's knowledge of the streets and Eli's hearing they had made it to the vehicle undetected. The ride in the vehicle had been a blur of seizing muscles and the burn of fields, with Megan's presence next to her. She couldn't quite believe they had made it, still expecting someone to find them at the cabin.

They had slipped out of the side door of the utility room at the moment Maria had been recognized, the soldier's shout unmistakable. Adams had rushed them forward, making for the break in the fence as the soldiers ran after Maria. The kids had already been running for the first building outside the fence when there was a burst of gunfire. She had stumbled, Adams half-carrying her to the cover of the building.

"It wasn't them," said Adams, Megan and Eli white with fear. "It was only the door."

It had helped them to keep moving but it had not helped with the fear. That iciness still ran through her veins, and warmth wouldn't return until she heard their voices or saw their faces.

She shoved her hands deeper into her pockets, wrapping the oversized coat around her before lowering herself into the faded Muskoka chair. The wood creaked as she sat back, only a few strips of red paint still clinging to the arm rests.

The night barely moved, the small waves within the shaft of moonlight the only discernible change. Adams shifted and the sand on the porch scraped beneath his boot.

"Have you known him long?" asked Storm.

He watched the water, trees, and the bare track they had driven in on, ever-vigilant.

"Eleven years."

"And Maria?"

"Not as long."

"Was she a good soldier?"

"One of the best."

That reality hung between them, that no one would have had a better chance of escaping than the two of them.

She tucked her feet beneath her, the chill of the night deepening.

"I remember you," said Storm.

The night settled closer, pushing up against the edges of the porch. "You were there."

Adams had a new stillness to him that was wary, protective.

He had been a face above her when she had been in agony. One of the men who had carried her after she had collapsed on stage.

A frog croaked in the darkness, another responding further away.

"I'm not wrong, am I? You were there?"

His attention was on the darkest part of the lake, his face turned from her. He nodded.

"You helped him."

She couldn't stop the accusation, the care she received more about experimentation than getting well. Adams had been outside the room where she had been held, guarding the door.

"My wife and daughter were in the treatment facility." His voice was flat and distant with a torrent of pain running beneath it. "Valerie said she met you."

Storm saw again the line of locked doors, felt the cold tiles beneath her bare feet and the blood running from her knees. She pushed out of the chair and walked to the opposite edge of the porch, away from that fear and panic. The boards creaked beneath her.

"Your daughter was there too," said Storm.

She had been curled in the bed, so small only her crop of black hair showed above the sheet.

"Camille."

It broke Storm's heart to hear the tenderness and the strained control in his voice.

"I'm so sorry."

She turned, had to at least have the bravery to face him. Valerie had been beautiful, with long black hair and deep brown eyes that made you want to believe that the world would be okay.

His gaze stayed fixed on the far end of the lake, as if he would find them there. A spider's web swayed above him, tattered strands hanging down.

"I thought it was the right place for them," said Adams.

A moth fluttered against the screen, desperate to get to the light of the oil lamp inside.

"It should have been." She could still feel the corrosive energy running through her veins after one of Wesley's injections, and the belief that she would die. "You couldn't have known."

"I should have."

Their shared guilt hung around them, as thick as fog over water.

"They knew you loved them."

He was so still he might have stopped breathing, and perhaps he had the moment they had died.

"They didn't say that."

"They didn't need to."

She took several steps towards him, stood half-way on the worn boards, her shadow stretching long and dark towards the lake.

He didn't want her coming close, his body turned away from her, his suffering his alone.

She stood with her hands at her side, unable to move forward or back.

"Thank you. For helping me."

A piece of the torn web broke free and drifted beyond the railing into the dark.

"Not everyone would," she said.

The barest of breezes blew off the lake, scraping a curled leaf across the porch.

"Will you be able to stop it?" he said.

She remembered the number of Gatherers in the city and their failed attempt to do anything about it.

"I don't know."

With Amanda gone and Maria not back, she couldn't see a clear path.

The screen door groaned and Megan stepped onto the porch.

"Is Hamel here?"

Adams pulled his feet underneath him and smiled, almost pulling it off.

"Could you not sleep?"

Megan swerved while she walked, her eyes half shut, more asleep than awake. She wore faded blue pajamas, her hair bigger and bouncier after the earlier bath.

Adams shifted his position and she climbed onto his lap, his arms folding around her as naturally as the air he breathed.

"I thought I heard someone," said Megan. She closed her eyes and leaned her head against his chest. Adams brushed a wayward curl from her forehead.

"Storm and I were just talking."

"About the Gatherer?"

Megan's voice was distant, sleep reclaiming her.

Adams kissed the top of her head and leaned back on the bench, pulling her close to him. His face was drawn, and haunted shadows lay below his eyes.

"I made his bed for him."

Megan suddenly sat up, pulling out of Adams' arms, and squirming off his lap.

"That was nice of you," said Adams, his now-empty arms falling back to his sides.

"And Maria too."

"Did you sleep at all?"

Megan shook her head as she bent to pick something up off the porch. It was a section of tree branch, a few dried leaves still attached. She twirled it, the leaves rustling, her energy breaking open the night.

"My mom and I waited for my dad when he was away. It's only if you fall asleep that they don't come back."

It was as if each of their losses trailed behind them, none of them ever free.

"We can keep watch for you," said Storm, but Megan was dancing past her, holding the broken branch above her like a baton.

A wave of fatigue struck Storm, like a sudden gust of wind. She retreated to the chair and perched on the edge, waiting for the dizziness to subside.

"Are you okay?" asked Adams.

Storm slowly inhaled, dizziness clinging at the sides of her vision.

"Do you need the water?"

Megan had stopped in front of her, the branch lowered.

"I'll be okay."

Adams and Megan stood over her. She didn't remember Adams arriving.

"Why don't you get her a glass of water?" said Adams.

Storm closed her eyes, caught in the tide of fatigue.

"Not a glass," said Megan. Her voice sounded far away. Her small hands pulled at Storm.

Storm resisted, wanting to sleep.

"Help me get her up."

Adams' arms were lifting her, and she envied his strength, and health. She felt the hopelessness of it, this fatigue that would never end.

"No, down here."

Megan was insisting and Adams refused, his voice low and rumbling in his chest.

"It's okay," Storm said.

He paused at the center of the porch, as Megan's light footsteps descended the steps.

"Come on!"

"You're so weak already," he said.

"It will help."

She rested her head against his chest, listening to the steady beat of his heart as they moved down the steps and across the grass, the air growing cooler as they approached the water.

Megan stood at the end of the dock, a thin silhouette against the gleam of the water.

The floating dock swayed beneath them as Adams's steps thudded on the old boards.

"Put me here."

He held her closer, his grip tighter.

"You're sure?"

"You need to be back at the cabin in case they come."

The glow of the cabin stretched down the slope towards them, a warm welcoming place she had to hope would draw Maria and Hamel back.

"Make sure you stay with her."

The wood was rough and cold under her feet when he set her down, and she let herself slump further until she sat on the uneven boards of the dock.

The vibration of his footsteps retreated, pausing mid-way to the shore as he looked back. She lifted a hand in reassurance, though didn't know if he would see it in the dark. When the vibrations stopped and he made his way up the slope, she breathed fully of the cool damp air, feeling the smallest return of energy.

Megan sat beside her, her legs hanging over the edge. Storm shifted her position, so her feet hung down, inhaling sharply as her toes touched the water.

Megan swung her feet, sending splashes over the water. Storm submerged her feet to the ankle, flexing her toes to let the water reach every area of skin. She felt a settling, that first spark of energy spreading, pushing back the fatigue.

"You know about the water," said Storm.

Megan's legs stopped swinging. Storm felt the heat of her small body next to her. She had one hand resting in her lap, the other casually on Storm's leg.

"Is that how you got better?"

Megan snatched her hand back, held both in fists on her lap. A gap of cold opened where Megan's warmth had been.

"I won't tell anyone," said Storm.

Megan crossed her arms as if that would hide the evidence.

"When did it happen?"

She had so many questions.

"My mom said not to tell anyone."

It would have been Megan's mother's final attempt to protect the girl, even after she was gone.

"Your mother was smart."

"I miss her."

Storm enclosed Megan's small fist with her hand.

"I'm sorry she died."

The remaining waves from Megan's feet lapped against the dock, the surface returning to its smooth, flat blackness.

"Me too."

Storm pulled her close. Megan's shoulders were so narrow, her arms and legs more bone than flesh. With her mane of hair, it was easy to forget how small she was.

She held her tight, the two of them a small spot of warmth in the darkness. The moon glinted off the water and the frog she had heard earlier repeated its call, and they sat, Storm's feet slowly going numb.

"You said you were going to fix it," said Megan.

Storm remembered her certainty when she'd told Megan those words.

She searched for words that might explain why she still hadn't. The obstacles they had encountered and her growing fear that it had gotten too big and that putting an end to it was getting further out of reach.

"It was harder than I thought."

"Because you're sick?"

She was tempted to blame the illness and the corruption of the larger Gatherers. In truth, she had been naïve, not understanding how far out of her control the Gatherer had gone.

"Other people control the Gatherer now. I thought it would be easier to stop them."

Megan pulled away from her and swung her feet through the water, the splash echoing under the dock.

"Isn't it the Gatherer we need to stop?"

Storm half-smiled at her use of 'we.' She re-adjusted and dipped her feet deeper in the water, the jolt of cold as strong as any current.

"They are making bigger ones and sending them all over the world."

"They'll still be connected to all the others," said Megan.

"Yes. Through the central hub. We tried to stop them that way, but we couldn't get in."

Megan pulled her feet from the water, folded them to sit cross-legged.

"Not the hub. The streaks between Gatherers."

Storm felt a wave of unsteadiness, as if her fatigue were returning.

"Hamel has them on his laptop. He can show you."

She sounded determined and miserable as if holding out for Hamel to show her these streaks would force him to return. Storm moved back from the edge and slipped out of her jeans and underwear and left her shirt and coat in a pile on top.

"Why don't you tell me about them? While I soak."

Storm lowered herself into the water, feeling its cold pressure rise around her knees and hips. Megan had freed herself from the disease and the possibility of it took the edge off the cold as Storm's feet sunk into the cold mud. She sucked in air and forced herself to stay in the water as the burn spread up her legs and reached her bones.

Megan sat quiet, the water rising to Storm's neck, the tightness in her chest making it hard to breathe.

"At first Hamel thought they were spokes on a wheel because they all ran back to a Gatherer."

Storm took short, shallow breaths.

"But he mapped them out and it's a web. Of all of them connected. It makes big white streaks on the ground where it comes to the surface."

"They aren't always at the surface?"

Storm spoke through gritted teeth.

"I can feel them underneath," said Megan, her face in shadow.

"And how do they feel?"

Storm weighted her feet in the mud, felt the silt slide between her toes.

"Like I want to see my mom."

TWENTY-FOUR

MARIA

MARIA HAD BEEN RUNNING for hours. The mind-numbing excruciating plod of three-hour training runs where you kept putting your foot in front of the next in hopes that it would end. Except no matter how far she ran her mind would never be numb enough to un-see her final images of Hamel. Shot in the shoulder, blood spreading out in a thick pool below him even as he pressed the flashlight into her hand and returned fire at their attackers.

He had refused to let her carry him, pushing off her hands. There had been no time for words, or a thank you, simply a look and a nod and she had plunged further into the seeping blackness, expecting at any moment a second shot to take her down.

She slowed to a walk, her breathing heavy. She had been following the stream for over an hour, the stream widening the further she traveled downstream and the forest at its edge clarifying into moss covered trees and dense ferns as the dawn arrived.

She paused next to a split cedar trunk, the still-living branches twisting above her. A bird cawed into the morning as a spider lowered on a thread at her shoulder. There was no sign of pursuers but there hadn't been since she left the tunnels.

She bent to drink from the stream, splashing some on her face to wash away her fatigue. Her stomach clenched in hunger. She broke off a piece of grass and chewed it. The growing light burned her tired eyes.

She spit out the mashed piece of grass and picked another, trying to calculate the distance to the cabin from Hamel's whispered instructions as they had moved blind through the tunnels, as if he had known what came next. A rush of grief stopped her bursting through the wall she had tried to build, her fatigue eating away at its foundation.

She splashed more water on her face and looked to the lightening sky until her breathing slowed and she forced her grief back to the place where she kept all her sorrows. She ran faster, trying to escape Hamel's and Amanda's faces, so that she knew only the scream of muscle and her labored breath.

She had slipped twice on the rocks, blood seeping through her pants at her knee and her palms scraped and bleeding when she finally slowed, squinting at the full brightness at the end of the stream where it opened onto the lake.

Would they even be there?

She stepped out of the stream, pushing through the low shrubs and tangled vines to a place where she could view the lake unseen. It stretched long and narrow, the conifers close at its sides, the area carved for the resort the only open space. A dozen cabins lay higher up on the slope, still boarded up for winter, except for one at the end. It was smaller, half-hidden behind a tree, the porch blocking her from seeing movement inside. The mini-van parked outside had its hatch open, and a bag leaned against one of the tires. It was an older model, light blue, and with rust around the wheel well.

She pressed closer to the tree as the screen door snapped open. She let out a long breath as Adams stepped onto the porch carrying a knapsack. He scanned the water and trees and the path that led to their cabin before he strode towards the van.

Eli followed behind him, the continuous pitch of his voice carrying across the water, though not the words. She searched for Storm, a renewed worry pushing into her exhausted veins. It eased at a slower movement on the porch, someone sitting up on the bench and a flash of red hair as she stood and crossed to the steps.

Storm scanned the same way Adams had, her attention hesitating for a moment in Maria's direction, before descending the steps, using the railing as support. She made her way to the van, slower than Adams, repeatedly looking back to the lake and the floating dock.

Maria almost waved and called out but saw the pick-up parked at the gatehouse and the door of the shed propped open.

She ran, ducking below branches and hopping fallen logs, circling the edge of the lake and keeping her sight on the van as Megan emerged from the cabin and skipped across the grass to the vehicle.

Adams called to her, and she said something back, the tread of Maria's feet and the crack of branches loud around her. The shoreline rose in a rock cliff next to the resort and she was forced to divert away from the water, catching a last sight of Storm as she climbed into the back of the van.

Maria's legs burned as she scrambled up the outcrop, gasping for air when she reached the peak and heard the dull thud of the mini-van's closing door. She slid down the opposite bank, landing in a patch of spiky stalks, the thorns scraping her hands and face.

In a few steps she was at the edge of the open area, the gatehouse and shed between her and the van. A man came out of the shed and searched for something in the bed of his truck.

Adams stood at the front of the van, looking across the lake to where she had been, waiting that extra second in hopes that the person who hadn't arrived suddenly did.

"Hold on," she whispered, willing the guy at the pick-up to find whatever the hell he was looking for.

Adams got in the minivan, the taillights glowed red, and the white reverse lights came on.

The guy at the pickup whistled as he opened the cab door, and took a long slow drink of coffee, as the van started down the track towards the gate.

"Come on," she said.

The maintenance guy walked painfully slowly to the tailgate, picked up whatever tool he had found, and flipped it once on his way to the shed.

The van flashed between trees, winding away from her on its way to the exit. She ran, reaching forward with her arms as she dug past the pain, past the fatigue, drawing every ounce of power into her failing muscles.

The van paused at the exit, still a hundred paces away. It turned into the wider road, the trees on either side closing around it.

She leapt the ditch, feeling the surge of fire as she reached full speed, her feet barely touching the ground. The van pulled away.

She called out, pushed harder as it drove faster, the dirt road opening between them. She yelled and waved her arms, and it didn't stop.

Her leg buckled and she stumbled, falling to the ground, gravel ripping into her palms. She hauled herself up, a pale face from the back window watching her. The brake lights glowed.

Adams was at the rear bumper when she reached them, catching her in a bear hug as she almost collapsed. The back hatch opened, and Storm crawled from under a copper blanket, stiff and shaky, but surviving.

"Hamel?" Adams asked as he pulled out of the hug.

She shook her head and grief distorted his face as he looked behind her to the empty road. Storm hung her head and then Adams was ushering her to the front of the car, as Storm lowered the back hatch.

"Where's Hamel?" asked Eli as she sat in the passenger's seat. He and Megan's frightened faces crowded over her shoulder.

"He took a shot," said Maria, realizing her error when the boy's eyes widened, taking over his entire face, and Megan's face collapsed.

"Will he be okay?" The pitch of Eli's voice was piercing, and he stared at her shirt and pants, stained with Hamel's blood.

The van picked up speed, stones flying up against the undercarriage, the racket a counterpoint to the quiet inside.

She exhaled, let her breathing slow.

"There were two groups in the tunnels."

She looked to Adams for guidance on how much to say but he had his own struggles, his knuckles white where he held the wheel.

"Hamel made sure they saw us."

She remembered the sounds of boots on concrete, and the beams of their lights flashing over them like spotlights.

"And they caught up to you."

It was Megan who spoke, as she handed Maria a bottle of water. Maria took a long inhale, the relief of the liquid exquisite. The boy's gaze didn't leave her.

"They'll look after him," said Maria. Because they would want to know everything he did.

"I want to see him," said Eli.

Adams unclenched his hands from the wheel and slowly flexed them. His voice was shaky.

"Right now, we're going to find a safe place. Then we'll decide what to do next." He squeezed Eli's shoulder as they drove deeper into the morning dusk still clinging between the trees.

"Do you know where that is?" asked Maria, feeling as if she would never stop running.

The motion of the vehicle undermined her focus, and she could feel the exhaustion gathering, strong enough now she wouldn't win.

"Yeah," said Adams. "We have an idea."

TWENTY-FIVE

STORM

MEGAN AND ELI TOOK turns leveraging the handle of the water pump and great gushes of water splashed on the drain set into the dirt. The campground was empty in the early season and they had parked well into the rows of campsites, out of view from the road and next to a rusted playground. Eli still wore his pajamas, the hem already dark with wet. During the drive, Megan's pink tutu had reappeared, the one she had worn when Storm had first encountered her in the dark zone, like an angel coming out of the dark. She had lost her wings since then, and the wand, yet in many ways she had become more ethereal, her props no longer needed.

Megan caught Storm watching and smiled before shrieking as an extra-large splash sprayed against her legs. Megan had been more resilient than she had expected after Hamel's death and she felt the draw to be close to her and her strange combination of fragility and strength.

"Look here," said Adams, turning the laptop towards Storm. He sat at the opposite end of the bench, the computer and the transceiver blocked by an aluminum shield and placed several meters from her. The setup had not been easy, and they all felt the absence of Hamel and Amanda.

"This is what Hamel put together?"

The map was hard to see on the small screen, the layout looking like one of those inter-connectivity ads where the world is covered by a network of bright nodes.

"This shows the north-west of the US and the west coast of Canada. Each of these—" He swirled the mouse around one of the bright points, "—is a known location of a Gatherer."

It was easy to find Rima with its high concentration of devices, the spot on the screen dense with small points. Adams zoomed in, going too close, the images blurred until he zoomed back out.

"Each of these lines is a streak?" Maria stood behind the bench, between Storm and the laptop, as if she thought she would need to step in and protect her.

Adams pointed to several lines in the north-west of the city.

"These ones we can confirm. The others—" He paused. "Hamel extrapolated from what we saw."

"So, they're all connected?" asked Maria. She had slept while they drove, but looked rougher now, her face pinched.

"It's what I felt at the commune," said Storm. It wasn't the afterlife, or nirvana, or any kind of higher power. It had been this interconnection of devices, forming a planet-wide web. "There must have been streaks, we just didn't see them."

"There was one," said Megan. She stood farther back from all of them, the line of clouds on the horizon a dark bank behind her. "It was at the bottom of the ramp."

"So they transmit energy?" asked Maria. "Like the electrical grid?"

Storm and Megan both shook their heads and Storm nodded for Megan to go ahead.

"It's pulling energy into it. From everything. The streaks give it more surface area to do it."

"And where does the energy go?" asked Maria.

Storm and Megan hadn't discussed it yet. Megan had wanted too much for Hamel to come back and show her.

She waited for Megan to respond. What Storm had seen in those brief moments in the commune had been infinite, terrifying in its boundlessness.

"Somewhere else."

Storm smiled.

"That's funny?" said Maria.

"No. It's true. It goes someplace else." To a place Storm could feel and be afraid of but couldn't understand.

"Can we get it back?" asked Adams.

Storm understood his desire to gather up the energy they had lost, return it to wherever it had been drawn from, and put the lid back on the box.

"It's not like that," said Megan.

Eli had come over from the waterspout, the front of his pajamas splattered with water. His cheeks were rosy, and his eyes bright. He was a contrast to Megan's solemn gaze, her chin lowered as if sensing the earth beneath her.

"My gran said that it knew her name," said Eli.

Storm had felt the same recognition, as if she had seen life in its purest form.

"It's like the tide," said Megan. Storm felt again the pull of it.

"So where does the energy go?" asked Adams.

He had zoomed out the screen, to show the countless number of nodes. The earth's crust had been pierced at countless points, and a line carved between them. Storm felt sorry for them as they struggled to understand something that was intuitive, and outside of what they knew.

"We don't know," said Storm.

Their earlier view didn't even begin to encompass the severity of what they were now seeing; a web that was drawing energy from all over the earth.

Maria had finally come to rest, her hands on her hips, her feet spread.

"It doesn't matter where it goes, we just have to stop it from getting there."

The slopes behind her were the pale green of spring leaves and the darker mix of conifers.

Adams rubbed his hands down his thighs. She could feel his unease and Maria's, their skills and experience far removed from where the Gatherer was taking them.

Adams changed the view of the screen, spreading and then condensing the grid of nodes, the full web displayed across the entire globe.

"If we destroy the Gatherers, would the streaks then be disconnected pieces, or would they reform?" said Maria.

Storm flexed her fingers against the residual ache. She had no sense of how the streaks would perform, this manifestation so far gone from what she had created.

"They would find each other," said Megan.

"How do you know that?" asked Storm.

"Because it's what they want."

Fear rippled across Storm's skin as real as if she had been burned by a field. Maria and Adams had gone still, the way they did when they sensed danger.

Megan stood and first walked, then ran to the old slide and teeter totter in the corner of the playground.

"Come on, Eli!"

Eli ran after her, his bare feet displacing dirt with every step.

Maria pushed the hair back from her face in frustration. "She is so much like you."

Megan was at the top of the slide's steps, launching herself down the slick surface as hard as she was able.

"She drops that on us, that the pieces of the Gatherer will be like some horror show limbs trying to reconnect, and then walks away."

"She gets bored," said Storm.

Maria dropped her arms in exasperation and Adams smiled.

"My point exactly," said Maria.

People didn't understand how suffocating the boredom could be, when something was so clear and people needed to discuss and question it as if it weren't the most obvious thing in the world.

Adams closed the laptop and started dismantling the shield.

"There has to be a way to stop them from reconnecting."

"What does that even mean?" asked Maria. "Is she saying they're intelligent?"

Storm stood, her leg muscles stiff.

"All energy wants to stay in balance," said Storm. "A negative to the positive. A force and its equal. Maybe that's what it's trying to do."

"And kill all of us in the process," said Adams.

He folded up the shield and tucked the transceiver under his arm.

"It doesn't have intention," said Storm. "It works on a different plane."

Adams called to the kids and waved them towards the van.

"So it doesn't even know we exist," said Maria.

Storm nodded.

"More or less."

TWENTY-SIX

STORM

AT THE SUDDEN DECELERATION, Storm slid forward on the floor of the van. She braced herself against the wheel well and lifted her head as they plunged into an overgrown lane, the overhanging tree branches close against the sides.

A sign flashed by, obscured by ferns and moss, and the letters too faded to read. She scooted towards the back and held on as they bumped over several large ruts, the screech of pine branches along the side overriding the sound of the engine.

Her hip ached from where she had lain on the hard metal, and she shook her head to clear the grogginess that lingered from sleep. Maria and Adams sat in the front seats, with Megan and Eli's silhouettes between them, they too woken by the sudden change in speed.

Adams swerved to avoid a pothole, and the van rocked from side-to-side, the dull, gray of the morning deeper beneath the trees. The smell of salt and ocean brought the memory of cold water on her skin and she rubbed her face, trying to wake the alertness she would need to enter this haven of the afflicted. She would have met some of them on her first visit to the dark zone, though Adams had said their relocation to this hospital had been abrupt, and not all had survived.

They passed a shovel leaning against a tall Doug fir before the trees pulled back and they bumped into a large clearing, the hospital looming over it. It looked to have been built in the early 1900s and had a high raised porch, its hard lines out of place in the lushness of the rainforest. The structure was square and block-like, the damp and moisture having left it wilted and worn.

On the grass in front of it, hundreds of people gathered in small groups, some lying on the tangled grass, others leaning against the columns of the porch. There was no mistaking their thin pallor or the beaten postures for anything other than the afflicted.

Adams had described a country retreat where the afflicted went to recover. This was something entirely different. More like a dumping zone for anyone who was audacious enough to show symptoms.

Adams stopped the van a few meters into the open area. A group of hollow-eyed teenagers closest to them looked their way in unison. A girl with dark skin and long braided hair stared at them, and her lack of response was frightening. Her lips moved, saying something to the group and a boy next to her, with a toque pulled low over long greasy hair, shrugged, his stare unrelenting. Another boy beside him, his shoulders broad and lean, slowly stood, wiping the grass from his pants. He seemed more capable than the others, still thin but having retained some of his strength.

Adams turned off the engine and the rattle of the wind pushing through cedars moved into the space. Carefully, Storm lifted the copper blanket and climbed out of the van. As her feet landed on the gravel, the side door opened and Megan bolted for the porch, Eli close behind her. They raced through the crowd, small points of energy moving freely on the bare patches between people.

Maria climbed from the cab and came to stand beside her. Adams spoke when he reached her other side.

"There are more than last time."

Faces turned towards them, as a slow murmuring spread through the crowd. She had a sudden rush of apprehension. These people would be angry, at best disappointed.

"We won't be safe here," said Maria.

The teenagers watched them warily.

"Storm will blend right in," said Adams.

Did she fit with this crowd of wasted souls, with hollow-eyes and sunken mouths? They were little more than corpses, their life force fading away.

"It would only take one of them to blow our cover," said Maria.

Adams's gaze followed Megan's progress as the kids reached the porch steps.

"There's no cell service."

"And anyone using a satellite would immediately have hundreds of angry afflicted hunting them down," said Storm.

With the number of prone bodies and the atmosphere of restless waiting, it could have been a rock concert or a sit-in. The physical weight of their presence felt like as good a protest as any.

Marty, the woman who had first helped her at the dark zone, stood in the open front door, her clothes the same worn jeans and faded plaid shirt, her gray hair pulled back in a practical ponytail. She bent down to welcome Megan as she leapt at her, the girl's arms wrapping tight around her waist. Marty had been one of the few to help the afflicted, providing them a haven inside the warehouse, and now here.

The tightness in Storm's chest eased, and the crowd transformed into what they were. People needing help. It might not be as hard to blend in after all.

Adams and Maria stayed close to her side as they walked through the crowd. The gravel drive swung in a long arc in front of the building and they loosely followed its path.

The teenager, who had seemed healthier than the others, had sat down by the time they reached him. Up close, the restlessness of his gaze spoke of mental distress. The young woman with the braids held his hand tightly in her lap, and her gaze only briefly met Storm's before she looked away.

The crowd was quiet, the few conversations in low tones, words of agitation mixed with words of comfort.

A woman held a baby against her large breasts and reached out with her free hand to Storm as she passed. Maria moved to interfere and Storm waved her back. The squeeze of the woman's hand was quick and strong, and Storm had only a quick look at raw red skin on the baby's face.

She nodded before looking away, unable to speak through the suffering that lodged in her throat.

An unshaven man with skin that matched the gray of the sky glared at her and said words that looked like a curse, but he didn't move from where he sat, his wife's head resting on his lap.

Maria drew in a long breath beside her, and Storm felt the same need to force calm in the face of this distress. The damage to these people was so much worse.

They walked in single file through an opening between a Korean family with three children and a couple whose hair had gone entirely white. The man nodded to her and Storm tried not to let her gaze flick to the shock of whiteness that matched the absence of color in his face.

"Who's going to save the world now?" yelled a male voice. Maria and Adams drew closer but when she turned her head, she couldn't see who had said the words, people's faces lifted to her reaction rather than to who had spoken. The clouds had grown darker, pressed closer above their heads.

When they had reached the steps, a man with a red turban spoke in a low murmur to the hands clasped in his lap, while a woman in a long dress lay stretched out on a step and could have been dead but for the blink of her eyes.

Storm tried to push down the panic at the level of the devastation. She wasn't going to blend in here, she was going to drown. She lifted her head, looking for a place to escape and met Marty's steady gaze. She had come to the top of the step, had one arm around Megan and the other extended down towards Storm.

The dry warmth of her soft hand was a life raft.

"It's good to see you again," said Marty, taking both of Storm's hands in hers. Above the press of people, Storm breathed. "You look well."

"I wasn't sure I would see you." Marty's pressure on her hands was firm and constant. "How long have you been here?"

"They cleared us out the day before your press conference."

Marty released her hands.

"That wasn't my——"

Marty held up a hand to stop her. "We never believed him."

Storm felt disoriented, battered and lurching from one crash of emotion to the next.

Marty turned to Adams.

"Megan tells me you've been doing a good job."

He smiled, and looked vulnerable somehow, younger.

"And I see you've found a new helper," Marty continued, as Eli moved close, and Adams took his hand.

"They have both been great helps. We wouldn't be here without them."

Eli beamed and Megan danced from one foot to the other.

"We rescued Storm," said Eli.

More people had taken shelter on the sides of the porch and Storm was aware of their bent heads and focused listening.

"She needs that a lot," said Maria, and then they were laughing. A woman with a shaved head close to them grinned.

"It's good to finally meet you, Maria," said Marty. "I've heard a lot about you."

"Likewise."

Maria had the peaked look of someone too long without sleep, the escaped hair from her ponytail lank around her face.

"I guess you didn't bring any supplies," said Marty, addressing Adams.

He shook his head and nodded at Storm.

"We got sidetracked."

Storm felt the exposure and the expectations that she would somehow make all of this right.

The door behind Marty burst open and Romero's tall, lanky energy filled the porch. His hair hung into his eyes and a frayed hole showed at the knee of his jeans.

"It's good to see you're still here," said Storm when he came to rest beside Marty.

"Of course." Romero waved in a grand gesture towards the crowded lawn. "We are needed more than ever."

Storm inclined her head in acknowledgement. She hadn't seen him since her first time at the warehouse when Maria had been missing.

"So how can we help?" said Marty.

The first splats of rain sounded on the grass behind them, accompanied by the louder strikes on the porch roof. The crowd rippled en masse, writhing as the weak struggled to their feet and hands reached out to assist.

Marty's voice rang loud and clear above the rain. "Come in, everyone!" She had one of the double doors open, Romero held the other. The crowd turned and flowed towards them.

They were carried through on the current, crowded on either side by the pale and weak. They pushed into a high foyer, a wide staircase leading up. The steps were already full, and there was nowhere for the crowd to flow, the pressure from behind growing.

"This way," said Megan, her hand slipping into Storm's and guiding her to the stairs. They picked their way through the sick who were trying to make room for those arriving. Maria stayed close behind.

They stalled a few steps up, those trying to make room unable to do so quickly, the rising voices echoing within the foyer. Adams and Eli were to the side, having met their own roadblock. The smell of sickness was thick, mixed with the stench of unwashed bodies. Maria was pushed up against her back. Storm looked to the high ceiling, tried to breathe as if she were in that space.

"Calm down!" Marty's voice cut through the echoes. "There's room for everyone. It will just take some time."

The pressure around them eased, Marty's calm creating space.

They were moving forward again, wending their way up the steps, a clear path open before them. At the second-floor landing, two dim corridors extended on either side, the shadows of the afflicted moving within them. Megan pulled her away from them to a large, empty room that opened off the landing. It was lighted by a single window, the light a stormy gray, and she had the odd feeling that she had arrived home.

Megan dragged her towards the center. She had to step over several wires laid along the floor. There were others, all running towards the center, in what appeared to be spokes. The area at the center of the room, where the wires came together, was open, the defined lines of the spokes all merging into the hub.

Maria stood with her legs straddling a wire, her frown directed at the device at the hub. She seemed unaware of the effects of the web. If anything, she looked more exhausted.

"This is why Hamel and I came back here," said Adams, from where he stood inside the door. "I thought it would be a cure."

They fell quiet at the mention of Hamel's name, their thoughts following the same path.

Eli followed one of the spokes and squatted next to the hub. Megan crouched beside him.

"Does it work?" asked Maria.

"We never got the same success as at the warehouse." Romero had arrived beside Adams.

The observation could have encompassed the entire place, for here the afflicted were not as well cared for as they had been at the warehouse.

"Marty said to get you whatever you need," said Romero. "We've had a large influx of new arrivals so she couldn't come herself."

"Where do they come from?" asked Adams.

Romero looked back towards the corridor and its press of bodies.

"Five buses came yesterday and three today. We don't even get warnings anymore." Romero had lost his idealism since she had last seen him, his inability to stop the tide clearly marked on his drawn brow and bruised gaze.

"A place to rest is all we need," said Storm.

Maria stood over a wire, not two steps from the hub, in the middle of what would be the strongest field.

"Do you not feel it?" asked Storm.

"What am I supposed to feel?"

"Not everyone can," said Megan. "It helps them but they don't always feel it."

"Do you?" asked Maria, directing her question at Adams, who shook his head.

Romero stepped around Adams so he could come into the center of the spokes. "I can't either. Which was why having Megan to help was so important."

"But you were never able to make it work?" said Storm.

"Given enough time?" Romero shrugged. "We might have."

Yet Storm's legs had stopped aching, her thoughts clearer than they had been in days.

Maria swayed, and Adams moved to her side fast enough for Storm to barely have seen it.

Maria brushed him off, almost tripping when she pulled away from him. She wasn't aware of the well-being of the web, but it still tore down her defenses and allowed her fatigue to move in. Adams didn't look much better, his exhaustion less hidden now that he stood near the hub.

She and Megan exchanged a glance. This was something they understood about the Gatherer. Even if you weren't aware, you were still under its influence.

"I'm sorry we can't offer you a bed," said Romero.

Maria's shoulders had slumped, and when Adams rubbed his hands over his face, the movement was slow.

"It's okay," said Adams. "We'll be fine."

"We'll take turns," said Maria. "Keeping watch." She scanned the room as if looking for the best place to stand guard. It looked as if it pained her to keep her eyes open.

"There's no need," said Romero. "You are safe here."

"She," said Maria, tilting her head to Storm, "is not safe anywhere."

"Eli. Megan," said Adams. "Come over here. We need to rest."

"We're not tired," said Eli, who was circling the edge of the room, taking giant steps over the wires. Megan was matching his route, closer to the center of the hub, so they moved in unison around the circle.

"I want to show Eli around." Megan looked wild and ragged and fully competent next to Adams' fatigue.

"We can do that later," said Adams. He was trying to grab Megan's hand but she side-stepped away from him, keeping her pace with Eli.

"It's only Storm they want. And Maria. No one cares about us," said Eli.

"I care about you." Adams' voice was rough. "Don't you forget that."

Megan skipped to meet Eli at the edge of the room, near the door.

"He just meant that no one is looking for us."

"So we'll be safe," added Eli. "And you don't have to worry."

It was impressive how quickly they disappeared. Smiling at them one second and then simply gone, the sound of their running feet following behind them.

"She lived here for months," said Romero. "This is like home to her."

"Even with all the people?" asked Maria.

Romero lifted his palms outward in a gesture of resignation. "I think she sees them as *her* people."

"People that are dying," said Adams. His feet still pointed towards where the children had gone. "Don't you think it's time we stopped it?" His words were short and raw. He waved in the direction of the stairwell, and the steady murmur of voices as people arrived and others tried to make room. "Is this not enough?"

His anger bounced off her like pebbles from a stone wall, the existence of the afflicted having already made her skin thick and hard.

"Why don't we all get some rest." Storm stepped carefully over the wires, feeling the energy of it, like warm water around her ankles. The window looked out towards the ocean, the drops of rain on the pane smudging the view of the back lawn and the edge of a cliff. The trees along the cliff bowed under the force of the wind. "I'll keep watch."

The window ledge was wide enough for her to sit, her feet dangling above the floor.

"We'll take turns," said Maria.

"I'll go first," said Adams.

Romero raised his eyebrows as he met Storm's gaze.

"I have work to do," said Storm. "If anything happens, I'll wake you. You'll be right here but you have to sleep."

"This is the only room the patients aren't allowed in," said Romero. "You won't be disturbed."

Storm lifted her feet so she sat sideways on the sill.

"You'll wake us if you hear anything at all," said Maria. "No being the hero."

Storm smirked and shook her head. The window was cool at her side, the patter of rain against it a low hum.

"No being the hero," Storm repeated.

"Do you want food?" said Romero. "We have a cafeteria."

"Sleep first," said Storm.

Maria moved to the open section of the wall next to the window. Her shoulders were sloped, her head bent, her whole body carried towards the possibility of sleep. She peeled off her jacket and rolled it into a ball, before she stretched out on the floor, using the jacket as a pillow beneath her head. Adams took an identical position on the other side of the window, his own coat wadded beneath his head. This wasn't the first time they had slept on a hard surface, their movements too practiced, the positions too similar.

"We only need an hour," said Maria.

Storm nodded and promised to wake them, though she wouldn't. This moment of rest was precious and their time here limited.

The sheer number of patients meant that something about the Gatherers had changed again. Right when she thought she understood, it twisted and warped, and tore another piece off what she thought she knew.

Romero leaned down to straighten one of the wires on the floor. The touch was careful and precise.

A gust of rain struck the window, the light in the room growing dimmer. Already Adams' breathing was low and steady. Maria's was quieter, though with the same regularity.

Even in repose they looked strong and fit, the full relaxation of sleep not yet taking over. It was easy to forget that they were human, that inside the training and the competence there was a person trying to survive.

Her gaze moved to the spokes of wire, thirty-three in all, some dropping through holes drilled in the floor, others tracing up the wall and disappearing into the ceiling. Megan had said it ran throughout the building, winding in walls and down corridors in an attempt to gather the whole building within it. And that it was strongest at the center.

She slid off the window ledge, the drum of rain on the window pushing into the room. Adams' feet had splayed apart, and Maria's jaw had a softness to it not seen while she was awake.

A woman with stringy brown hair poked her head through the doorway and, after seeing Storm, drew back.

She used to regret that separation, her fame and the Gatherer forever separating her from others. Yet now as she followed a wire into the middle, she thought maybe that was how it was meant to be, her first encounter with the miracle that was the Gatherer collecting process already drawing her away.

She crouched at the center and placed her finger on the tiny device, aware of Romero's quiet scrutiny. The device was warm and the faintest dusting of white surrounded it on the tiles. When she tried to rub it off, it stayed.

She held her hand over one of the wires, the way she had seen Megan do and felt that tiny pull. The faintest of replica of what she had experienced at the commune. All of it pulling. Drawing things away. Yet what healed here, destroyed on a larger scale.

Footsteps sounded in the corridor, running, and then stopped. Megan and Eli stood in the door, their faces flushed and looking the way children should: happy, as they explored what was new.

Megan's expression changed from child to adult as she approached the hub. She kneeled next to Storm, careful that her knees did not touch the wires.

Storm still held her hand above the wire.

Megan held hers above a different wire, her hand dirty and scuffed and completely steady.

"It's the same as the others," said Storm.

Megan nodded, moving her hand over each wire.

"It wasn't until we came back here that I realized," said Megan. She looked up as Romero and Eli came closer and stopped several steps away.

Storm knew what she would say but at the same time, didn't believe it. The pull was there; she knew there was a transition of energy. What she needed was confirmation of the other piece. The one that didn't make sense with anything that she knew.

"They all go to the same place," said Megan.

Storm drew in a long breath, concentrating on what she felt in her fingers, the draw that was moving into her hand. Because it wasn't about direction, it was about a destination.

All the Gatherers and the streaks and even the benign whiteness, all pulled to the same place.

"Do you know where that is?" asked Storm.

She already knew the answer, had known subconsciously with almost every breath since she had first recognized she had discovered something new.

"Back to the beginning."

Storm closed her fingers into a fist as if she had decided against picking something up.

And then Megan was gone again, running in step with Eli, her curls bouncing behind her.

Romero hadn't moved from his spot near the wall, his hands clasped in front of him as if pleading.

"Can you explain it to me? And how you got better?"

She stood, the building alive with the movement of the afflicted, that endless restlessness that wouldn't let them stop. She understood it now. Recognized it in her own nerves. She put her hands in her pockets and carefully picked her way out of the spokes.

"I can try."

TWENTY-SEVEN

MARIA

MARIA SAT WITH HER knees bent, her back against the wall. Her head hurt, and her arms and legs weighed a thousand pounds. She hated sleeping after a long period of wakefulness, her body taking the opportunity to protest what she had put it through. Adams snored softly against the opposite wall, his black stubble approaching a beard. Storm sat on the wide windowsill, scribbling in a notebook and doing a good job of impersonating a mad scientist.

"Why didn't you wake me?"

She had slept most of the afternoon and outside the window the day had started to fade. She pulled the elastic from her ponytail and ran her hands through the tangled hair before retying it at the base of her neck. She leaned her head against the wall, letting her eyes close, lingering in the lull of sleep. She was back in the endless tunnel with the brightness of Hamel's flashlight guiding them forward. They'd been walking for hours, the blackness never wavering. A sudden burst of rapid fire came from every direction, and a bloom of blood flooded the back of Hamel's uniform as he toppled to the ground.

She started awake, her heart pounding and mouth dry. For an instant, she couldn't place where she was, until the room resolved into the outline of wires on the floor, the scratch of Storm's pencil and Adams' quiet snore.

She stood, couldn't stand the quiet of it, or the peace. She paced to the far side of the room, her heart still hammering as memories of Amanda pedaling away alternated with Hamel's final words urging her to *Go*.

She stood with one foot on either side of a wire, her breathing fast and shallow. How long had she been standing there? The room was darker, the light from the windows turning to dusk.

"Are you okay?"

Storm's pencil was poised above the page, her head turned to Maria.

"Yeah." Was she? She still couldn't catch her breath. "I just need some air."

The corridors were emptier than before, but she still strode past a dozen people before she reached the stairwell. Many of them watched her haste, the whites of their eyes gleaming in the dimness, their voices dropping as she passed.

The heavy smell of food rose up the stairwell, and her stomach contracted in hunger and nausea. Dozens of patients crowded the steps. She caught the gaze of a boy of ten or eleven and had to look away from his suffering.

She burst through the double doors to the outside where two groups of patients huddled on the porch. Their attention was fixed on the middle distance. The tangled lawn held nothing but growing dark and grass soaked from the earlier rain.

She ran down the steps, her footsteps on the gravel drive marked in the quiet. She was running by the time she turned the corner of the building and slowed at the relief of the cold wind off the ocean. She drew long deep breaths into her lungs and leaned against the flaking wall.

She shouldn't have left Hamel behind, shouldn't have let Amanda go. She'd put the needs of the mission first and all she had gotten in return was loss. The web of Gatherers was stronger than ever, and what had they achieved?

A man sat on the wood bench by the garden, huddled within the oversized jacket of a fire fighter. It gleamed in the fading light making him easy to see, yet she hadn't noticed.

She rolled her shoulders; her chest was too tight, panic threatening. "It's Maria, right?"

His easy kindness reminded her of Havernal, her commander and the first person she had lost to the Gatherer.

She leaned over, with her hands on her knees, feeling as if she might throw up. Pebbles had been pushed into the dirt, only their sharp edges above the surface.

There was the creak of wood and then the careful slow shuffle as he moved towards her.

Not now, she thought.

She saw Amanda's back retreating into the night, and Hamel's eyes filled with fear that wouldn't leave.

The man stopped beside her, and she couldn't bring herself to lift her head. It was too quiet, the distant wash of waves too calm. The world should reflect everything she had lost, not simply continue on.

She turned away from him, but not before she registered the dark beard and hollow cheeks, the chest that must have once filled the coat. He wasn't much older than her, and he had the same pained walk as Havernal.

"It takes a while to adjust," he said. "To this place."

He didn't say to the suffering, but she filled in the words, the murmur of pain and the smell of sickness still with her, despite the bite of the air.

"When did you arrive?"

"About ten days ago."

When they had still been at the cabin, naïve as to what they were up against.

"How long since you fought?" she asked.

His hands were crossed in front of him, holding the coat close around him, his chin lifted to the wind. Maria ran a hand over her face, still feeling as if she would break apart.

"A while." He held the words close.

"I'm sorry."

Night was moving in, and it felt like they were in their own private space with the ocean and the sky.

"Not your fault." He could have been a younger Havernal, with that steady calmness.

"It is." The words were out before she could think, her voice raw, her pain too exposed.

Two women supported each other as they walked along the edge of the cliff, their path meandering, their legs unsteady. She had to look away, had a burst of anger at their weakness. A ball cap that had been left on a picnic table fell to the ground in the wind.

"All you can do is your best," he said.

She clenched her fists. She didn't need his empty platitudes.

"It's not enough."

The beam of a lighthouse blinked on at the top of a distant cliff, the sweep of its light slow and steady.

"I sometimes lost people when I was fighting." He spoke with a depth of pain in his voice. "I always thought I could have done more."

He followed her gaze to the lighthouse, and they watched its beam cycle and sweep.

"What I learned, was that my job was to fight the fire. To do whatever I could to stop it."

She wanted to run from his calm certainty, even as he seemed to re-arrange the pieces of her back into where they belonged.

"I was there at the beginning," she said. "I could have stopped it."

The reflective strips on his sleeves shimmered when he moved his arms.

"Did you set the fire?"

The first day she had met Storm in her lab, the Gatherer had been a rough outline within the enclosed test area. Storm had already tapped into its limitless energy and was experimenting on how to channel it.

"It's gotten too big."

The air grew colder, the darkness within the trees deeper.

"Even the biggest fires are put out eventually."

His certainty was compelling, and she so wanted to believe it.

"Have you seen the streaks?"

He shuffled his feet and there was a slight protectiveness in his shoulders that she recognized as him pushing through whatever pain he was experiencing.

"I saw some before we left Rima."

"And you still think we can put out the fire?"

The yellow light of an oil lamp appeared from behind the building, its glow illuminating a patch of grass but not the faces of those that held it.

"You'll have to."

It was as if he had laid the final piece of her back into place. All that was left now was to act. She settled into the simplicity of it. The relief.

He turned from her and shuffled back to the bench with pain in every step.

"Can I help?" She moved to support him.

He leaned heavily on the back of the bench before he lowered himself onto it.

"I've survived worse."

She could see the dim outline of his cheekbones above his beard, the line of his brow. She hovered, not knowing how to help.

"Can I—"

He pulled his coat tighter around him.

"I'm not the fire."

Could it be that simple? His suffering was not something she had time for, and she hated it.

He hunched further into his coat, the reflective strips catching bits of light from a lantern in a window above. Otherwise, he was undefinable, his outline lost within the coat's folds.

She stayed for a moment, hearing the rustle of wind in the pines, and the occasional drip of water. It was a recognition of him, and Hamel, and Amanda. Of all those she would carry as she moved forward.

"Thank you."

He looked up briefly and nodded. His eyes were sunken and in that instant the skin below his right eye twitched. He looked away, self-conscious of that show of weakness.

She rested her hand on his shoulder, felt the sharpness of his bones. It would be torture for him to not be able to help to not do something to put things right.

She let her hand fall and walked into the wind, stopping in the long, trampled grass at the edge of the cliff. She wasn't the first person to stand on this precipice. It was a steep slope rather than a cliff, tufts of grass and small, weathered trees growing out of the slope. A narrow path led down a few paces from where she stood.

She had thought the cliff would at least provide some protection. Stanton, or whoever he sent, prevented from approaching from the ocean. She still didn't believe she had gotten away. She had been out-numbered and had to have been seen on the surveillance network as she fled the city, despite her best efforts.

She looked back towards the hospital, trying to pinpoint the window where Storm sat and Adams slept. They would leave in the morning, no matter how safe Romero claimed the place to be.

She retraced her steps, past the bench where the firefighter had sat. She hadn't even gotten his name. She looked to see where he might have gone but despite his slow movement, he had managed to disappear.

The van was where they had left it, on the gravel drive, only a few meters from the tree line. She climbed in the driver's seat, the cab holding the dampness from the rain. When she started the engine, the groups on the porch actually looked in her direction, sound at least able to break their comatose state.

The old frame creaked as she drove it closer to the porch, sliding it into a spot beside the building where it was at least less exposed. It wasn't much but she at least felt she had done something to protect their only way out of there.

She was grabbing Megan and Eli's bags out of the back when headlights appeared at the entrance to the drive, bouncing as the vehicle struck the potholes and trenches in the gravel. Another bus arrived from the city. She grabbed the SIG from beneath the front seat.

The bus settled at the point in the driveway closest to the porch, the reflection in the windows preventing Maria from seeing inside.

One of the afflicted from the porch, a girl in her early teens with a bright pink shirt, rose and walked slowly to the bus.

With a hiss the door opened. The driver, who was rail-thin with a beak nose, turned to wave his passengers forward.

Her heart sank as the first patients shuffled down the steps. They looked lost and bewildered and struggled to stay upright. Six adults descended, then three children, a line of others following behind. They spread onto the grass, staying close to the bus as if it could provide them protection from this unknown place.

Maria waited, needing to see everyone off the bus before she went forward, as frozen as the group on the porch that simply stared. There were over fifty people outside the bus and still more descended. Every color and size and age all blended into a mass of the sick and suffering, no different than those already crammed inside.

She slid the SIG into her pocket and crossed the lawn to the first couple. They were exhausted and anxious, their eyes lifted to the looming façade of the hospital. She pointed them inside, assuring them they were at a safe place. The people kept coming, asking for explanations and help, and their need overwhelmed her so that all she could do was respond to the next and the next. Soon she was aware of Marty beside her and Romero, both offering comfort and reassurance. She took strength from their patience and capacity to care for these people, mimicking their words and condolences so that eventually she made her way to the base of the bus steps, and the few stragglers that were still getting off.

"You go ahead."

The voice came from inside the bus, someone out of sight organizing from behind. It sounded too familiar, too much what Maria wanted to hear. She turned away from it, her mind playing tricks on her until a silhouette caught her eye, the head tilted in defiance, the hair falling in a wild wave.

Her breath stopped, even as her body moved, responding without her, not waiting for her mind to catch up. She hurried a man with a walker off the steps. Squeezed past a frail woman with a cane so that she stood at the front of the bus, looking down the empty aisle to where a woman leaned over a patient who trembled so violently, she was unable to stand.

"Amanda?"

Amanda looked up, confusion, recognition, and relief crossing her face in quick succession. She had the patient half out of her seat, the woman veering to one side.

Maria caught the woman's other side, lifted her out of the seat. She smelled of sweat and pain.

"What are you doing here?" Amanda asked.

Maria held tight to the woman who lurched from step to step, even as she longed to wrap her arms around Amanda.

"We—" But how to explain where they'd been?

Amanda held one hand against her ribs, holding the woman with the other. They made slow progress down the aisle, each of them supporting the trembling patient as they had eyes only for each other. Amanda hopped on every other step.

"You're hurt."

Amanda shook her head and tossed her hair the way she did when she wanted to blow something off.

"It's fine."

When they reached the front of the bus, Romero stood on the steps.

"I can carry her."

Maria moved out of the way as Romero ever so carefully scooped the woman into his arms, like he had done it a thousand times before. The driver followed him out, telling him there would be another load the next morning.

And then it was just the two of them, the space between them too far until Maria had wrapped her arms around Amanda's waist, and Amanda's arms were around her shoulders. She pressed Amanda hard against her, so tough and real and euphoric.

"I'm so sorry." Amanda spoke into Maria's hair, and Maria shook her head, squeezing tighter.

"It doesn't matter."

"You were right—"

"Shhhh." Maria leaned away and pushed the hair back from Amanda's forehead. "It's okay. We didn't know."

"You did."

Amanda's eyes were wide and dark brown, too open and too scared.

"What happened?"

Amanda kept her hand away from Maria, and only weighted one foot.

"It doesn't matter."

Maria pulled her close again.

"It does matter."

"I'm just happy you're here." Amanda's voice was soft, low, and Maria's heart lurched at the vulnerability.

The voices outside reached them as dusk descended into dark. Maria drank in Amanda's warmth, pressed as much of her to her body as she could.

"Don't leave me again," said Maria.

"As if I could."

Amanda's attempt at humor only partially worked, but Maria still smiled.

"Is Storm—"

Maria ran her hands over Amanda's waist, felt the sharpness of her ribs.

"She's here. We made it out."

Amanda had that look she got, asking Maria for forgiveness, again, for something she had done.

"I'm so sorry. I—"

She pressed her finger to Amanda's lips.

"We're safe now. We all made it. It doesn't matter."

Amanda's gaze searched hers, looking for truth.

"Did Stanton do this?" asked Maria.

Amanda looked away but not before Maria saw the flash of fear. Maria's rage rose hard and sharp.

"He wanted to know where you were."

Maria carefully took Amanda's wrist and moved her hand to where she could see it. It was badly swollen with dark bruising blossoming out from the swelling.

"Is it broken?"

There was a sound on the step behind them.

"Is there anyone else?"

Marty had one hand on the rail, her foot on the step. Maria held Amanda's gaze for a long second before lowering her hand.

"Just one," said Maria, taking hold of Amanda's uninjured hand as she turned. "A friend of mine arrived on the bus. Amanda, this is Marty. She runs things around here."

"And where is *here*?"

Of course: Amanda didn't know where she had arrived, as blind as the others.

"This is the Great Bear Hospital," said Marty. "Or it was. Now it's a haven for those fleeing pain."

"Sounds like the perfect place," said Amanda.

"You better come in then," said Marty. "It's crowded but we can find a place."

Maria squeezed Amanda's hand where she still held it. Amanda looked at their joined hands and raised her eyebrows at the outward display.

Maria shook her head once, annoyed at Amanda's need to point it out and elated she was still herself enough to do it.

"Just leave it alone," said Maria. "For once in your life."

"Why would I do that?"

In response, Maria ushered Amanda ahead of her. Amanda used the seat back as a crutch with her good hand and hopped forward, her injured foot not touching down.

Maria's anger flared at an intensity that threatened to overtake her. She heard the firefighter's steady voice in her head, *Our job is to fight the fire.* She forced herself to turn from the temptation of her rage.

At the top of the steps Amanda paused, and Maria stepped forward, ducking beneath her shoulder to support her and wrapping her arm around her waist. They took the steps slowly, Amanda leaning hard enough on Maria that she almost carried her.

"Can you make it to the porch?"

The lawn had cleared, the new arrivals already absorbed into the building. A few lanterns flickered in different windows, the darkness having settled the restlessness of the place, increasing the illusion of safety.

"I can manage."

Before Amanda could protest, Maria lifted her up, her core and back engaging at the added weight.

Amanda cursed her as she looped her hand around Maria's neck. "I could have made it on my own."

"This is faster and you know how impatient I am."

Amanda's hand gripped harder as they mounted the steps.

"Yeah. I do."

TWENTY-EIGHT

STORM

STORM'S PENCIL CAME TO a rest at the end of the page, the cramped muscles in her neck releasing and the final period on the page an ending point for what she finally understood. Calculations covered the page, a convoluted meandering trail through what she had known before and what she knew now. The room had grown dark, the scratching on the page illuminated only by the fading light of the sky but she could still see the logic clearly. She sat with it for a moment, Adams snoring in the background, the agitation she had carried since she had first gotten sick finally clearing.

She wanted to shout, a loud cry of relief, and tell the world what she had found. Yet the legacy of the Gatherer stopped her, for she had once freely announced the miracle of the device that would save the world. How strangely ironic that that hubris would be what slowed her now, at the exact moment when she had discovered something even greater.

Through the window, an oil lamp followed the edge of the cliff, the outline of the figure carrying it barely visible. Adams' breath moved slowly in and out, and in the hallway, there was a quiet, unexpected burst of laughter. Out on the point, the beam of the lighthouse turned and swept, a slow, steady pattern within the darkness.

She squinted to see the final calculation, re-tracing the steps she'd made to get there, knowing from each scratch of the pencil that she had got it right. She hugged the notebook to her chest, the pages feeling too flimsy to carry what they held. Yet it didn't matter, for it was in her head now and she understood what needed to be done.

She should have seen it sooner, the simplicity and logic of the solution so clear now that she had found it. It had been Megan's confirmation of what they sensed, of the energy flowing to a common place, or in this instance, a common point.

Voices rose up the stairwell from the lobby. They seemed louder, though she had been so immersed she hadn't been aware of anything around her. Adams shifted and muttered something beneath his breath as if he had heard them too, though didn't wake.

How long had it been since she had been able to think clearly enough to perform deep calculations, an intricate dance between the formulas and the secrets the universe was willing to reveal? She didn't dare move, this place too fragile and yearned-for for too long.

The glow of the lanterns in the stairwell filled in the shape of the door. She should see if the voices were anything to worry about, but not yet.

Footsteps sounded as two voices drew closer. One was Maria, sounding strained.

Storm slipped off the window ledge, wishing she had a light to confirm what she was hearing. An outline filled the doorway, a swinging lantern hanging in front of the shape.

Maria carried Amanda in her arms, Amanda holding the light. Storm's relief soared, above the euphoria she already held. She rushed forward and took the lantern from Amanda's hand.

Amanda grinned at her. Storm clasped her hand briefly before Maria pushed forward, carrying Amanda to the windowsill.

Adams had woken and sat bleary-eyed, as Maria deposited Amanda on the sill.

"Are you hurt?" said Storm.

She laid the lantern beside Amanda to see her better. Her thumb was swollen and bruised, and she grimaced as Maria turned her so she could rest one foot on the ledge.

"What happened?"

Amanda inhaled through her teeth as she tried to adjust her foot. Maria lifted the leg carefully and placed her rolled-up jacket beneath it.

Storm bit down on her questions. Amanda was here, safe, if damaged; all things that could be fixed.

Storm touched Amanda's shin, reveling in the hardness of the bone, her appearance fueling Storm's certainty that they had finally found the right path.

Amanda leaned her head back against the wall, her gaze drifting to Adams who had come to stand beside Storm.

"This is Amanda," said Storm, introducing them.

"That was my guess," said Adams, reaching to shake Amanda's uninjured hand.

"Gently," warned Maria.

"It's good to finally meet you. I'm glad you made it."

"So am I."

Amanda winced as Maria lifted her injured hand, examining it from all angles.

"I have something for you." Adams dug in his pocket and handed Amanda a silver lighter that Storm had seen Amanda use a thousand times.

"How did you get that?" asked Storm.

Amanda accepted it with confused gratitude, her fingers curling around it.

"Eli found it near the barn."

Amanda wiped her thumb across the inscription and lifted it to show Maria.

"How did you know—"

Adams held up his hands. "I knew it couldn't be either of them."

Maria grunted and Storm couldn't help but smile.

"Thank you," said Amanda, tucking the lighter into her pocket.

Maria placed a finger on the tip of Amanda's swollen thumb and moved it ever so gently. Amanda hissed.

"Probably broken," said Maria.

"I could have told you that." Amanda pulled her hand protectively against her chest.

"What happened?"

Amanda half-smiled yet didn't achieve it, her eyes haunted.

"Turns out I'm not as tough as I thought."

"You made it here, didn't you?" said Maria, the brusqueness in her voice a contrast to how gently she adjusted the jacket beneath Amanda's foot.

"I got lucky."

Maria carefully untied Amanda's laces. "You got smart."

"We're just glad you're here," said Storm. "Were they watching the house?"

Amanda ran her good hand down her thigh, smoothing the creases from the dirty jeans.

"Maria was right."

Through the pitted window, the sky was a study of gradations, dark blending with the last light on the horizon.

"They took my workstations and my security system." She still seemed stunned that they had invaded her home. "They found everything."

She exhaled.

"I was only there a few minutes before they came. They were military."

Amanda had been speaking to her feet, not looking at them, but she turned her head purposely to see Storm.

"Your mother was with them."

Storm's thoughts skipped before she understood what Amanda had said.

"She was at the house?"

"And the compound. Where I was held."

The room sharpened as Amanda recounted her mother's arrival and her time held captive in the office tower that had once been Storm's domain. She would have been in the room where Amanda was held, had walked the halls.

"She's helping him?"

Her mother had sworn she had stayed for damage control, as determined as Storm to rectify her part in the Gatherer's destruction.

Amanda sucked in through her teeth as Maria supported her calf and pulled off her boot and sock. Bruising surrounded Amanda's ankle bone and had settled along the edge of her foot.

"Did he do that to you?" asked Adams.

"No." Amanda relaxed as Maria set her foot back down. "That I did to myself." She held up her thumb. "*This* I didn't."

She told them a story of plenums and air ducts that hardly seemed possible. Storm's fear and certainty rose when she talked about the lobby and the whiteness that spread from the original Gatherer. It confirmed what she had expected, banished any questions as to whether she had got it right.

Maria and Adams blanched at Amanda's description of the soldiers at the gate. Those personnel were not far from who they were, and in another life could have been them.

"I made it to the copse of fir trees, which is when I did this." Amanda pointed to her swollen ankle. "I hid in the underbrush, watching the movements of the guards. There weren't enough of them to cover the full perimeter so I waited until I could see which areas they weren't covering. In the end it was easier than that. A guard came in to relieve the man at the side gate. When he didn't move for fifteen minutes, I went closer. I went slowly so I wouldn't startle him, but he didn't even look up."

"You walked right by?"

Maria's alarm was the same as when she had tried to prevent Amanda from leaving for the house. Never happy when Amanda took risks.

"He was so still for so long I knew something wasn't right. And by that time, dawn wasn't far off."

There was a change in Amanda. Trauma and pain, yes, but not the cowering or withdrawing you might have expected. If anything, she seemed stronger, less broken.

"Do you think anyone followed you?" asked Adams.

His worry crowded into their small space, fed on and reflected by Maria.

Amanda laughed, quick and bitter.

"The guards are barely functional. There is no one there capable of following anyone."

It was what Storm had expected that anyone within the compound would have suffered irreparable damage in such proximity.

"There's something else," said Amanda, and even before her attention again turned to Storm, she knew what it would be. For her mother had been there longer than anyone.

"She's sick," said Storm, and felt a strange falling away when Amanda nodded.

"And Stanton," said Amanda. "Both of them are severely weakened." She paused as if considering holding something back. "It's as if they're in its thrall. Like some of the addicts I've seen."

Storm's elation deflated, struggling under the weight of Amanda's announcement.

"How bad?" She would be too late, the end of this a forever receding target.

Amanda shrugged with a resignation that fueled Storm's fear.

"She's convinced you will come to them. That you will save it."

Storm gripped the crumpled notebook, remembering the power of the calculations. The murmur of patients flowed around them, the quiet sounds of the hospital settling in for the night. It was a shadow of the devastation they would encounter at the compound when they got there.

"I'm so sorry," said Amanda, and Maria and Adams made similar noises of condolence.

It didn't make sense that her mother was still there. After all this time.

"We're going back there though," said Maria. "Aren't we?" She nodded at the notebook.

Storm's hands were sweaty on the cardboard cover. The colors were washed out, a faded, bleached section over half the cover.

"You've had two hands on that notebook since I got here," said Amanda.

Storm thought she'd been hiding her excitement, waiting for the right moment.

"You know how to stop it," said Maria.

It wasn't a question, Maria's certainty and understanding were clear. There was also an undercurrent of motion, Maria's energy gearing up to get going.

Storm held the notebook in front of her, waiting for the doubt to arrive. There were marks on the cover where she'd made side calculations, and a piece torn out along the top edge.

"Yeah. I do." Her elation had faded, tainted now by the news of her mother, but the certainty remained, solid and steady. "And everything you've told me—" She nodded to Amanda, "it all fits."

They paused, each of them recognizing the significance of the moment. The hours they had spent trying to get here and now they simply … were.

The lamp lighted their faces, a small pool of yellow connecting them. After all the talk and false starts they had made it to that final silence. Their bodies and minds shifted to a new direction, a new task to be done. She would never be closer to anyone. Even Daniel and her team had never understood each other the way they did.

* * * *

Storm waited for Adams to arrive back with the first aid kit, and, despite Amanda's protests, splinted her thumb and pressed an ice pack to her ankle. Maria stayed close while the others, including Megan and Eli, who had arrived with Adams, had spread out through the spokes.

"It was Megan who first noticed it," said Storm. "She, or we, have always been able to feel the pull of energy by the Gatherers. It may be from the original contact that altered us somehow, but even before the Gatherer I had always been more aware of energy than others."

"Why weren't we altered?" said Adams, pointing to himself and Maria. "We've been just as exposed to others that—" He didn't finish the sentence, his face flushing, but they understood he meant others who had died.

"We may never know. Energy is variable and so much of it is hidden, there is an infinite number of ways humans can be affected."

Storm moved to the edge of the room where the wires disappeared through walls and the ceiling to spread out throughout the building. Bits of wood mixed with the dust on the floor below where the holes for the wires had been drilled.

"The Gatherers have always been connected. Firmware updates are sent through secure channels and each Gatherer is connected back to the hub at the headquarters much the way these wires are."

"It's what should have made them so easy to stop," said Amanda.

"It wouldn't have worked, even if we had gotten in," said Storm. "The Gatherers have formed their own network, outside of the manufactured channels." She held her hand above the small wires, felt the faintest pull.

"The streaks," said Adams.

"Hamel made a map of them." Megan stood on the opposite side of the room, her outline blending in with the shadows along the wall. Storm moved towards the middle, and they followed.

"The white streaks we've been seeing and even the white patches have all been co-opted to form a massive network."

"Even this one?" asked Eli. He had bent down beside Storm and was rubbing his finger over the faint whiteness around the minute Gatherer.

Storm wiped her finger along the tiny edge of a crystal. "Every single one of them."

It was what held them all together, the common element in the smallest to the largest.

"It's all the same crystal," said Maria.

Storm nodded slowly, not surprised that Maria had figured it out. She had been there at the beginning, seen the original design.

"How does it supersede the physical network?" Amanda spoke from the windowsill. It would be hard for her to grasp a network that existed outside of physical nodes and wires.

"It doesn't," said Storm, before Megan interrupted.

"The physical wires are still there except the Gatherer doesn't care about them. It only wants to connect to all the other crystals."

"Through the streaks," said Storm.

"It made its own network?"

"It's not a network," said Megan. "The flow is only in one direction."

"Back to the center," said Adams.

"Not exactly." Storm nodded for Megan to continue.

"They all go to the same place, but it isn't at the center."

"So where is it?" Maria was impatient, her hands on her hips as she straddled a wire.

"Can't you guess?" Storm imagined she could feel the destination, broadcasting from the room's small network. It was so clear now, all the flows converging into the final river. "You were there."

Maria frowned as she checked memories of every place they had been. The glow of the lamp cast their shadows against the wall, making them all seem larger.

"Shit." Amanda moved to get off the windowsill but stopped at the pain.

Maria turned. "You know?" She helped Amanda reposition her leg.

"I don't believe it," said Amanda.

"It makes sense," said Storm.

"Yeah," said Amanda, shaking her head. "It does."

"Did you want to enlighten the rest of us?" Maria crossed her arms.

Storm stood, the regret of it strong and clear, the sadness sharp.

"It's the original Gatherer. The one that birthed all the rest. It's pulling all the Gatherers back to it, and the energy with it."

The small network gave even as it took away. She knew that she had been altered, that the reason she still functioned was that her body had adapted to whatever change the Gatherer had done.

"So we stop the original Gatherer and we stop them all?"

Maria stood by Amanda, unwilling to move away from her. Storm wondered whether she would be able to leave one final time.

Megan and Eli hopped between the spokes, their feet sharp points from the shadows. The adults stood in a circle around Amanda, each of them contributing their hope and fear and ultimately their resolve to the maelstrom of emotions that whirled between them.

"So what do we do?" Amanda's hair was a tangled mess. It suited her, and the place.

Storm lifted the notebook. She flipped to the first page, briefly following the process that had led to her conclusion. Once she had found the thread its simplicity had been beautiful.

"The lattice of the original Gatherer crystals was what allowed it to access a kind of energy we hadn't known existed. Something that was invisible but in fact supported the rest of the energy chain." She pointed to one of her calculations. "I started with the original function, looked to see what would happen when I extrapolated—"

She could feel herself warming up, a tumble of words gathering in her head.

Maria touched her arm. "We only need the conclusion."

It was Maria the soldier who looked at her, focused and efficient. Storm marveled at the precision of it, as she closed the notebook.

Three pairs of expectant eyes watched her. Adams stood straighter, the circles beneath his eyes faded below the intensity of his gaze.

"It's simple, really. If all the energy is being drawn through that first Gatherer, we just have to stop it."

Maria and Adams frowned, each of their expressions distorted by the lamp at their feet.

"The original Gatherer opened the door," said Megan, from the darkness behind them. "So we need to close it."

Storm broke away and moved around the edge of the room, giving some distance to the plan forming in her head.

"It has to be disrupted," said Megan. "Even if the lattice were destroyed, the gate would still be open."

There were voices in the hall again, the incessant shuffling that signaled the end of dinner. A bent group of three passed the open door.

"And how do we do that?" asked Maria. Her impatience vibrated off her and Storm felt it too. They were so close.

"The corrupted Gatherers," said Storm.

Their expressions shifted with the first flicker of understanding.

"A distorted version of the original device would operate in the same place, except just a little bit different."

Adams was looking from one to the next, trying to keep up.

"We kill a Gatherer with a Gatherer?"

"Exactly." Storm beamed, the symmetry of it made so much sense.

"Both of those are in the compound," said Adams.

The first touch of fear slid within the group.

"We have to go back to the source," said Amanda.

"We were always going to end up there," said Maria. It was the words Storm had said to Maria when they had first returned to Rima. There was only one place this was going to finally end.

Storm hadn't looked away from Maria. They could both feel it now, the certainty of what they would do. The relief showed in the clearing of lines on Maria's forehead, the easing of her shoulders.

Storm felt the same relief, uncertainty running off like water from the previous rain and replaced by a clear and simple purpose. Even if it all went wrong, they at least had this moment, when they could see clearly despite the darkness.

TWENTY-NINE

MARIA

THE CLANG OF POTS and the sleepy murmur of voices came from the other side of the wall, as Amanda leaned heavily on Maria. She had been insistent that she needed to get out, desperate for the cigarette Romero had found for her.

Their passage echoed on the hard tiles, the smell of must and damp rising from the mildewed walls. Amanda's complicated scent flowed over it, of stale smoke, almond shampoo, and a stubborn refusal to back down.

Maria held the door as they stepped into the sharpness of the cool morning, the wall of trees that blocked the view of the road still holding the early dusk.

Several patients wandered the grounds and a tall, lanky man stood at the edge of the cliff where she had stood the night before. She slowed, trying to read his body language, afraid he might take the step that would send him off the cliff.

"Not everyone needs your help," said Amanda, following Maria's gaze.

"You'd be surprised."

A voice called out from behind the building, muffled by the mist off the ocean. The man lifted his head and shuffled towards it.

Amanda smiled as they followed the stone path that led to the overgrown garden. Maria started to lower her towards the bench, but Amanda resisted, pulling Maria towards the expanse of grass, much of it still bent from the crowd of new arrivals.

Amanda balanced on one leg as she lighted the cigarette with the silver lighter.

"Can you still see the inscription?"

Amanda held it out so Maria could read the faint letters.

No looking back.

"It still applies," said Maria.

Amanda blew smoke away from her, her body relaxing on the exhale.

"Do you think there will be a time when it doesn't?"

The coat Amanda had found in the donation bin didn't meet in the front, and she had only one arm in a sleeve, the splinted one in a sling.

"I hope so."

Amanda combed her hand through her tangled hair. Maria reveled in the characteristic gesture; didn't think she would ever tire of watching her.

"You called out in your sleep last night," said Maria. It had been a long, unintelligible streams of words as if Amanda were terrified.

"You talk in your sleep all the time." Two of the residents came out of the door they had just exited. "Come on, let's get to the trees."

Amanda had already started a painful hop across the lawn and Maria slipped back under her shoulder.

"You shouldn't be hopping around."

She braced herself under Amanda's weight, wishing they could stay this close forever.

When they were within the trees, Amanda pulled away and steadied herself on a trunk slick with wet. She took a long drag on her cigarette. The sleeves of her coat left her wrists exposed, the pants that were too large cinched tight around her waist.

"So you're going to leave me here?" She gestured back towards the hospital.

"You can't come with us."

"I'll be fine in a day or two. It already feels better."

Amanda's toes barely rested on the ground, and she hadn't weighted her foot once on the way over.

"We can't wait that long."

Amanda tapped ashes in frustration, letting them fall over a splintered stump.

"I can't just stay here."

It was all so familiar, Amanda's anger, and her refusal to do what Maria asked. She couldn't remember a time when Amanda had waited for anyone. She'd either been beside Maria or two steps ahead.

"You've been through enough."

Amanda carefully touched the band of green moss on a trunk. "Hasn't everyone? Haven't you?"

"I knew what I was getting into."

"Did you?" Amanda's voice was derisive, a poor camouflage for her pain. "When you got on that train and headed out to find Storm, to find a cure for Havernal, this is what you imagined?"

She made a large sweeping arc with her arm to take in the ocean, the sky and the hospital.

"Of course not. But at least I signed up for it."

Amanda picked a pine needle off the sleeve of her coat, the movement precise and controlled. Maria braced herself for her anger but when Amanda finally did speak it was low and disappointed.

"You are so thick sometimes."

Maria crossed her arms.

"It's not like that's a new thing."

It was darker within the trees, the dusk blocking the view of the road.

"So, I just wait here for you to come back?"

Wings beat overhead and Amanda lifted her chin to watch the path of a solitary gull towards the ocean.

"You'll be safe here," said Maria.

"But will you?" Amanda's voice broke. "I don't want—"

The words fell between them.

"Anything to happen," Maria finished.

The brown of Amanda's eyes was dark and clear. A wave of mist floated between them, the coolness taking the heat from Maria's skin.

"What if you don't come back?"

Amanda dropped her cigarette into the wet leaves. Maria put her hand out to steady her and the coolness of Amanda's fingertips was on her neck and the burn of her lips on hers. Maria slid her hands inside Amanda's coat, drawing her in, needing the pressure of her body on hers. She felt as if she were drowning and finally able to breathe.

"No promises," said Amanda, when they came up for air, her forehead pressed into Maria's.

"I will come back," said Maria.

Amanda kissed her again, and Maria leaned into it, drinking long and deep. She wrapped her arms around her waist, felt her lean hardness yield.

"Just don't do anything—" Maria said, her chin lifted to the sky as Amanda's lips traced her neck.

"—Stupid?" There was a playfulness underneath.

"Risky."

Amanda traced her finger along Maria's jaw.

"I want you here when it's over," said Maria.

A gust blew across the tops of the trees and a burst of water fell around them.

"Will it be? Over?"

Maria ran her hands over Amanda's ribs and followed the muscles along her spine.

"One way or another."

A cluster of cedars lay behind her, and Maria carefully drew Amanda within its shelter. Water seeped through her coat and dripped around them, and Maria knew only the touch of Amanda's skin and the heat of the fire beneath it.

THIRTY

STORM

S TORM JOLTED OUT OF sleep at the sound of shouting. A high-pitched woman's voice yelling at someone to "get away."

She crawled to her knees, stumbling as she rose to her feet, her mind still caught in the sound, obliterating sleep.

A struggling light filled the room. Maria's rolled-up coat lay on the floor and Megan's blanket was near Adams' pack, yet none of them were there. Storm paused, checked to see if she was still dreaming.

A deeper voice swore back at the woman in the hallway, sounding all too real. Storm staggered towards it, bracing herself on the door frame at a wave of dizziness, yet acknowledging that she felt better this morning. Rested.

The corridor was filled with patients, some standing, some lying, others huddled against the wall, the air stuffy with the nighttime breath of a crowd.

A few paces away, a haggard man held one end of a mattress that you would use on a camping trip. The other end was clutched in the hands of an emaciated woman. As she watched, the man wrenched the mattress, pulling it out of the woman's hands and stormed off down the hall.

As he passed his eyes met Storm's, fierce and unapologetic.

"You'll pay for this!" the woman shouted. Yet there was an edge of defeat in her words, the energy trailing off by the final syllable. She stared after him, her arms loose at her sides, as if he had taken more than just her mattress. And maybe he had.

No one comforted the woman and Storm moved towards her. Before she reached her, the woman turned to the wall and a worn cloth bag of her belongings.

Further down the hall, two couples argued over who had staked out the small space of concrete first, reciting their various ailments to see who deserved it more.

Below the argument, and she couldn't pinpoint the source, was the sound of a man crying, a heartbreaking soundtrack to their pointless battle.

She retreated into the room, feeling guilt at their abundance of space. Romero had said the patients weren't allowed close to the wires for fear of damaging them. It might be time to reconsider.

She retrieved her notebook and a towel Maria had found for her and picked her way through the crowded bodies in the hall. Brighter light flooded the stairwell, highlighting the increased crush of bodies, the cry of a baby and the countless conversations echoing in the tiled walls.

She descended the path that had been left open along one side of the staircase, the space barely wide enough for her feet. Occasionally she caught someone watching her, the intensity of their gaze between awe and resentment, confused as to why she would be here. Her own restlessness reflected this, that this was no longer the place she needed to be.

Her stomach turned at the smell of burned oatmeal at the bottom of the steps. The cafeteria, previously a place of space and quiet, sounded like a gymnasium full of children, the din assaulting her ears.

At the door to the kitchen Marty spoke with one of the kitchen staff, a tired looking man in his sixties who shook his head at Marty's questions. Her shoulders looked more stooped than the day before, the curve of her spine deeper as it struggled to support the increasing burden.

Storm got Marty's attention by stepping in front of her on her way to her next impossible task.

"Storm. I didn't see you." Marty's eyes spoke of exhaustion. "Did you sleep well?"

She said it by rote, the inquiry of someone eternally caring for and concerned about those around her.

"Yes. Thank you." Storm had slept well, despite the noise and the hard floor, the certainty of a solution having finally let her rest.

Marty seemed barely to have heard her.

"Is everything okay?"

Marty exhaled, with the first hint of frustration Storm had seen. Marty led her away from the foyer, through a metal door and into a musty corridor that smelled of onions.

"The latest shipment of food didn't arrive."

She watched the congestion of the lobby through the window, a presence that threatened to boil over.

"By tomorrow—"

She didn't say that they wouldn't be able to feed people. That the situation was about to get so much worse. Storm saw it in how she watched the crowded foyer and the pinched sides of her mouth.

"Every load of patients is sicker. With so many unable to function. We have no place to put them."

Marty's expression was grim, her usual calm fraying at the edges.

"I might be able to help you. It won't solve the food problem, but it will calm them, relieve their pain."

She was a good six inches shorter than Storm, and her hair parted straight down the middle, the hair gone white along the edges. Storm startled for an instant before she recognized it as a light gray, a natural color for her hair.

"Is that how you got better?"

Marty's eyes were hard as flint, and piercing, the transition from her usual compassion startling.

"Stronger, but not cured."

Storm explained about the ocean, how it had relieved the worst of the pain, and – she believed – repaired some of the Gatherer's damage.

She held up the towel. "I'm going there now."

"The water is close to freezing."

"I went in every day, multiple times. It's how I'm still able to function."

Marty scanned Storm's face and hair.

"They won't believe me."

Dampness filled the corridor, a seeping ancient wetness.

"They'll believe anything you tell them."

Marty looked over Storm's shoulder to the stained wall behind, seeing how it could be done, the same way Storm followed the thread of an idea.

"Romero said you had found a solution."

Marty took her hand, the skin soft and dry. Her gaze searched Storm's.

"I have."

Marty lifted Storm's hands to her lips and kissed them. Storm tried to pull away, cringed at the inappropriateness of it. She wasn't a saint or the pope, she was only trying to fix what she'd done.

"Don't!" It sounded like a croak.

Marty wouldn't let go of her hands. "I wish you could see yourself, how strong you are."

Storm couldn't say anything, the rush of emotion in her throat so thick it welled into her eyes.

She looked at the scuffed tips of her boots, felt about ten years old.

"Can Megan stay with you?"

It was easier to discuss Megan, veer away from the emotions of Marty's belief.

Marty's expression softened.

"And Amanda too?"

Storm nodded. "Yes. Maria will need to come with me."

The older woman squeezed Storm's hands and it felt as if the pressure of it made her stronger, the healing capabilities of this place coming from this woman rather than any small network.

Marty withdrew her hands as she sighed. Storm tried to return some of the energy, to help her do what she needed.

"I need to make some calls. See if I can find some supplies."

"It won't be long now," said Storm, wondering if she was telling the truth.

Marty smiled though there was a heaviness to it, Storm's promise not yet real.

Marty slipped back into the foyer and Storm listened to the sound of the waking hospital. It was no longer the subdued hum from yesterday but the unsettled turbulence of those suffering.

Storm reached the door to outside in a few strides. The air was heavy with dew, and a mist hung over the ocean. She turned towards it, droplets clinging to her skin. It smelled of brine and salt and took her back to the endless times she had immersed herself in the frigid water during the winter. She had come to dread the immersions as much as she craved them.

She moved towards it now, the grass wet on her ankles, the wash of waves growing louder as she reached the edge of the cliff. It wasn't as steep as she expected, with more grass than rock. A narrow dirt track led off at an angle, hidden by low shrubs and gnarled trees after the first switch back.

She hadn't expected to be able to descend, had wanted only to breathe in and feel its mist on her skin. The idea of touching it drove her down the narrow path, the steep slope almost touching her shoulders at times, the path more suitable for mountain goats than people.

Halfway down, a crouched figure appeared in the mist. She had thought it was a stump but as she drew closer Eli's small, hunched body emerged.

He looked startled when she arrived as if he had been caught in the act. The first hint of a breeze made the air cut deeper and he wore only a t-shirt.

"What are you doing here?"

He had built a cairn out of stones, balanced on a boulder. His lips held the faintest hint of blue.

"Listening. And waiting."

The mist shifted, became more threatening as she recognized the work the others did to keep her safe, while she scratched notes on paper. She looked to where the ocean should be and the path that led down to the water.

"Do you hear anything?"

He shook his head, the goosebumps on his arms visible up close.

"Is Megan down there?"

He nodded and added a flat stone to the cairn.

"Does she know you're here?"

The stone fell and he picked it up again, tried to rebalance.

Storm laid a hand on his shoulder, at some level aware he might not welcome the touch.

"She's lucky to have you," she said.

The branches of a cedar appeared and disappeared in the mist.

"I can keep watch," said Storm. "I need to speak with her."

He hesitated and she saw he was shaking, the frequency of the shaking so different from the minute trembles of the afflicted.

"Go get warm. I'll make sure she comes in."

The slope became more sheer as she continued down, the earth replaced by exposed rocks, so that at times she used both hands and feet to navigate the ledges and cracks. The occasional ancient tree clung to the cliff and she took solace in their ability to survive.

A gull swooped down the side of the cliff, disappearing below her feet.

She traveled more carefully, tucking the notebook into her waist and the towel around her neck. She gripped tufts of grass as hand holds, the rocks and earth slippery with wet, the boulders that lined the shore rising as she descended.

It felt good to touch the earth in a place where the Gatherer had not yet been. She imagined she drew energy from it that she would use to sustain her, but mostly she used it to dampen her fear.

The crash of waves reverberating off the rocks, grew louder, the noise and breadth of the water transporting her so that it was possible to believe she had stepped away.

Small pebbles covered the narrow beach and her boots crunched on the rocky band, the sand giving beneath her feet. The slime on the rocks had built up over centuries of ceaseless waves, the arch of barnacles on the rock face a thousand shades of gray.

Megan sat amid it, crouched on a flat rock that poked above the water, a bent stick in her hand. Her head turned as Storm approached.

The girl's expression was unreadable, half-sage, half-vacant. Eli's absence was marked, his natural exuberance made for this place.

Storm stopped at the water's edge, the waves lapping at her boots. Megan's rock was several meters from shore, the bottoms of the girl's jeans wet, her shoes discarded in a pile among the pebbles.

"Does Adams know you're here?"

Megan drew the stick several times through the water, tracing a pattern in the waves.

"My mom and I came here."

It wasn't so much a pattern as repeated slashes. Storm unlaced her boots and slid them off, placing them beside Megan's and the towel and notebook on top. The water was icy when it touched her toes, small shoots of pain already running through her feet.

"I can see why she liked it here."

High boulders lay half-submerged, their surfaces marred by green sludge and the ubiquitous barnacles. They spread in a wide swath that could have been the Milky Way. You wouldn't notice the passage of time here, every wave holding a promise you held your breath for.

"Are you going to die?"

The question was like a jolt. She waded deeper into the water, her toes already going numb.

"I hope not."

Megan swung the branch again, cutting fierce, violent Xs into the waves. The breeze blew back her curls, exposing the fragility of her cheeks and the thinness of her neck.

"Everyone dies eventually but some people die before we want them to," said Storm.

"Like Hamel."

Beyond the boulders, the ocean shifted in slow rolling swells, the water the same dull gray of the mist and clouds.

"Yes. Like Hamel."

The water had passed her knees, the bottom of her pants soaked. She should have stripped down, left her clothes on the beach, but she couldn't leave Megan now, perched on this place of pain.

"I want him to come back."

"And your mom too."

Megan slashed furiously, the stick bending under the force.

Storm thought Megan's sorrow would break her in two. After all the death and suffering Storm had witnessed, it would be Megan's pain that broke her.

"I had a friend." Storm walked deeper, her legs encased in burning cold to her thighs. "He helped me create the Gatherer." She saw memories of Daniel at his desk, close beside her in bed, and of his final stillness when they had left him. "He died too."

"Did the Gatherer make him sick?"

The icy waves rose higher, the burn on her legs receding between swells, her feet gone numb.

"Yes."

The gull appeared to hang above them, floating on the breeze. Megan stopped slashing, the stick hanging limp in her hand.

"Hamel, and my friend Daniel, and even your mom, all died trying to stop the Gatherer. And that shouldn't have happened." She stood beside Megan's rock now, close enough to touch. "So I need to stop it. Even if—"

The interruption of the Gatherer's energy flow would be catastrophic. Anyone near it likely wouldn't survive, or the buildings around them.

"I could help you," said Megan. "So you wouldn't have to die."

She spoke softly, barely above the waves, yet Storm heard each syllable clearly, as if Megan whispered in her ear, and she was suddenly aware of Megan in an entirely new way. The girl's body had transformed into a frenzy of electrical signals so she perceived Megan as only energy. She was disoriented as her own energy joined with it, rising from the foundation of the water, so that they flowed freely, melted fully into one.

Storm stared wide-eyed as they joined with the solid charge of the rock, the sopping slime on its surface, the motion of the breeze and the beat of the gull's heart. All of it a single pulsing, living thing. It could have lasted a second or an eternity and it wouldn't have mattered. She knew every piece of it, the loss of it excruciating when it stopped.

"What was that?" Storm was off-balance, her voice raw, as if it had been decades since she had spoken.

Megan shrugged, dragging the stick slowly through the water.

"It happens sometimes."

Storm looked to the rocks and the gull, where moments before there had been only energy and flow. It was a vision of what she had known was there but had never been able to see. She had felt it with every cell, her life inseparable from everything around them.

The discovery of the Gatherer had been an infinitesimal blip compared to this awareness. The door to a universe they had only guessed at.

Waves pushed against her legs, her flesh part of the incessant pound of water against stone.

"How long have you been able to do that?"

There was a weariness to Megan's expression as if she had lived a thousand years.

"Did your mom tell you to keep it secret?"

"She didn't know."

A patch of mist cleared and for an instant she saw beyond the boulders to the full breadth of the ocean. There was a moment of energy again, this time rising through the water. It left her breathless, this so far beyond what she could have imagined.

She should gather Megan up, take her somewhere far away. Yet she knew that wouldn't be her role.

She touched Megan's shoulder, marveling that the barrier of their skin had reformed.

"Marty said you could stay here. When we go back to the city."

A small splash rose where Megan tossed the stick into the water, the drops landing on Storm's arm.

"I want to come."

Storm crawled onto the rock, water streaming off her pants. She should be cold but felt only exhilaration, this child far beyond the miracle of the Gatherer.

"You need to stay here."

Megan's frown was dark and angry. Storm didn't flinch from it, or the power this little girl held.

"If I don't come back, you need to still be here. You understand so much more than I do."

She drew Megan towards her, and it felt as if the cliff grew higher, the ocean expanding outward, the warmth between their bodies hardly registering in the expanse.

"I don't want you to die."

Storm wondered if Megan could see her death, or if it was only the fear of a young girl who had seen too much loss.

"I don't want to die either." She felt the pull of the Gatherers again, an energy so different to what Megan had shown her. "But if I do—" She tilted her head so Megan would have to look at her. "I'll still be here with you."

THIRTY-ONE

ADAMS

ADAMS PAUSED OUTSIDE THE room, the quiet of the ward filled with sickness and pain. Three rows of cots extended the length of the room, only a narrow path between rows, less between each cot. It was the space reserved for the worst of the afflicted and every cot was filled.

He smelled the lab again where he had found Valerie and Camille, the stench of death and decay that never left his nostrils. He shook his head, trying to free his mind from the memory.

A woman wearing a hijab came towards him, moving silently between rows. He felt as if he knew her, from a forgotten time or place.

"Can I help you?"

She was in her mid-twenties, her brown skin glowing with health. She watched him calmly, as if accustomed to long pauses before responses.

"You're not sick," said Adams.

"I arrived with my aunt." She gestured to the far end of one of the rows. It was impossible to know which of the still forms she waved at. "And offered to help."

She extended her hand.

"I'm Lida."

She was at home amidst this suffering, exuded a calm competence that reminded him of Marty. Her hand was warm, the grip strong.

"I'm Benoit," he said. "Are you a nurse?"

"A nurse in training."

Her face was open and kind, her skin unbearably smooth. He felt ragged beside her, and unkempt.

"I was told there was a soldier."

There was a flicker of concern in her brown eyes.

"He came in on one of the buses," he added.

She folded her hands over her belly, and he realized she was pregnant. The small mound of the baby was only just beginning to form.

He paused, distracted by that point of new life.

The patient's combined breathing was quiet and tentative. His own breathing calmed, as if Lida orchestrated the breath for all of them. A slow steady in and out.

"You came in the van."

She spoke clearly, not whispering, the closest patients undisturbed. "Yesterday."

"So, you know Ms. Freeman." Her voice was melodic, like the song of a single bird. "And Ms. Kowalski."

Gray wool blankets were draped over each bed. There was an orderliness here, a steady point in the building. Each blanket had been tucked at the end, and an old grade school notebook had been lain beside each cot, the same kind as the one Storm had used for her calculations. The patient's names were written in block letters across the top.

"They are my heroes," she said.

"Even though Ms. Freeman caused this?"

He expected more resentment, with the consequences lying before them.

"But now she is trying to stop it. She is sacrificing everything."

"You've made charts for them."

She shifted her feet, seemed to stand taller.

"I thought we should keep track, in case there are any changes."

"Storm – Ms. Freeman – is always taking notes."

Her face glowed, making her shine brighter.

"You should talk to her," he said.

She shook her head. "I am needed here." To watch and wait and guide this room of strangers back to the living. "Is she as brave as they say?"

He thought of Storm shepherding Megan and Eli ahead of her when they had escaped the dark zone, flinching when they passed within range of an electric field but not showing her pain until she had finally collapsed at the resort, pale and shaking on the porch for hours before she finally slept.

"She is."

The eyelids of the closest patient fluttered and the man's arm dropped off the cot.

Lida gently re-positioned the arm, the white line of a scar showing through the rash on the man's shaved head.

"Are they drugged?"

She pulled the blanket higher up on his chest, leaving it below the rash. She touched her hand to his neck, feeling for his pulse.

"Being with the others seems to help them." She looked at her watch counting beats. "It takes them awhile to settle after they arrive but once they do, they seem grateful."

"So their symptoms are … mental?"

She lifted her hand from the man's neck, seemed satisfied. "That's what this room is for."

He could barely hear the din from the overcrowded floors.

"Is the father here?"

He let his eyes fall to her belly, felt the tear of pain at the memory of Valerie.

She looked away, to the brightness of the single window.

"No."

The father wouldn't be welcome, even if he was there, that much was clear.

"I'm sorry."

"No need to be."

Her fierceness belied her calm exterior. He would have liked to stay with her longer.

"Is the soldier here?"

She hesitated, watching the room as a shepherd would her sheep.

"He was very agitated when he came in."

"Is he dangerous?" he asked. He would be able to manage him. He knew what crazy was.

"Not to others. But he was very distraught."

Adams had only felt tinges of despair when he had been at the compound. Most of it not registering through his grief.

"I need to see him."

She nodded, though walked with less serenity as she led him between the rows. She stopped halfway down, beside a Middle Eastern man whose face and shoulder had gone white. One of his legs was off the bed, the gray blanket crumpled at his feet. He twitched twice as they watched, tortured by whatever his dreams delivered.

"Will he wake?"

"He will. But there's no guarantee what state he will be in."

The man had a barrel chest and forearms the size of stovepipes, a soldier at the peak of fitness. He would be hard to hold down and he marveled that Lida had even got him to settle.

He moved to the side of the bed, adrenaline flushing into his arms and legs, his body preparing for a confrontation.

"You should stand back," said Adams.

Lida stood, brow pinched, her hands folded across her belly. The elderly patient in the cot beside her had blue translucent skin.

"His name is Theo." She pointed to the notebook beside the bed.

Adams gestured for her to move further back. She stayed where she was.

"Theo."

Adams spoke as if Theo were someone he knew and touched his shoulder. Half of one eyebrow had gone white, the hairs coarse and standing up.

The man's eyes opened slowly, and his gaze slid up to meet Adams. There was confusion there, and exhaustion.

"This is Benoit." Lida leaned over to where Theo could see her face. His confusion eased. "He wanted to speak with you. Would that be okay?"

Theo scanned Adams from head to toe, his gaze slow, reluctant.

"I know who you are."

Lida helped him sit, the strength in her small frame impressive.

"Have we met?" asked Adams.

Adams couldn't place him. The big man shook his head, infinitely weary.

"We were told to keep a look out for you." Lida helped him turn his legs so he sat on the side of the cot. The border of white with his darker skin formed a diagonal line across his nose and cheek. "Before it all went to shit."

"Can you give me specifics?"

Theo's gaze darkened as he met Adams'. The one eye encased in white didn't move, the other looking up at him from a dark, bruised skin.

"You're going back there?" said Theo.

Adams had a moment of disorientation, a sudden fear before he could shake it off.

"It looks that way."

Theo exhaled a breath as large as his chest.

"You should question those orders."

Theo clasped his hands but not before Adams saw the shake.

"How many soldiers are left?"

Lida glanced at him quickly, a warning.

"A dozen. Maybe two. But it's not organized. It hasn't been for a long time."

"So they're rogue?"

His white eye was rimmed red, as if it bled.

"There are no operations or role calls. It's everyone for themselves in there. I don't even know how I got here."

A thin sweat spread over Adams' skin. It confirmed what Amanda had described; the compound consumed by the white.

"And is Stanton there?"

Theo shrugged, and it startled Adams. Soldiers either feared Stanton or revered him.

"He looked bad the last time I saw him. If he's in there, there won't be much left."

Theo lowered his head into his hands, his brown fingers were dark against the white of his face.

Lida stepped between them, deftly maneuvering Adams back from the bed.

"He needs to rest."

Lida spoke quietly to Theo as she eased him back on his cot and a rush of frustration pushed back Adams' fear. He had been so certain that Stanton would be waiting for him.

It was why no one had come for them. Why there hadn't been a pursuit. They hadn't outwitted Stanton; he hadn't been looking.

The loss of focus was disorienting.

The gray blankets became the black body bags. The quiet, the silence of the morgue. His grief rose wild and uncontrolled, as fresh as the day he found them.

He turned, searching for a way out.

Lida touched her hand to his arm, her brown eyes pools of endless calm. Words flowed from her lips that he couldn't hear.

She guided him to the window, and he squinted against the brightness. Lida stayed beside him, her hand resting lightly on his arm. She got him to breathe and then again, his breath slowly matching hers and the rest of the room.

THIRTY-TWO

MARIA

ARIA CLOSED THE DOOR behind her, easing the latch soundlessly into place. The hospital lay in a rare moment of quiet, most of the patients asleep, and she didn't want to be the one to break the silence.

The dawn air was cold, heavy with dew, and she breathed in long gulps, grateful for its freshness after the crowded stuffiness of the hall.

Mist floated by in clouds of damp, smudging the outlines of the trees and the driveway into a wash of gray. No wonder everyone had crammed inside. The edge in the air made her lower her chin into her parka, and shove her hands in her pockets, as she moved towards the cliff.

Storm had gone down to the water, and while Amanda had said she would be fine, Maria was irritated with Storm for going alone.

The wet grass soaked the bottom of her pants and drops of mist condensed on her cheeks. Storm could have been completely immersed in the mist and saved herself the trip down the cliff. Except she needed the ocean; the reality of this had been confirmed each time Maria had carried Storm to the water at the cabin, and later supported her as she walked.

"Will you be able to let her go?" Amanda had asked.

It hadn't been said in anger or jealousy, and Maria hadn't known how to respond. This wasn't about her and Storm, and a relationship. It was about taking the Gatherer out of the world.

"It's not like that."

"I know," Amanda had said, as she had trailed her finger along Maria's forearm. "But at some point, she won't need your protection anymore."

Maria reached the top of the cliff, and looked down into a shifting, flowing sea of mist.

Her worry grew.

The mist obscured the path, only a few meters visible before it disappeared. The completeness of it bothered her, as if Storm had been swallowed up.

"Storm!"

Her voice barely traveled, snuffed out by the moisture in the air.

She started down and had taken only a few steps when there was movement on the path ahead. A figure emerged out of the mist, forming into Storm's long, angular body. Maria stopped, caught in the pulse of her worry, the peaks of it ebbing as Storm's face became clear. She had a towel draped over one shoulder, wore a loose shirt and pants, and her hair was wet.

"How was the water?"

Maria tried to keep the worry from her voice, though knew Storm would hear it.

Storm walked slow and steady, only partially winded from the steep climb, a calmness to her that was unexpected.

"Cold."

The path was wide enough for only one and Maria turned back up the cliff. They walked in time, with the sound of Storm's raised breathing behind her.

"Everything okay?" asked Storm when they reached the top. They stood at the cliff, looking out into the mist to where the ocean should be.

Maria hesitated but they were long past the point when they would keep things from each other.

"I'm not sure about Adams."

It felt wrong to say it, like it was some kind of betrayal.

Storm rubbed the towel over her hair.

"Because of the despair."

More strands of Storm's hair had gone white. The damage of the Gatherer was slowly winning despite the ocean and the distance, every exposure taking a little more out of her. "It could destroy him. With Valerie and Camille, and his attachment to the kids. It could be too much."

A gull cried in the distance and Storm looked towards the sound.

"It could be too much for us as well."

Maria didn't know what to fear more, the white or the despair that came with it.

This place was so calm, so certain, she couldn't imagine it being stripped away.

"What does it feel like?"

Storm stopped rubbing her hair and let the towel rest around her shoulders. A tendril of mist moved around their ankles, the cloud starting to break up.

"Like every single good thing in your life is gone and not coming back. I never got used to it, even when I knew it was happening. It's worse than the fields, that certainty that there is no hope left in the world."

"At least this time you won't be alone," said Maria. "That should make a difference."

Storm cocked her head. Crow's feet spread out from her eyes, her cheeks hollow beneath her cheek bones. She smiled.

"I never did thank you."

"Yes, you did. A million times. Besides, there's no need."

Maria pulled her parka closer around her, willed the sun to rise faster and burn away the chill.

Out of the mist came a gull, gliding straight for them, its wings making no sound. It skimmed over their heads, the first flap of its wings snapping above them.

Storm laughed as Maria ducked, turning her head to watch it flap up above the cedars, to the clearness of the morning sky.

"Do you think it's trying to tell us something?" said Storm.

"Like what?"

"That we're on the right track?"

The gull flew south over the trees, disappearing into the tops.

THIRTY-THREE

ADAMS

DAMS PULLED TWICE ON the blades of the paddle, before laying it across his knees and letting the kayak cut through the dark water. Maria and Storm glided beside him in a tandem boat, their faces and the occasional flash of their paddles visible against the backdrop of the ocean.

They had left the van at a boat launch further up the coast and had been paddling south for half an hour. Most of the houses sat high on the shore, perched above the rocks. Occasionally he saw a lighted window, but most sat in darkness, only the reflection off glass indicating they were there. He searched for the white outline of a Gatherer tucked beside a shed or garage, but the few he saw were too far away to see whether the area around it had turned white or a streak stretched towards the next device.

He braced his knees against the inside of the kayak as the boat rose and fell with the swell, the motion pushing them in towards shore so that they paddled on a diagonal, pointing out to sea.

"There's no one here," he said as their bows dipped in the waves. He had expected there to be people, even a handful of those lucky enough to be immune.

A tattered flag hung at half-mast, not moving in the still air.

"You still okay with this?" asked Maria.

It took him a moment to realize she was asking him.

"You look after Storm. I'll find a corrupted Gatherer."

The despair would do its best, make him feel as if the world were ending, but it wouldn't matter. He had survived the end of the world once before.

Maria and Storm stopped paddling. The houses on the shore had turned to low-lying warehouses with extensive docks, the cast-off nets and traps of the fishing trade piled at their side. They coasted in parallel past the empty lots and the unbroken pools of light beneath streetlamps.

"We'll be able to see it when we come around the point," said Storm.

Their paddling slowed, all of them stealing a final moment.

"Can you feel it?" asked Maria.

Adams felt only a strange unsettling, like he needed to run. It could have been fear or an awareness of the compound.

"For the last ten minutes," said Storm.

Her shoulders were hunched, her paddle laid across her lap.

He wanted to say that they could do this, no matter what they faced, but it was Maria who spoke, stealing the words he had used each time they had started a mission.

"Let's go save the world."

His stroke faltered, the blade striking the side of the boat. Her voice had been flat with just enough irony to expose their naivete. They had had no idea then what it meant to save the world and he hoped to God they did now.

He surged ahead, engaging the strength in his shoulders and back, the kayak slicing through the inky water.

The docks and wharves gave way to large boulders along the shore, the buildings set far back from the water so that overgrown grass and shrubs formed a wild, unordered border before the yards, where parked forklifts and tire sized rolls of metal shone beneath weak light.

One yard held a Gatherer the size of a small car, and Adams' fear notched up, feeling as if it watched each paddle stroke, warning the rest of its network that they had arrived.

It's not sentient. He heard Storm's voice in his head. *Unless you think the continual flow and balance of energy in the universe constitutes intelligence.*

He would have believed it capable of anything, with the way that Gatherer glowed and no other person in sight. He pulled harder, aiming the bow of his kayak to the end of the point. It was more rocks than dirt, the weathered boulders glistening with wet, a white shape caught between two boulders turning to a washed-up bottle when they drew close.

He pulled ahead, breathed in the last few seconds of being within the point's protection.

The compound extended south, a mix of rocks and beaches that had once been the most coveted place to work. The headquarters rose like a glowing tower above the firs, the upturned hands of the logo visible at its top.

He couldn't look away from the lawn where it sloped to the beach or the firs that stood as statues before the headquarters. They glowed with a dull luminescence that came from the reflected light of the city – or he hoped it did, because otherwise the whole compound glowed white in the moonlight. A landscape hostage to whatever held it.

He heard Theo's voice. *It's everyone for themselves in there.*

Maria and Storm slid past, paddling in time towards where the fence extended out into the waves, a thick guide wire holding it in place.

He checked the shore again, the stillness deeper. There should have been troops or activity, not this haunting emptiness.

They arrived at the guidepost together, the metal icy, inseparable from the cold of his hand. They floated together, Maria holding the tip of his boat to anchor them.

"It's all white," said Storm in almost a whisper.

Fear prickled through him, the white of the grass and trees not the glow of the city after all but the flat dull of the white that had overtaken it. Doubt followed his fear, that they could ever achieve this.

"Can you still do it?" asked Maria, her demand returning him to the boat and the cold water on his hand.

"We have to try," said Storm.

"We'll have to separate," said Maria. She shook Adams' kayak and he looked away from where the retaining wall had gone fully white at the top, still gray at the bottom where the waves washed against it. "Do you remember what to do?"

He inhaled sharply and shook himself, letting the cold push back the weight of his thoughts. He let go of the post and let the waves push him along the line of the fence until the bow of his boat crunched onto a small bit of sand next to the outlet of a canal.

He leapt out of his kayak, his pack already secured. He crouched beside the retaining wall of the canal, his view of the grounds blocked by the slope of the lawn. The grass was brittle beneath his feet, breaking rather than bending. The concrete of the wall was just as altered, its surface hard but brittle, as if he could poke a hole with his finger.

He had a sudden memory of Valerie and Camille, laid out like specimens in their body bags, their eyes forever closed, and his life gone with them.

He steadied himself on the wall, remembered how weak Valerie had been the last time they spoke, and how Camille hadn't woken up. He had let Wesley pull him away from them. Who was he to think that this would make a difference? Stopping the Gatherer wouldn't bring them back to him.

The sand gave way beneath his feet, the lapping water indifferent to him and their suffering. What did the world care how much he struggled?

Maria and Storm's boat knocked into his as they landed. Maria was out of the boat immediately, her face close to his, framed by her black hat and coat. Her wet hand grabbed his chin, and she forced him to look at her.

"It's not real. We talked about this. It's the despair. It's an effect of the Gatherers."

He could feel it now, a dark current that had overtaken him. Storm had warned him, yet he had fallen right into it. He removed her hand, held it for a moment to steady himself.

"Got it."

It had been so easy to slip in.

"Can you do this?"

Her voice cut through him. He remembered Theo's jittery eyes trying to focus. The anguish that followed him.

"Yes."

"It will always be there, trying to pull you down."

He'd discounted it, hadn't believed them, had thought it was something only weaker people succumbed to. Yet it had found his Achilles heel in moments. And walked right in.

"Should we change the plan?" Maria was pulling up the boats.

"No. I'm good."

They crouched in a tight circle, the black of the ocean behind them, their toes touching the white sand, and Maria's calm unaffected by the river of hopelessness surrounding them.

Storm lifted one foot, then the other, retreating to the water with her heels submerged. Her shoulder had curled further and she held herself rigid as if warding off pain.

Maria stopped him when he moved towards her.

"Get going. I'll look after her."

Would she even be able to, in this sea of white?

He poked his head up, checked the route to the test facility, and was surprised by the movement of a soldier along a path thirty paces inland, his back to the ocean. He held his assault rifle at ready position, which didn't make sense for a long night on patrol. Adams hadn't seen him while he was coming in since his pants were as white as the ground, and his bare back the same luminescence as the trees. He signaled to Maria to stay put. The man shuffled three paces to the right and took up his position again, facing inward as if that's where the greatest threat would come from.

Adams crawled up the slope, flat on his stomach, cursing his black hat and clothes that carved a clear silhouette against the glow. The distance opened between him and the beach, and the current of despondence hovered around him. He had never felt the pull of the Gatherer, had thought it was a metaphor to help people understand it. Yet this unhappiness felt too real, like it came from inside him. No wonder Stanton had wanted it.

You could debilitate whole armies with despair. Simply get them to lie down with no will to live.

The night hovered around freezing, yet the soldier stood bare-chested and didn't move. No wonder Amanda had been able to sneak by. Adams could probably walk right by him, yet Theo had warned him of the volatility of those who had stayed too long.

He approached slowly, eyes and ears tuned for the scuff of a shoe or an exhaled breath. The night was still, his footsteps quiet on the deadness of the white gravel path. The moon had just risen in the east so that the landscape shone brighter, the white dominance unavoidable in the cast of the moon.

He had almost reached him when the soldier finally turned. First his head, then the slow pained follow of his body. He moved to lift the rifle and Adams stopped it halfway. His hands were a healthy pink compared to the man's death-like skin.

They stood with their hands on the half-raised rifle. The man's eyes in the moonlight were wild and panicked, not because of him, but like an animal unable to escape. Adams felt his resistance against the despair harden, its power the real danger here.

He lifted the rifle from the man's hands and laid it on the ground. It had changed form, most of it the same dead white as everything else and wouldn't work as it was intended. The soldier raised his hand to strike. It was a movement so slow that it pained Adams to watch. He closed his fist over the man's hand and, turning him so that he faced away, struck him in the back of the head. Not enough to kill. Or injure. But enough to free him from his suffering long enough for Maria and Storm to get through. He laid him carefully on the ground

The test facility lay in front of him, a carved block sketched out of white. The air hummed and the bottom of his feet were pins and needles.

He turned back to the ocean, to where Maria and Storm hid. He gave the signal that they were safe to come in. Or as safe as they were going to be.

THIRTY-FOUR

MARIA

ADAMS DISAPPEARED OVER THE retaining wall and Maria turned back to Storm. She stood with her feet in the water and looked stunned, unable to even verbalize what was happening. She had her face lifted to the whitewashed tower of the headquarters in the distance and the wonderland that lay between them.

She remembered Storm's words of caution, that it wasn't intelligent, but it sure as hell felt like a presence hovered around them, waiting for the kill.

"Storm!" It was a hiss in the quiet.

Storm tried to focus but her attention rolled away, forever returning to that high tower.

She turned her back to Storm.

"Get on."

Storm remained fixed in the sand. Maria had thought they would have longer before she was overtaken.

She looped Storm's arms around her neck, scanning the chilling whiteness for movement. Adams stood behind the soldier, who hadn't noticed him.

Storm didn't resist and didn't help, her arms loose and floppy like someone unconscious. Maria leaned forward, forcing Storm onto her back and breaking her connection to the white ground. Storm gave a small huff and Maria was already moving, hunched low, carrying Storm piggyback along the beach.

"So powerful." Storm's mouth was close to Maria's ear, her voice clearer.

"So you're back?"

Storm's arms tightened around her neck; her legs pressed her hips.

"Even the tiniest potential, it wants it all."

"How long until it overtakes us?"

"Don't know."

Maria could feel it. For once, understanding what Storm was saying. Her feet burned, the lower half of her calves aching as if something pulled at her flesh.

At the end of the beach, where a second fence reached into the water, she paused. Adams had disappeared. It was part of the plan, but it made her uneasy.

The waves lapped behind them, yet it was as if nothing emanated from the compound, the flow only in one direction.

She adjusted her grip, holding Storm's legs tighter against her, hoping the place where their bodies connected would be a barrier the white couldn't break. She started along the fence, the most direct route to the tower.

There were small trees along the perimeter, part of a manicured garden, the trunks ghost-like in the moonlight, the undergrowth a blur of white. Dead, but somehow still used as a channel by the Gatherer, sustaining the structure even as it stole.

She caught movement out of the corner of her eye and a soldier rushed at them from behind a clipped white shrub. Maria lunged off the path, her legs straining under Storm's extra weight.

The woman missed them, and Maria had time to let Storm down and spin to face her before the next attack.

The woman had no weapon, her skin marble in the moonlight. Her training was military, the moves performed in excruciating slowness, her face locked in a grimace of pain and terror.

Maria stopped the attack with one hand. Twisted the arm behind the woman's back, her resistance wilting so that it was like subduing a rag doll. Maria lowered her to the ground at the base of a tree, the woman making no effort to rise.

Storm lay on the ground, her whole side exposed to the white. She looked dead, the white of her face blending with the grass and leaves. Maria shook her. Slapped. Storm's eyelids flickered as she lifted her and carried her across her shoulders.

Maria moved slower, second-guessing white shadows beneath trees and outlines that warped in the moonlight. She skirted around a pair of motionless soldiers guarding the side entrance. It stood open and the soldiers faced inwards, their eyes not lifting to follow her or recognize that she was there.

The bulk of the tower rose ahead of them, visible in the openings between trees, the siding seeming to shine brighter than the rest. Storm mumbled constantly, the words indecipherable, her body jerking as if hit by electric shocks. Maria stopped within the boughs of a willow.

"You still with me?"

Storm was groggy, unable to lift her head, and Maria's legs shook, her feet an agony of firing nerves, every cell screaming to turn around. She adjusted her grip and held Storm tighter.

An open lawn stretched to the headquarters. Every blade of trimmed grass was devoid of color, the entire scene sculpted in white. A gravel path led to the back entrance, the concrete overhang heavy and worn as if it were thousands of years old.

She waited for the hopelessness, the pain she had seen in Adams' eyes, yet there was only the threat of this whiteness and the fear running through her.

Silence overwhelmed her, the entire world blotted out by white noise. There were no animals in the trees, no insects in the underbrush, the distant sound of the city absorbed into an utter stillness.

Her feet ached and the fire rose to mid-thigh, the pins and needles having turned into knives and hammers. She had a sudden memory of Amanda walking away from her, the feeling fresh and raw, and her own panic at losing her thick in her throat.

She let the image fall away. This was the despair. She was briefly elated at finally being like the others until the feeling was snuffed out by the effort it took to look away from her worst fears.

She moved forward. One step in front of the next, the effort excruciating, like she had the flu and a fever and had just completed a full day's training run. There were no more soldiers, no people, just wading through the thick painful soup towards the tower, her body throbbing with the ache.

The headquarters seemed to shimmer, yet each time she looked towards it the shimmering stopped. It was there, in the corner of her eye, waiting.

It was hours, or days, before they reached the corner of the building, her sense of time marked by pain and the creeping loss of energy. Storm hadn't moved since Maria picked her up and her fear spurred her forward, around the corner so that they faced the sidewall. The bricks were as aged as the entrance with chips of mortar fallen from between bricks. Her feet crunched on the fallen pieces, the noise catastrophic.

"We're almost there."

Storm's head lay heavy on Maria's shoulder, her arms loose around her neck.

"Adams?"

Storm's words were slurred, struggling.

The drive to the main gate lay empty, the landscape frozen, the walking path to the test facility wide and clear. The soup would have been worse for him, laced with his own tragedy.

Maria shook her head.

Adams wasn't there yet. But he would be. Had to be.

She paused at the front corner of the headquarters. Sweat soaked her shirt and hair, her body's efforts to keep moving crashing up against the pull of the streaks.

The statue of the upturned hands sat in the center of the circular drive, its luminescence otherworldly, as alien as the light from a different sun. It held the same shimmer, the same threat, seen only when she looked away.

She lifted a foot, the same way Storm had. It didn't break the connection. They were too immersed now: this the Gatherer's domain.

The lobby entrance was sun-bleached like a battered sailboat. The rotating door was an ivory carousel that no longer spun. Patches of the glass were opaque, not allowing her to see within the lobby.

She adjusted Storm's position, the shoots of pain moving from her legs to her hips.

She took a step. The concrete under her feet flexed beneath her. She turned away from the impossibility of it, her focus on the rotating door.

She saw an image from the war, of civilians shot on the streets with their eyes turned towards her. She shook her head, refused to see it, and took another step. The despair flashed horrible images, real and imagined, across her mind. She latched onto Storm's weight and the certainty she was real. She stumbled, and caught them before they fell, the door a warped mess of flowing energy before them.

As she held Storm tighter, she heard the faintest whisper.

"So beautiful."

THIRTY-FIVE

ADAMS

THE MAN, THOUGH HE was more of a boy, collapsed against Adams, and he carefully lowered him to the ground, unconscious from the blow to his neck but free for a moment from his mental torture.

The young soldier had been sitting on a bench, rocking front to back, coming after Adams long after he had passed. He had telegraphed each strike well in advance as if he had wanted Adams to stop him. And perhaps he had, looking at his young face, relaxed now from its frantic terror.

Adams stood before what had once been the treatment center, where he had taken Valerie and Camille in hope of a cure. The building was smaller than he remembered, only two storeys high, its exterior bathed in white so he stood in a glowing landscape, the moon his only light.

There was the single door where he had stood guard, believing that he was protecting them, so pleased with himself and his connections that could give them this coveted opportunity. It stood empty now, the building and the ramp that led to it abandoned.

He breathed in, pushing back the sadness that threatened to overtake him.

"They have all the best resources, and they are getting results," Stanton had said. And Adams had believed him. He imagined he could hear Camille calling to him, the only sound in the dead quiet, her voice high and clear.

He took a step forward. They weren't there. Had been dead for months. Yet he couldn't stop himself moving forward, the pain unbearable.

He flexed his hands, wiped them across his eyes. It was so hard to hold onto what was real. His body vibrated as if every nerve had been activated, the commands originating outside of him. He struggled to remember why he was there. Was it for Valerie and Camille? To finally bring them home? Yet they weren't there.

The compound was etched in black and white, as dead as a stone statue and as lifeless. The headquarters lay beyond a grove of stark white firs, Maria and Storm somewhere in that whiteness. He turned his back to the emptiness of the treatment center, the test facility filling his view, waiting for him.

Its matte black exterior had gone white, yet its presence was as formidable, and more frightening. The ground pulsed beneath him, a steady ominous beat. The strength and force of it was out of sync with the deadness of its exterior, that looked as fragile and thin as ice.

He found the ever-present rage inside him and fueled it with gasoline. He remembered Stanton's smugness and Wesley's dismissal of Valerie's treatment, how they had kept them from him so he hadn't seen that they were dying.

He ran to the test facility's main entrance, recognizing the fatigue that was already settling in. He fought against it. Remembered how they hadn't even written their names on their charts, hadn't informed him of their deaths.

He surged forward, a sharp painful pulse of energy ripping into his arm when he touched the handle. He pulled back, pausing long enough to pull the neoprene gloves from the pack.

The door led to a vestibule with several facial recognition portals in the wall, beside a fortified locked steel door. Something ran over the surface of all of it, like a swarm of insects. It was energy, impossible to see when he looked straight at it, but a continual flicker in his peripheral vision.

He backed out the door, retreating to solid ground — except it wasn't solid, the thin veneer of energy touching everything. He knelt in the coolness of the colorless grass. There was no inertness, only the flow of power towards the headquarters. The logo on the tower seemed to glow brighter, his fear and the despair distorting what was really there.

He ran to the loading dock in the shadow of the building. Two large doors had been pulled shut and the main door bolted. A single delivery truck was parked outside, its tailgate backed up to the dock. Adams used the truck's handle as a foothold and climbed onto the roof of the cab, only recognizing when he stood on top of the main box that the charge was less there, the low-lying agitation a lower frequency.

He didn't stop to understand, using the box's roof as a springboard to reach a vent protruding from the wall and leveraging it to jump for the edge of the building. He flailed briefly, his legs swinging until he was able to smear his boots against the wall and roll onto the roof. He jumped to his feet at the jolt of energy, the rubber of his boots protecting him, but barely.

He searched for a way in, an elevator bulkhead or a utility door, his running footsteps coming to a halt before he reached the end of the building. A wide, exposed blast had opened the roof, the inward flare of the tar paper showing the blast had come from above as if a bomb had dropped cleanly through the roof.

The damage wasn't new, the edges damp with moisture. Feathers from a bird were caught in a twisted beam, and a rough coating of salt covered all of it.

He approached the opening carefully, testing the roof for strength. It looked down into a large space, with undefined blobs that circled out from a blackened central patch, the blobs slowly forming into the bleached corpses of dead cows.

The blackened patch stood out like a blight on the surrounding whiteness. Whatever had caused this destruction had pulled into itself, its remains a melted, unidentifiable ball of goo. A rush of static raced across his skin, like the aftershock of an electrical fire. Exactly as Storm had described. This had been one of the corrupted Gatherers, the implosion drawing too much energy into itself, so it destroyed itself and everything around it.

Disappointment reared up, underlain by a wave of hopelessness. He felt the despair hovering, waiting to pull him into its despondence, as if sensing that moment of weakness. Instead, he funneled the disappointment into his rage. He'd lived on rage for months; he knew how to block out all else.

He strained to see further into the space. A charred smell floated on a warm draft, but the moonlight didn't penetrate inside, his view of vague shapes in the white, none of it moving.

He reached for his pack and found the flashlight strapped to its side. He pointed it into the hole and turned it on, the brilliance of the white world blinding in the moment before the light failed. He shook it, flicked the switch on and off, but there was no charge, its energy already gone.

He drew the rope from his pack and looped it around the elevator bulkhead, tying a figure eight with both ropes. His harness slid on easily and he clipped a rappel device to the harness and the rope. He had a flash of Hamel making a joke at ropes training and he took strength in the belief that Hamel was with him, standing by his side.

He moved back towards the edge, one hand on the downward rope, feeding it slowly into the device. At the edge, he looked up at the sky, the few stars visible beyond the brightness of the moon.

He pushed off, the rope running freely through his hand so that he plunged down, the rope cracking and breaking against the lip of the opening, his feet hitting the ground as bits of the broken roof fell around him.

He disconnected from the rope and spun, alert for movement or attack. He stood in the brightest spot, the moonlight pouring in, the cavernous space the size of a football field.

There was no movement of air. The patch beneath his feet was ashes, still dark gray, the white seeming to flow around it. Dead, the implosion rendering it truly not alive. He moved off the ash onto the white and his toes tingled, then his heels.

He jogged across the empty warehouse. His eyes adjusted to the dimness as he ran, the space cast in a strange luminescence, the energy burning where it touched and all the time probing and testing as if gauging his potential.

"Not a chance," he said out loud, setting rules for at least himself. It may not be conscious but whatever this had created was as alive as him and wanted more.

Light reflected from the smashed windows of what had been a control room. Blank monitors covered one wall, and workstations torn from their connections crowded up against a metal wall in the direction of the implosion. The door had been torn from its hinges.

He stopped at the threshold. There were at least three bodies tangled among the workstations, their bodies inseparable from the technology, and just as devoid of color and life. He moved further into the room, searching for the outline of a corrupted Gatherer. One body wore what looked to have been a uniform, the others were too broken for any details.

The corpse's hair hung to its shoulders, the emaciated body that of an old man. He pulled the body from the wreckage and felt the energy flowing through it. It was the same forehead, the eyes closed: Stanton's suffering permanently preserved by the whiteness.

The injustice caught in Adams' throat. He wanted to kick or throw him, inflict some of the vengeance he had craved for so long. He hated that he had been robbed of that. His one chance to avenge his family.

He clenched his fist and the bone of Stanton's arm snapped, the pieces crumbling to the ground, white flesh caught on his palm. He gagged and whipped his hand away.

He raked his palm across the wall, using the edge of a terminal to scrape it clean, the futility of it threatening to overtake him. He shuddered. The absence of revenge left nothing but exposed pain he would never overcome.

Anger saved him, a deep roaring rage that refused to be calmed. He kicked at the corpse, let the fury race through him. Stanton's expression was of agony and he was glad for it.

He turned away, there was a flash of angular edges beside the body. He pulled his mind back, turned from the temptation to surrender and peered closer, hoping for the hard edges of the crystals that formed the heart of the Gatherer. When he pulled it out, it was the remains of printouts, whatever had been printed there erased by the white. He tossed it away and turned his back to the bodies and the debris.

By the time he reached the opposite door, he had grown weaker, his shins aching, the swirl of energy stronger. The door opened onto a corridor that bent in a long curve, the wall metal, the floor luminescent tiles. He hesitated, couldn't shake the idea that the floor moved. When he looked at it, it was solid and white. Only when he turned his head did it appear to shift, like a fast-flowing river.

He touched down lightly as he ran, willing himself to float above it, the curve of the hallway long and smooth. He was breathing hard when he was forced to stop, surprised at the soldier standing outside a closed door and that he was still alive.

The soldier lifted his head. He had a full beard, his hair hanging around his face, his uniform torn and white and his feet bare. A New Age Jesus to go with the New Age suffering.

Energy vibrated in Adams' head and along his nerves, playing with him.

"Hi," Adams said, though the words didn't sound right, the waves they should have traveled on distorted.

Adams had known this soldier, had stood guard with him at the treatment facility.

"Caleb?"

He had been a recruit, excited to be at the compound.

Caleb's brow furrowed and cleared, the name only the briefest interruption in the static that must be constant.

Adams strolled forward. Caleb didn't react when he reached him, other than a strange sigh. "How's Caley?" There had been a twin sister.

The boy's blankness collapsed into strained sorrow. Adams spun him and pushed him down the corridor.

"Go home to Caley."

The boy didn't move. He shoved harder, his feet burning. Finally, the boy shuffled forward, a slow effort of putting one foot in front of the next.

Adams listened, before carefully opening the door, and using it as a shield. He waited for gunfire, or hands reaching for him. A bird fluttered in the ceiling, a point of life that shouldn't exist there.

The space was as large as the one he'd first entered, the luminescence of the floor and walls reflecting off rows and rows of cages laid out in concentric circles. Close to fifty rows spiraled out from a Gatherer that sat at the center without its case, the guts exposed. He thought he could see the crystals, though they looked black and tarnished. The white flowed around it, showing more intelligence than Storm gave it credit for.

Small, furry bodies lay within each cage, rats, or squirrels, it was impossible to know. The despair ran thick, threads of it nipping at his thoughts, so the suffering of each dead rodent became Camille's, her helplessness reflected in theirs.

Before he could think or feel, he plunged between the cages, counting the seconds to the Gatherer, and the time when he could turn and run.

The pain was everywhere, a deep physical pain at his core, triggered by a despair as deep as the end of the world. He curled inwards in a vain attempt at protection. He stumbled, landing hard on the ground within reach of the Gatherer. There was no flow here, no current, only a hardness to the tiles that spoke of absence, and the inertness of something gone.

The rat in the closest cage stared at him from unseeing eyes, the small body petrified. There was no decomposition, its natural process disrupted, and no smell of rot, only a faint burnt smell of something charged.

He put one hand forward, felt Valerie's dead weight in his arms, saw her bloodless lips that would never smile. He put his other hand forward and grasped at the memory of her fallen asleep on the couch, her book laid across her chest.

On hands and knees, he moved impossibly slow as he fought against the futility.

Storm and Maria were waiting for him. He clung to the hope of that thought and searched for the memory of Megan holding tight to his hand.

He rose to his feet and staggered towards the Gatherer.

The lattice will come out as a single unit. He clung to the memory of Storm's voice in his head. *Disconnect it in three places.*

The crystals were burned, black on the outer layers where they had been pushed to their limit, clearer further in.

He found one connector on the side of the lattice, fused by the force of the energy that had once flowed through. He sliced the cable with his knife, his movement the painful flow of molasses. The second connector was the same. The outer coating of the wire was intact and the insides had melted to a solid mass.

The final connection was underneath, the group of wires hanging beneath it the artery Storm had described. He fought against the fatigue, longed to lie down.

He sawed at the mess of wires. He cut through one, then another, and still had hundreds to go. It was pointless. He would never succeed. He kept sawing.

He was halfway through the wires, his movements slowing, with pauses in between as he struggled with the futility of continuing. He remembered tucking a stray hair behind Camille's ear, saw Valerie smile.

The wires in the center were tougher, the fusion worse in the middle. He shook the lattice, checked to see if it would give but the wires held it in. His strength waned. He would die here, as forgotten as Valerie and Camille. What was it she had said to him, holding his face in her hands?

Take us home.

He had failed. He should have protected them and never let them near this horrible device. A plague on the earth.

He used his fury to rip the lattice from the Gatherer. The final uncut wires were still attached, so he brought the connecting cables with it. With a single slash he cut through the remaining wires. The Gatherer was light, despite all the damage it had caused. The pain in his legs eased, the frenetic firing of his nerves stopped, the white keeping its distance now that he held the corrupted Gatherer. It no longer touched him, a path of inertness beneath his feet.

He turned towards the exit. The relief and a sense of victory fueling muscles that no longer had their energy drained. He moved faster. The white separated in front of him, flowing around his feet so that he walked in a moving bubble, free of its creeping draw.

When he reached the corridor, the agitation of the white grew stronger, visible in his direct vision, no longer just in the corner. Yet it still divided, no matter how fast he placed his feet, the floor it landed on held no charge, as inert as a piece of driftwood.

He pointed his feet in the direction of the white flow, holding the blackened crystals between his hands, so they formed a circuit. The white energy writhed and twisted around him, never touching, wild in its need to absorb his energy but stopped by the corrupted lattice that was now part of his own network of nerves and synapses.

He ran, following the flow, the white parting under his feet. He had to hope Maria and Storm would be at its end, and one way or another all of this would finally end.

THIRTY-SIX

STORM

STORM CLUNG TO THE place where her chest connected to Maria's back. It was a calm point in a tornado of energy, the frame of reference of the world so fluid and changing that she struggled to recognize the entrance to the headquarters. One moment the doors stood solid and real, the next it was a flow of energy through the shell of what had once been the entrance.

The torrent pulled at her skin and gut, and there was nowhere to escape from it except in that small part where she and Maria still connected. A great river raged around them, its static as loud as any river in high flood. They were being pulled towards a plummeting waterfall, already past the point when they could save themselves.

Maria stumbled and their shoulders briefly touched against a pillar. The pain was a scream inside her, the current of a thousand tasers running through her.

Maria pulled them away, staggered as she shuffled towards the entrance. Storm couldn't differentiate between the door and the flow. There was so much potential racing around them, all pulling and dragging her with it.

This was the Gatherer, its original delicate structure resting inside the door, no longer delicate or new but a mutated and morphed device that knew only its hunger for energy.

Maria had stopped in front of the door. Their position became a point of stillness, a rock in the river that the energy flowed around, even as it wore it away.

Storm squeezed her legs tighter around Maria.

They had to go in, to the point where it all converged. The edges of the doors disintegrated and collapsed inwards, so that what had been reality disappeared leaving only a shimmer.

Where was Adams? As if the thought conjured him, he appeared beside them, a human shape in the churning white, remarkable for his intact edges and solidity. He gripped the charred remains of a lattice between his hands.

He shoved the lattice towards them, and Storm struggled to grab it, her signals buried in the fevered hiss of the white as it refused to let her touch it.

The part of her awareness she still held soared at its resistance. She had been right. This was what had to be done.

The white flowed thick and fast over her and Maria so she didn't know where they started or stopped. Storm felt it taking her, eating away at her most protected energy so that she would cease to exist. She screamed in frustration, and it rang in silence, her voice no longer there, her awareness slipping away, caught in that rushing roar. She was being pulled apart into two states, one physical, the other energy.

She was dimly aware of Maria reaching out with one hand, breaking through their cocoon of energy so that her hand contacted the crystal.

The world stopped, the white dropping away so that they stood as a quiet point in a frenzy of static energy. Storm could see the outline of Maria's hand where it touched the lattice, could feel the strands of her hair that brushed Storm's cheeks.

Maria let go of Storm's leg and Storm dropped to their island of inertness, still clutching Maria's arm. She felt the real connection to Maria and Adams. The warmth of flesh, their living breath. She wanted to marvel at it, laugh in its wonder, yet the edges of it were too fragile.

The sides of the door trembled, the walls of the building warping with the force of the energy, its point of focus the brightness where the original Gatherer had once been, now the top of a waterfall pouring energy into a vast hole where it would never return.

Adams pointed towards the vortex and then simply let go.

The rush of the energy up his body was quick and violent, so that he lifted his chin before it consumed him, his outline slipping into the white as it moved away.

Storm couldn't move. The roar of the flow deafening like water falling a thousand storeys. Maria laid her hand over Storm's, both holding the lattice. It surprised her to feel her skin, that it could still exist. Maria pulled her towards the door.

Storm resisted, pointing Maria to where Adams had disappeared.

Maria shook her head, though Storm also heard the *no*, a signal communicated through the crystal they both held.

I can do this on my own.

Maria loomed close, her brown eyes fierce and frightened.

Together.

Storm shook her head. If there was even a chance of escaping, Maria needed to try.

Maria frowned, her eyelashes a thin blonde fringe.

I'll be okay.

A frenzied stream of energy ran behind her.

Come back to us.

It was Maria's response, not words. A plea that hardly made sense anymore. Come back to where?

Storm pulled at the lattice and Maria opened her fingers. Storm didn't even know if she meant to let her go.

Maria's takeover was more violent, her face distorted as the white swarmed up her torso and encased her head. A white writhing outline of Maria moved away, a ghost in the flow.

Storm checked in with her awareness, and the part of her that was still untouched, and crossed through the streaming energy of what had once been the rotating door.

The first crack of the pulsing lobby came into view, or awareness, for there were no lines to it or any definition of structure, the steel and glass and tiles all merely conduits.

Her eyes burned at the brightness of what had been the Gatherer. A writhing funnel that flowed not down or up but in.

Something touched her. It was more of an exploration, an inquiry, the energy testing her potential. She held the lattice tighter. The energy tested and probed but never advanced. Not intelligence as they knew it, but this force had understanding.

Storm stepped towards it, a crash of power, drawing all things into it. Her bubble of protection grew smaller. There were tugs on her arms and back, and she knew parts of her were being stolen, bits of energy at the edge of her system. She let the flow pull her, the pain excruciating and ecstatic as it sought to absorb her. She had flashes of the expanse of it, moments when a part of her nervous system connected to it, the flow pushing closer. It was glorious, and she was aware of the potential of a seed and the dissipated flecks of an imploded star. She was part of a common stream that surged and waned, and that she had always been part of. It would be so easy to let go yet she clung to the hardness of the lattice, holding on so Maria and Adams had time to get away.

The energy took larger parts of her, cutting them off from her larger system so that she and her awareness contracted to the limits of the lattice, the energy unwilling to flow through it. She stood at the top of the waterfall, a boulder in the torrent. It pushed at her and tore at her skin.

A scream rang in her head.

She no longer had a shape. There was only the crash of potential through her as she drew closer. There was so much power in it, so much awe.

She clung to the last memory of herself, forcing the energy to come close enough to have all of her and making it reach too far. She felt the instant when a sliver of current took the last piece and rushed down the path to the lattice. It found the corrupted crystals, a sudden jarring shock that turned the flow back onto itself, the polarities reversed.

The ripple of the wrongness was catastrophic, the harmonics caving in on themselves, corrupting the entire flow.

Storm let go in that moment of achievement, rode the tsunami of devastation, beyond the lobby, beyond the compound, rippling out in a sonic boom of connectivity.

THIRTY-SEVEN

MARIA

MARIA ROSE AND FELL in the incessant rocking, each movement accompanied by a gritty scrape. She groaned, trying to get whoever was rocking her cot to stop. Her head pounded, a deep, throbbing pain that originated in the middle of her skull.

A hard ridge dug into her back but when she tried to turn, she couldn't move. She opened her eyes, pissed at whoever was playing the prank, and looked into the brightness of the moon.

The ocean stretched to a dark horizon and the rhythmic knock and scrape was her kayak bumping against a tiny patch of sand. Had something gone wrong? She couldn't find the threads of it, her mind slow to engage.

She pulled herself from the kayak. It felt as if she had been beaten to within an inch of her life. She was on a narrow bit of sand, boulders coated in algae and slime rising on either side, their faces impossible to climb.

The night was old, the moon low on the horizon, and the air calm, sedate. There was relief in that, as if it hadn't always been. Further down the coast, a crumpled fence stuck out into the water, the posts twisted and bent, the waves washing through. She remembered the cold touch of metal, and her need to protect someone.

She caught her breath, the memory of their struggle to the headquarters rushing in. They had reached the corner, seen the upward hands of the statue.

She scrambled back into the kayak and pushed off, using her hands to propel her forward, the paddle gone, the water burning cold. There had been a door moving and Storm's weight on her back. But where was she now?

It was hard to make headway, the waves pushing the boat towards the rocky shore and her arms so fatigued that she scraped along rocks, using them to pull forward.

She found Adams only a few paces from where she had landed. He was slumped forward, the tandem kayak jammed between two rocks, the front seat empty. She drifted in beside him, finally releasing her breath when she felt the warmth of his neck, and a low, steady pulse.

She shook him. He had a gash on his head where he had been knocking up against a boulder. The blood was a shock of red against the white of his skin.

"No, no, no,"

His face and most of his hair had gone white, the wedding band he still wore a strip of white gold on alabaster skin.

She shook him harder, pulling her hands from him as if burned. Her hands were as white as his. She touched her face, could feel her fingertips on her skin. She flexed her fingers, the muscles sore and the skin tight, all in order except for the white.

She struggled to pull him to sitting. He kept slumping back down, too heavy for her to hold.

Matted piles of seaweed lay in the crevasses of the rocks, and she pulled out clumps, her hands aching, searching for intact stalks until she had several long enough to make a makeshift rope.

It took several tries, balancing on a submerged rock to free his boat. Once it was free, she scrambled into her own, and looped the seaweed through the ring on his bow.

It was slow going. Adams' weight continually pulled her off-course, and several times she had to readjust his position so he didn't teeter into the water.

She was aware of every pull through the water and every flex of her muscles, relieved they still responded and terrified she was being consumed.

It took time to come out of the shadow of the rocks, the night calm and attentive as it cradled them. She didn't trust the peacefulness of it. It felt too much like the silence of destruction, the quiet she knew once a battle was done.

She half-hoped to find Storm caught on one of the rocks, battered but alive, her indomitable spirit once again pulling herself upright. But when Maria rounded the final point her paddling stopped, and her hands dragged in the water.

Open space stretched where the compound had been. The tower, the trees, the test facility, all of it no longer stood. A scraped section of earth lay where the warehouses had been, the dock pilings poking up above the water, the docks themselves gone.

She held on to Adams' kayak as they floated into shore, her other hand in the water, despite the cold. For what else had protected them from this devastation? An entire section of the city wasn't so much flattened as simply gone.

She searched for the place where they had landed, or the fence she had used as a guide but there was no distinction between one point of barren land and another.

There was a bump against the bottom of the boat and she started, the severed end of the guide wire they had rested at still attached to the remains of the post.

She closed her eyes, her head aching, disappointed when she opened them to the same flat emptiness where the test facility and the shining hands of the headquarters had once been.

At the shore, the scrape of their boats on the sand was the only sound in the world. She dragged the boats onto shore, struggling with the weight and the idea that this deadened place had once teemed with energy.

Adams didn't wake when she pulled him from the kayak and laid him carefully on the dirt, but his skin was warm and his heart still beat.

She lifted one foot and then the other, the energy and the despair that had flowed there gone, as if it was never there. It was her own loss that consumed her now and her understanding that Storm was not there to be saved. For she had a shadow of a memory of Storm telling her to go.

She walked over stripped land, needing to look even though as far as she could see buildings, trees, and fences had been swept clean. The ground held no grass, only earth left behind.

She walked in the direction of where the tower had been, unable to stop herself. It was the uniformity that truly frightened her, so different from a battleground where debris was left behind. Nothing had been spared, the guardhouse gone, no fence to mark the boundary. It was miles before a building broke the surface, the first glow of the rising sun behind it.

She stepped over a rock outcrop, its surface dark from being buried, now freshly exposed.

At the tower, or where it had been, she dared not go further. There was no shimmer, no disintegrating edges, simply a patch of earth that had once held the home of a miraculous invention and was now a grave.

She knelt and touched the earth, hoping that there would be a shift, or a pull, anything to let her know that Storm still lived. Out there somewhere, if not here.

The breeze flowed, and in the distance the ocean rolled, the earth beneath her fingers cool and damp.

THE END

Thank you for reading

THE STORM

Please consider reviewing this book on:

Amazon
Goodreads
Social Media
Or your favourite book site

ACKNOWLEDGEMENTS

EVERY NOVEL HAS ITS own path and *The Storm* seemed determined from the beginning to be a harder creature to handle than its two previous siblings, *The Gatherer* and *The Disruptors*. It could have been the pandemic or the fact that it is the third book in the series and required a believable, satisfying, emotionally gratifying completion with all the storylines wrapped up in a nice, tidy bow. I will leave it up to you, my readers, to decide whether I succeeded in this task. For me this was the most challenging and by far the most satisfying book to complete to date, and I am happy to be able to share it with you.

As with every act of creation, there are many people to thank. Some were involved directly in the development, while others provided much needed support during the many times when I was unsure whether the final book would see the light of day.

First and foremost, I'd like to thank my writing mentor Sherry Coman for being the encouraging, supportive voice and image at the other end of an endless number of zoom calls as we both struggled to keep going during the pandemic. Your wisdom and support are a big reason this book exists. I'd like to thank my beta readers Bella Howden, Colleen Gaffney, Philippa Campbell, and Adam Hamdy for their much-needed input on the ending (any complaints can be taken up with them ☺). Thanks to everyone who agreed to an Advanced Reader Copy and placed reviews in all the bookish places online and helped me get the book out into the world. My gratitude to Design for Writers for carrying the heavy load on the design and formatting of the print and eBook and doing such an amazing job. Thanks to Lori

Twining, Jeanette Winsor, Paul Frazier, Bruce Hanson, Eric Bishop, Deborah Levison, Beth Green, Linda Laforge and all my other writerly companions on this crazy, self-imposed journey we call the writing life. It would be a lot less fun if you weren't along for the ride. I'd like to thank my extended family for being enthusiastic and enduring cheerleaders since the beginning, and of course Ron, Bella and Elise for being my greatest joy. Thank you everyone!

ABOUT THE AUTHOR

As both an electrical engineer and a former journalist, Colleen Winter has one foot in the world of technology and the other in the world of words. Her stories reflect her fascination with technology and how it intersects with our lives.

She was short-listed for the 2020 Rakuten Kobo Emerging Writer Prize in Speculative Fiction, has received two Writer's Reserve grants from the Ontario Arts Council, won the Best First Sentence Contest at Thrillerfest, won first prize in the CAA Leacock/Simcoe Erotic prose contest, received a SLS Fellowship from the Unified Literary Contest, and is an alumnus of the Humber School of Writers.

When she isn't writing, Colleen can be found hiking or climbing the beautiful places of the world or sneaking out for early morning swims in whatever freshwater lake is nearby. She reads to get inspired by Martha Wells, Becky Chambers, Veronica Roth, Blake Crouch, Mur Lafferty, and Matt Haig. She is a member of Science Fiction Writers of America, The Writers' Union of Canada, and International Thriller Writers.

Colleen lives in Ontario with her husband Ron in their empty nest with their loveable, psychotic, reactive dog Kira.

You can find her at:
Website: https://colleenwinter.ca/
Instagram: winter_colleen
Facebook: https://www.facebook.com/ColleenWinterAuthor/
Twitter: @ColleenWinter3
Goodreads: https://www.goodreads.com/colleenwinter

www.ingramcontent.com/pod-product-compliance
Lightning Source LLC
Chambersburg PA
CBHW051127190726
48290CB00006B/1723